cyclamen

a journey of hope

CHADIA CHALMERS

Cyclamen: A journey of hope © Chadia Chalmers 2026

Second Edition

ISBN: 978-1-7644268-0-0 (paperback)
ISBN: 978-1-7644268-1-7 (ebook)

1st edition published in Australia by Chadia Chalmers 2021.
cyclamenstory.com

2nd edition published in Australia by Chadia Chalmers 2026.
cyclamenstory.com

A catalogue record for this book is available from the National Library of Australia

For Martin Chalmers

And for our children,
Samantha and Alex

Contents

Prologue

Find her! You HAVE to find her!

My heart beats impossibly faster with every step as I cross the threshold of a bombed out, ruined building, and begin climbing the rickety stairs. Without the moonlight to guide me any longer, the pitch darkness closes in from all sides and I can't see anymore, although I can sense rats scurrying between my feet and the sound of bats is paralysing. Adrenaline bounces my heart out of my chest as it tries to outrun the terror trembling through me and my veins fill with ice and shiver along my skin as my chest constricts, sucking the breath from my chest. When my eyes adjust somewhat to the darkness, I begin breathing again and inch my way up the broken staircase.

'Okay, calm down! Just calm down,' I whisper to myself. 'Just feel your way and don't lose your footing or make a sound. Oh God! Please help me.'

A massive hole stares hungrily at me, as though it will devour me should I set one foot wrongly. Steeling myself, I raise my gun in front of me, alert to the slightest sounds, and creep through it carefully. The acrid stench of burning and rancid food nearly asphyxiates me and everything around me takes on a surreal, supernatural quality until even the familiar bats begin to seem oth- erworldly.

Abject terror, or the biting cold, set me to shivering again as I continue to tiptoe through this living nightmare in search of poor, helpless Josephine and—suddenly—I round the corner and my throat constricts in a guttural scream...

I sit in the street, holding my mother's blood-soaked head in my lap, smoothing her hair and praying she will live. Looking around, I see more blood—a crimson river flowing all around me—and everywhere I look are the bodies of my friends and neighbours. To my left, I see a woman I don't recognize huddled over the body of a small girl. The woman's wailing suddenly pierces my ears and I realize the bomb blast temporarily removed my ability to hear, but now that I do, chaos and terror and grief penetrate my senses and snap me into the moment. Our street has been bombed and my mother has been caught in the blast. Everywhere I look is carnage. Bodies and body parts—some still twitching—lay scattered around me amidst the rubble and glass and gore. People wander around, covered in dust and blood, dazed and silent. A child cries, lonely and bewildered behind me and the lamenting cries of the beautiful people I know and love, fill my heart with a grief and sadness that is, again, all too familiar. I look down at my mother and call her name, but she doesn't move or respond. No! Please! Not my mum. Not like this. Please, God! In the distance, I hear the sirens approaching, although I'm unsure if they are ambulances or bomb sirens, and I bow my head over my mum and begin to pray…

"Please stop!" I plead as I huddle in the corner of our bedroom, covering my head to protect it from the large onions my 'loving' husband is hurtling at me. "Say you're sorry, Chadia!" Jerry taunts as he hits me with another onion. I can already feel my cheek and eye swelling from his wayward fists and my body aches from fresh bruises. I wonder how this has happened, how I was so easily tricked by his charm and his declarations of love—how I could have possibly believed he loved me. This isn't love! This is possession, ownership. I have to get away from him! But all I can do is lay on the floor and cover my head, waiting until he gets tired of the game…

My eyes pop open and, shuddering, I try to shake off the nightmare as an unreleased scream dies in my throat, but it's no use—I'll never be able to shake it because this nightmare stems from my very real and very vivid memories.

It doesn't seem to matter to my brain that I'm not living through the civil war anymore, or that I escaped my first and very abusive husband, or that it's now more than thirty years later. Never-ending visions of death, destruction and lost innocence continue to torment my sleep, even half a lifetime later. The senseless bloodshed during the civil war in Beirut has left a permanent scar in my mind. My memory is tainted by the sound of bombs exploding, rockets whizzing by, automatic weapons tapping out an unforgettable tune of carnage mixed in with the sporadic echoes of sniper rifles distantly shuddering.

All these memories still plague me today. I still feel the heavy thud in my chest of their impact upon our country, city, homes and, especially, the innocent. Vivid recollections—of lifeless bodies lying in the streets, injured children and adults writhing in pain and fear in a river of blood, and the ghosts of once-beautiful, but now ruined and abandoned buildings—they all haunt me. So many bright and beautiful places that were once filled with the happy voices of loving families, now dark and silent—capable of evoking only vividly traumatic and sad memories.

To say that the civil war in my home country had a significant influence on my life is an understatement. To say that marrying an abusive, violent and manipulative man who was my first husband didn't deeply affect me or traumatize me for many years would be a lie. My life has been a series of traumatic, soul-chang- ing experiences interspersed with heart-wrenchingly beautiful, hope-giving moments and all of it has taught me that we can all make this world a better place if we open our hearts to accept and embrace our differences.

This time, waking up from these familiar nightmares feels different and, even though it's only 5:30 am, I cannot convince myself to drift back into that uneasy sleep, so I escape my bed, driven by an overwhelming need to express myself and the pent-up memories I've been reliving for so many years. I wonder if perhaps purging my emotional past might lead to the end of my nightmares. Peering through the curtains of our bedroom window, I witness the beginning of what promises to be a most spectacular sunrise over the city skyline of the Gold Coast. Determined not to wake my husband, I take a moment to exhale a deep sigh, realising how grateful I am to live in this beautiful home, with these lovely views of the city and hinterland, where my entire family is finally safe, happy and comfortable.

I tiptoe downstairs as quietly as possible and head directly for the kettle to make myself a cup of coffee—something I never begin a day without—and, as the kettle boils, I know instinctively that today is somehow significant.

I take my coffee to our outdoor veranda and sit on a wooden bench I'd painted years before. Taking it all in, I absorb the beauty of the day—birds chirping from all directions, a gorgeous view of the city, and our lovely garden filled with orchids, vegetables and fruit trees, all backed by our sparkling swimming pool. Slowly, I shift my attention to the birds chirping as they drink and bathe in the birdbath and a beautiful dove catches my eye—a sign I have always believed represents a visit from my long-gone mother—as she flies gracefully from the birdbath to our pool fence. She sits there staring at me, as though she knows me or, perhaps, as if we share a secret or a memory and, in that moment, I think, God is great, and an incredible sense of peace, calmness and joy washes over me.

I smile to myself as I turn to look towards my favourite flower—a cyclamen—that sits on the glass table across from me. Suddenly, as if to symbolise my appreciation of freedom, the dove flies away as decades of memories come flooding back to me, pulling me under and carrying me towards the place where it all began.

PART I

1

Cyclamen Girl

The cyclamen—named for the ancient Greek word for circle (*kyklaminos*)—is a beautiful perennial plant native to Europe and parts of the Mediterranean Basin. Cyclamens are well known for their ability to survive and thrive through all sorts of weather in harsh, and often unforgiving, conditions.

Springtime was always so warm and beautiful in Marjeyoun where I was born. A town with only a few thousand people, Marjeyoun still had many schools and a college, a hospital, a Red Cross centre, a hotel, social clubs and a cinema.

Marjeyoun means 'Meadow of Springs'—named for the fifty-four springs found in the area—and it is surrounded by gorgeous expanses of woods, mountains and meadows and carpeted greenery. Most beautiful of all are the wildflowers, including the star of them all, the cyclamen. So strong and resilient, the cyclamen's subterranean bulb sets up deep roots (so it can survive all year round), and stays perfectly camouflaged and safely hidden until spring arrives and it can bloom again.

In Marjeyoun, the cyclamen is called Skukaa and when I was still an infant, my mother, Raifa, began calling me '*Em Skukaa*' (Mother of Cyclamen) because I was so drawn to the cyclamen plants around our home. One of my family's fondest memories of me as an infant was from when I had just begun to walk and, as though driven by a compulsion within my soul, I would toddle my way over to collect cyclamen flowers from the fields and woods surrounding our home. I would then hold these flowers like a baby, with great care and adoration. Unlike most toddlers, I wasn't interested in chocolates, sweets, treats, dolls or toys—it was the cyclamen that made my heart content. For as long as I can remember, I have been mesmerized by these intoxicatingly sweet and fragrant flowers and their enchanting beauty. More than that, though, I have always been drawn to the cyclamen's hearty resilience and ability to survive and bloom in the most adverse conditions.

In nearby Beirut, the cyclamen is called 'The Shepherd's Stick' because it resembles the stick similar to the kind many shepherds carry. This seems quite fitting as Jesus was a shepherd and I have always looked at Jesus and the cyclamen as symbols of love and hope. With the cyclamen's heart-shaped leaves and ability to withstand whatever the world throws at it, it's no wonder that it has always reinforced my faith that He has always had His hand in my life.

My mother was lovingly raised by my middle-class grandmother, Afifa, after my grandfather, Boutros, was tragically killed by bandits. Before my grandfather was killed, he and my grandmother devotedly saved one 24-carat solid gold coin (a gold lira) each year—hiding the coins in a metal box in their garden—and promising each other that the coins would be used toward the education of their children. When my grandfather was killed, my grandmother was thirty and pregnant with her fifth child and had four others under 10. Despite this seemingly impossible hardship, Afifa proudly provided for her two sons and three daughters, working tirelessly to tend their modest home on two acres, which was filled with numerous fruit trees and a large vegetable garden. She also baked bread for people in the area to support her family and used the fruits, vegetables, and bread to trade for other supplies. Even though she never asked for any financial support from others, she never surrendered to her situation and—through one means or another—kept the promise between her and my grandfather, ensuring all of her children received a good education.

Perhaps it was through watching my grandmother struggle to raise all of her children, and helping her as often as possible, that my mother grew up to be so sweet and humble with such a truly beautiful soul. Not only was she kind and loving and generous, my mother also grew into a petite beauty, with gorgeous brown eyes, full lips, and long, wavy dark-brown hair that tumbled softly over her clear olive skin. It made perfect sense that a tiny beauty like my mother caught the eye and, soon after, the heart, of my handsome father, Karim—even though he was nearly twenty years her senior.

Even though my father had been married previously and had fathered two children—my half-siblings—irreconcilable differences drove him and his first wife apart. In the end, though, everything worked out as he was still able to see his children regularly, but was also free return to Marjeyoun, where he eventually met, fell in love with and married my mother.

My father Karim, just like my grandfather Iskandar (whom I never had the chance to meet but have seen in photos), was quite a distinguished looking man. He had a tall and robust athletic stature with a light complexion, a full head of neatly-combed thick dark hair, and piercing green-blue eyes accentuated by a defined nose. He was a good-looking man who came from an upper-class family so he regularly wore smart suits with tailored waistcoats and neckties, which perfectly enhanced his image of being both graceful and in control. When he and my mother were together, his prominent stature nicely complemented her petite beauty and the two of them made quite a striking couple—not for the obvious reasons of their pleasant looks—but more for their personalities and energy. Even though my father came from a wealthy family and was an extremely attractive man, it was his deep faith and humble nature—that of a true gentleman—that my mother was drawn to. They connected on a level that made their deep love radiate outward to everyone, wherever they went. When the Second World War ended, my mother and father exchanged their vows, sincerely declaring they would be together until death parted them. Following an enormous wedding attended by 300 guests, they honeymooned in Beirut before returning to their home in Marjeyoun and settling in to raise a family.

My father was born in Bethlehem in the early 1900s. At the time, the economy there relied on tourism, agriculture and education and there were no borders between Lebanon, Syria, Palestine and Jordan. My father's parents were born in Lebanon and both came from wealthy families who owned many properties and businesses. My grandfather Iskandar was a pastor, based in Jerusalem, and the head of the Lutheran Church in four countries.

Not uncommon for the time, my father hailed from a large family of twelve children who all benefitted from high levels of education and who all developed respectable careers as doctors, engineers, business owners and a school principal. My father had a quick wit, a sharp mind and an insatiable hunger for all types of information and education. Therefore, it wasn't surprising that he not only obtained a degree in business from the American University of Beirut (AUB), but also went on to become a veterinarian and became fluent in both the written and spoken words of many languages.

So it was my father's love of animals that brought him and my mother to his beloved family home in Marjeyoun to work as a vet while he and my mother raised a family. Since my father harboured a sincere love of all animals, working as a vet was a natural vocation for him, and, as such, we were lucky that we had plenty of land to allow room for family pets, as well as animals that came to him for care.

My father's ancestral lands were extensive, with many estates covering hundreds of acres in the South of Lebanon. The land where our family home was built was known by locals as *Jannit Aden*, or 'Paradise of Eden', because it was renowned for the variety of unique fruit trees in our spectacular orchard. The lands were lush and green—populated with groves of pine forests and our famous fruit trees—with breathtaking vistas overlooking the rolling hills and valleys below and the snow-capped mountains visible beyond them. From my perspective, the distant towns dotting the landscape in the valleys always reminded me of clusters of beautiful doll houses. Everything in the area was lush, green and joyously beautiful—a perfect reflection of the joyous and beautiful life we lived there.

Thirty-five people worked on our estates and, from my earliest memories, our home was always open to family, friends, animals and even strangers. My father's beloved family home (which was an architectural masterpiece built in the mid-1800s by my paternal great-grandparents who were both born there and had loved the area) had whitewashed archways that encased an elongated dining table which was regularly filled with food and surrounded by visitors enjoying life, love, laughter, family, friendship and camaraderie. The rest of the main dwelling was constructed from sandstone with displays of pointed arches held up by a façade of Corinthian columns. There were six bedrooms, multiple living areas, a pool (also constructed out of stone) and welcoming fountains that glistened pristinely in the sunlight at the entrance.

It was a warm and inviting place, brimming with the joy and laughter of good health and a loving family.

Following a seemingly well-constructed two-year plan, my brother Antoine arrived two years after my parents said their vows, followed—in two-year intervals—by my sister Nada and my brother Walid. Unfortunately, even the best-laid plans can be thwarted and thrown off course by nature—as they were when my mother then endured the heartbreak of two miscarriages—so it wasn't until several years after Walid was born that I finally made my way into the world.

According to my family, I was a beautiful baby. Perhaps my favourite photo of myself as a toddler is one where I'm wearing a light-pink dress as I joyously run through the surrounding gifts of nature—a cyclamen field peppered with perfectly-petaled white, light-mauve and light-pink flowers that have become such a potent symbol for my life.

As I said before, from the time I could walk, my love of the cyclamen made my family think of me as the 'Cyclamen Girl'. Ironically, just as the delicate appearance of the miraculous cyclamen flower hides its hearty and stoic roots, so would my creamy complexion, rosy cheeks and piercing green eyes hide the strength and solidarity of my soul through the unfolding destiny that fate had in store for my family.

2

Paradise Lost

The troubles that would eventually fall hard on my family began shortly before I was born, when the owner of an adjacent property to our family home—a lawyer and an obviously vengeful man—declared that the property line between our lands was wrong. He brazenly declared that he and his family would move the fence over, substantially reducing our acreage. My father was normally a peaceful man and did not wish to enter into a conflict, but he refused to allow the neighbour to move the property line. As a result of my father's refusal to comply with the neighbour's unreasonable demands, the neighbour pulled him into a lengthy court battle.

By the time I was born, the problems with the neighbour had escalated and signs of strain and struggle were beginning to tarnish the shine of our family's core. The expense of the lawyers my father had been forced to hire to defend his rights, his home, his property, and his family were taking a tremendous financial and emotional toll on everyone, even the workers on our property. During a particularly difficult month where our finances were stretched past their limit, my father was late in paying our workers' wages and our previously strong foundation of welcoming love and respect for everyone who visited our lands began to break down.

A lasting lesson my parents taught me while growing up is that we all have the ability to choose how we react in any given situation—with compassion and understanding or otherwise.

Unfortunately, many people don't have the ability to take a step back and see the bigger picture in stressful situations. They live their lives in a limited bubble, so-to-speak, where they only see what they want to see and believe what they want to believe and if somebody bursts that bubble, it turns their world on its head and they react in vindictive and destructive ways.

Such was the case for many of our workers when my father was late with their wages. They conveniently forgot about how well they had always been treated by our family and reacted by becoming angry and destructive.

Some of our workers chose to exact their pound of flesh from our family by stealing items from our home and outbuildings, while others chose to be destructive. My family's heart bled as we were forced to witness deliberately lit fires hungrily licking at the bark of our beloved ancient fruit trees and barns—soon reduced to cinders around our precious property.

My mother even witnessed one of our workers inexplicably hitting a pregnant cow with a stick as retribution for his anger at being paid late. Why the man thought inflicting pain on an innocent creature would alleviate the anger he felt is quite beyond my ability to understand, till this day.

The court case ran over a long and gruelling year and the devastation was dramatic in heart, mind, body and soul for all of us. Still, we kept our chins up and did our best to be happy and see the good in people, even in challenging situations.

One of the upsides of the ordeal was that during that year, my grandmother Afifa—who lived about two kilometres from our home—came to help look after my siblings and me, allowing my parents to focus on preparation and attendance at court. We loved having her around.

Endeavouring to alleviate some of the financial strain during the court case and pay off some debts, my mother sold half of her jewellery (gifted by my dad years before) and then decided to take a quick dressmaking course. She then began working as a tailor's assistant, earning a modest income to help pay our workers' wages hopefully to prevent any further damage or theft to our property.

The outcome of a lawsuit is often not based on the actual merits of the case, but is decided by who can afford the most convincing lawyers. Luckily for my family, in this instance truth and justice prevailed and the courts ruled in our favour. Victory, however, was bittersweet as my father won the battle, but lost the war and despite the legal triumph, by the end of it we were financially drained—asset rich but cash poor.

And we all felt the pain of the loss, even me and my siblings. It is remarkable how children, though young and seemingly oblivious, can still be so in tune with their parents' struggles. It wasn't until years later that my mother told me that when our neighbour first made his demands, my brother Walid—who was about seven—began digging a hole next to the property's fence. When the neighbour's wife asked what he was doing, he replied, 'I'm digging a grave for you and your husband because you made my dad very upset and you're going to make him lose all his money.' God bless the innocence of a child. We may not have comprehended the facts of the case or the true extent of the toll it took on our parents, but we children could sense the pain and struggle they were going through. Such callous cruelty and blatant ignorance affected all of us and, ultimately, changed the course of all of our lives.

3

A New Life

After the lawsuit, the deliberate destruction of our lands and loss of our workers, my mother declared it was time for a change. At the time, in Lebanon, it was considered dishonourable to sell your ancestral lands, so it was with heavy hearts that we abandoned our family home and left everything behind to move to Beirut to start a new life. After living on a spacious rural property, moving to the city was a big change for all of us. Fortunately, the humble two-bedroom, ground-floor apartment we moved into—in an average area of Beirut—blessed us with a large backyard as well as trees and woods close by. It was the 1960s and Beirut was not yet a crowded city, so the abundance of room and green spaces helped us adjust to our new lives.

The neighbours in our four-apartment building were also a blessing and they welcomed us with friendly smiles and cold drinks, coffee and sweets. This hospitality is a normal part of Lebanese cultural practices and it really did help us with the transition to our new environment. It didn't take long until we all became like one big family with all the mothers in the building visiting each other daily for morning coffee and to cook and share dishes with one another. They would also babysit each other's children and help and support each other where required. Our new neighbourhood was so full of love and care that it helped us settle into city life, especially our mum, who appreciated it all so much.

Our lives had radically changed, but where the sun rises there will always be a tomorrow. Even though I was under three when we were forced to leave our home in the South, I still experienced some residual trauma from our time there. I suppose some of the pain and suffering I'd witnessed had been locked away in my mind, protecting my young psyche from the deliberate destruction of our family's estate. Once we moved to Beirut, however, a key somehow materialised, found its way to the vault inside my mind and unlocked it.

The release of my toddler trauma materialised when my entire family, including my cousins, returned to Marjeyoun to visit my grandmother and watch my first-ever movie at the cinema. The little boy's name in the film was Bruno and early in the plot, thieves descended and kidnapped him as a fire blazed through his house. As the drama unfolded, I screamed and ran up to the big screen on the stage, yelling, 'No! No! Don't take the little boy. Please leave him alone!'

To me, this was a documentary of my life gone by—the barns burnt, the loss of our home, the loss of our security and safety.

No matter what anyone said, and despite the chastising looks I received, my pleas continued. 'Please! Please, God, don't let him take the boy. Bruno is a nice boy. Please! Please!' Of course, I was told to quiet down, but I wouldn't be silenced. 'No! No! We need to save the little boy. He's going to die! Look at him and the fire and everything,' I protested in my continuing hysteria, pronounced in my toddler lisp.

Suddenly, everyone in the cinema stood up and started clapping. As I was clearly inconsolable, the entire audience decided to hug me, not understanding that my heartbreak for the little boy in the film was triggering a childhood trauma I had witnessed with my own eyes—something I was also too young to truly comprehend. Who knew that simply watching a film could so easily trigger such pain hidden deep within a young child?

Despite the new beginning, filled with welcoming neighbours and love, our family was still struggling to maintain its legacy and regain a solid financial footing. It became too much of a financial strain to keep all of us under one roof, so my parents made a hard decision to send my two older brothers to a boarding school in a different region of Lebanon, while my sister went to a girls' boarding school in Jordan, where my paternal aunty was the principal. And so, it was with heavy hearts and questioning minds that my parents said farewell to three of their four children that year. Antoine and Walid would be able to come home on all of their school holidays, but Nada—being so far away—could only make the trip during the summer holiday.

My mother, with another child on the way, then began working as a dressmaker and my father managed to gain employment as a security guard, working for an employer who— years before—had been the beneficiary of my father's support.

My father was a brilliant and visionary man so it didn't take long for him to rent the unit next door, which meant we had the entire ground floor to ourselves; however, this wasn't just for our comfort, but rather as a business opportunity. Most of the buildings in our area were between two to seven levels—some connected to each other, others apart. Close by was a drycleaner, a butcher, a fruit and vegetable shop, a pharmacy, a newsagency, two convenience stores, a clothing shop, a hairdresser and more. Using his excellent economic foresight for bolstering our family's income, my father used space in the neighbouring unit to open up a local convenience store. This was also very welcome as it gave us a total of three bedrooms, two living areas, two bathrooms and two kitchens. My mother also helped in the shop when she was home with us because by this time, my fifth sibling, John, was about to enter the world.

On an extremely cold winter day in January 1966, my beautiful bouncing baby brother, John, brightened our lives by entering the world. Winter was bitterly harsh that year, so when John was a mere ten days old, we were running both the gas heater and the coal heater to thaw out the chill in our freezing bones and, tragically, our newest addition—such a tiny and fragile newborn—inhaled the carbon monoxide fumes of the heaters and nearly died. By the time anyone realised what had happened, he already looked dead.

Tiny baby John was blue and not breathing.

Time stood still as my innocent baby brother's lifeless body lay before us and, in grief-stricken horror, my grandmother wailed, 'The baby is dead. The baby is dead.'

And then time seemed to suddenly speed up and pandemonium broke out—screaming, wailing, chaos, helpless hands thrown in the air as shock and disbelief overtook us. With nearly all of us believing that this fledgling life had been lost to the world, my father refused to give up hope, attempted to and, incredibly, resuscitated my baby brother. Our disbelieving eyes witnessed a miracle as John started to breathe again and though at first there was only the faintest movement, soon there was no doubt that life still coursed through his veins.

My parents immediately rushed him to hospital where my baby brother was kept in an incubator for more than a month until he had completely recovered and miraculously—although it started out rocky—he survived and thrived as his part in the story of life was only just beginning.

Even before we knew he would survive the experience, my father (as the son of a pastor), baptised my baby brother the moment he regained breath.

Thank God and by His grace, John survived.

Since my mother now had two young children to care for while trying to help my father make ends meet, my loving and caring Grandmother Afifa—a simple lady with such a beautiful soul—would regularly come to visit us in Beirut to help my mother and care for my younger brothers and me. I was always happy to see her because she would sing us lullabies, was incredibly funny, and was renowned for being an amazing cook. We also had a couple neighbours with children of a similar age to me, so we all used to play together. These friendships kept us children occupied and content, but I loved my other siblings so much that I still missed them terribly while they were away at boarding school.

When I was around six, I cherished the times Walid would return from boarding school and I would get so excited as we planted corn together in our backyard unit for the next season's harvest. Those ears of corn, like me, thrived in our new environment, some of them growing up to my waist while others towered over me.

On his visits home, Antoine used to go bird hunting in the woods close by and it still makes me smile when I remember him insisting that I go with him to help. Instead of 'helping' though, I would run through the woods picking wild flowers—naturally my beloved cyclamen—and I was really no help at all, but Antoine still allowed me to join him on his expeditions.

One cold day when we returned from hunting, I did something extremely foolish and nearly had a very serious accident and, to this day, I still have no idea why I did it. My mother was outside cooking lamb kebabs on a rectangular metal grill over coal, known as a *manqal* and, with a stick, I started moving the burning coals around. One of the glowing coals dropped into my black gumboot and burned through my sock and into my flesh as the gumboot started melting. Horrified, my father rushed me to hospital as I screamed in unbearable pain. I still have a scar on the top of my left foot about three centimetres in diameter because, that one time, my childish curiosity got the better of me. Ever the type of people to bring light from dark, my parents made me feel better by telling me this made me unique and special, and I chose to believe it.

While we never regained the wealth we had once enjoyed, our finances improved with the ever-burgeoning business of our little convenience store. Due to this, when it was time for me to start school, my parents could afford to send me to the Lutheran primary school in Ashrafieh, about four kilometres from our home. The school was considered expensive—Sixty Lebanese Lira (equivalent to twenty American dollars) per month—but my parents wanted the best education for me, so they were thrilled that we could afford it. It was very exciting to ride to and from school each day on a yellow school bus—it reminded me of a bug-eyed monster—with twelve windows on each side of the vehicle and doors that swung open and I really enjoyed my days at school, learning and playing with the other children.

There was, however, one particular mishap during my school years that will stick with me forever and often reminds me of how strong and resilient I have been from a very young age. At one point, my mother was so consumed with keeping up with the hustle and bustle of day-to-day life that she forgot to pay my school fees. Sadly, for me, at the morning assembly, the principal announced that any student who had not paid their school tuition should remind their parents to do so.

I was a proud seven-year-old at the time and I took this to mean I had been unceremoniously dismissed by the principal because my fees hadn't yet been paid. So, holding my chin high, I left the school grounds—during a torrential downpour and without informing my parents I was leaving—and started trudging the four kilometres home.

Thoroughly soaked through and carrying my school bag over my shoulder, I walked down the hill until I reached The Low Bridge (locally known as *Jisr al-Wati*). I could see that the rains had all but washed out the road and the bridge was completely submerged and invisible. The river had also burst its banks to the point where cars were sliding across the road surface in the current and people considerably larger than me were being swept away and people were trying to climb on top of buses—either from the windows or via the metal ladder at the back—to save their lives.

I can't explain why I kept plodding on. The sensation—which felt as though I were floating on top of the water or walking on clouds—was akin to an out-of-body experience and felt like God was protecting me. While the deluge destroyed much of what it touched, inexplicably I survived the experience of crossing the submerged bridge and returned home unscathed. The moment my mother laid eyes on me, she erupted in a rage I had rarely seen in a woman I knew to be so kind, loving and gentle. Now that I am a mother myself, I understand that fear from seeing me arrive home unannounced and knowing I could have been killed was what triggered my mother's anger.

The following day when the waters had finally receded enough to allow safe passage, my mother returned with me to school (in a taxi) and marched straight into the principal's office. The principal—a tall, elegant lady in her forties—was mortified when my mother berated her for putting my life in jeopardy. Profuse apologies were forthcoming as news on the television and radio explained that lives had been lost due to the flood on the famed Low Bridge the day before.

I have no idea how I survived—a young, small girl—when so many others perished. Perhaps, I was emulating that wild cyclamen flower I identify with so profoundly, and I found a way to survive in the harshest and most extreme conditions. With a resilience so deep that it is only shown during the hardest of times, survival has clearly been ingrained in me since birth and my life has attested to this, time and again, as I grew up.

Happily, and despite the mishap at the bridge, my parents kept me in the same school until I concluded year seven and, from that point on, my mother was forever mindful of always paying my tuition fees on time. To help her remember, she kept an envelope of cash in her dresser drawer with the words SCHOOL FEES written in black capital letters and she took money out of it each month to ensure payment to the school. I was grateful as I really enjoyed school, particularly the creative arts of singing, dancing and acting.

I always looked forward to spending summer holidays at my grandma Afifa's home in the South. My grandmother was a profoundly humble woman—she never wore makeup or attempted to dye her long grey hair. She was proud of who she was and always joyous when surrounded by her family. Afifa was a glorious storyteller who, through use of her narratives, taught me truths about life, love and hope. Her wise words had a profound impact upon my life, so much so that I still recall and pass them on to my own children today.

I especially looked forward to helping her harvest the abundant fruits and vegetables from her beautiful gardens that bloomed as far as my eyes gaze could reach. One of the special jobs I shared with my grandma—something I still cherish in my memories— was picking the mulberries and walnuts from her trees. As I loved to wear white T-shirts, this always ended with my shirt, face, hands and legs in a dark purple mess of stains. My grandma would just smile and indulgently shake her head, even though she had to spend ages bleaching my shirts to get rid of the stains. Back in the day, she would bleach clothes by soaking them overnight in a mixture of plain yoghurt mixed with lemon juice and then scrub them with soap the next day. It was a lot of work, but still, she would always smile and laugh at the sight of me.

My grandma was an absolutely amazing cook, preparing wholesome meals (like zucchini and vine leaves stuffed with rice and meat, as well as chicken or vegetarian dishes) on a round clay barbecue (known as *manqal teen*) that she'd made herself. Grandma always proclaimed that slow cooking was the best and she would often begin preparing meals in the wee hours of the morning and then cooking them all day on the manqal teen. Her small house was always fragrant with odours of saj (flat) bread, labneh, cheese and jams, all of which were, naturally, homemade.

One of my favourite pastimes during those summers was picnicking twice a week with grandma's friends at our family's abandoned property. While many would think it would be hard on the heart to return to a place that held such sorrow for our family, I loved being back where so many wonderful memories also existed, mixed in with the sadness. We would undertake the twenty-minute journey on foot and then spread ourselves out under the remaining trees where I would entertain everyone. I would frequently dance and sing and play the Lebanese drum (*derbake*) for the audience of women and make my grandmother and her friends dance with me. I was ever the entertainer and loved both the attention and the praise and laughter.

Aside from tending to her gardens and fruit trees, cooking and enjoying picnics with her friends, my grandmother was also a gifted potter who crafted stunning pots and other creations— for her enjoyment and to supplement her income. Much like her days as a young widow, she was never one to ask for financial help, so selling her pots to willing customers afforded her a means of retaining her independence. My grandmother was as clever and resourceful as she was loving and humble, so nothing ever went to waste if it could be helped.

Grandma Afifa had a small pool at her home with the edges around it adorned with her stunning pottery planters that were equally as gorgeous as the blooms which sprouted from them. My siblings and cousins loved to swim in the pool, but since she had no salt or chlorine to keep it fresh, we had to change the water every week. Not to let anything go to waste, when the water was ready to be refreshed, we emptied it in her gardens and planters.

Of course, the summers rarely went by without some sort of childhood shenanigans or mishaps. We were children after all and bound to get into scrapes here and there. I recall one such incident when two of my cousins enthusiastically leaped into the pool to cool down on a particularly hot day, but I decided to get a drink of water from the old tap at the corner of the pool instead. No sooner had my lips kissed the welcoming liquid than a swarm of bees descended on me from all directions and I was stung on every exposed area of skin. Apparently, the bees took offense when I boldly ventured too close to their flowers and decided that a full-scale attack was necessary to teach me to pay better attention. My face was peppered with quick-swelling, angry marks and I was quite sure it would be impossible to tolerate—let alone survive—such excruciating pain.

Screaming like a banshee, I ran to my grandmother, angrily wailing that I had been the victim of an unprovoked attack. Of course, my grandma, with great wisdom and finesse, immediately started cutting small pieces of fresh garlic to administer to each of my acid-like inflictions. Fortunately for me, these were not venomous bees and, after my grandmother's ministrations, the swelling began to subside the following day. Having recovered somewhat, I immediately insisted that I wanted to return to the safety of Beirut. Despite my love for the country and my roots, I was definitely a city girl at heart.

Notwithstanding the incident of the bees mistaking me for Winnie the Pooh trying to steal their honey, visits to my grandma's remained something I always looked forward to. She was an incredible woman who taught me so much and always filled me with an indescribable and joyous love.

4

Family

My three eldest siblings—Antoine, Nada, and Walid—all went to boarding schools and were all studying three languages (Arabic, English and German). They were all intelligent and did well in school and my parents were very proud of all of them. Antoine was rapidly becoming an adult—a time of life that brings with it both opportunities and challenges—and was developing into a strappingly handsome young man of medium stature with neat dark-brown hair and brown eyes. He was very fit and had a magnetism that attracted people to him. Upon completing school and with decisions to make, Antoine decided to become an electrical engineer and so he pursued a degree at a Lebanese university. My parents were very happy with his decision because since he'd been a young boy he'd always been interested in science, especially the invention of electricity.

Nada was also growing up quickly and, when she returned from overseas at seventeen, after she completed her studies, she decided to undertake a diploma in the city for office and secretarial skills. Nada was beautiful, with brown eyes, a delicate nose and full lips, all complemented by a gorgeous mane of golden-brown hair. She turned heads wherever she went, but didn't seem to notice because despite having studied and lived overseas, she remained extremely innocent, unsuspecting and sincere.

By the age of eighteen, Nada was beginning to attract would-be suitors, but my father was quick to tell them that she was far too young to think about marriage and that she was concentrating on her studies for now. However, one of these *admirers*—a particularly handsome twenty-one-year-old who worked for the Beirut Police Internal Security Services Division—would not be dissuaded by my father's firm assertions.

The moment Nada crossed his path, his mind, and his heart were set on having this woman and ensuring she became his wife. Initially, he came to our home with his parents to propose marriage, but my father was still of the opinion that Nada was too young to marry and politely told this hopeful young man not to open the subject again.

By this time, Nada had finished her secretarial course and she began a placement in one of the local firms. Her amorous admirer discovered where she was doing her training and, one day just before close of business, went to her workplace. The receptionist called my sister to advise her that there was a gentleman who needed to see her urgently.

Somewhat surprised after having seen this man only three times in her entire life, Nada very reasonably asked what he was doing there. The young man had a clever and deceptive plan in place. With feigned sincerity and concern in his voice, he told her, 'Your aunt Ratiba is in the hospital and your parents asked me to come here and take you to see her.' As my aunty didn't have children, she was someone we considered to be a second mum, and she cared for us like a mother. Aunty Ratiba (who lived in a unit in Ashrafieh) had met this young man twice at our home, and she had really liked him and wanted Nada to marry him one day.

My sister was extremely upset to hear about the misfortune of our aunt and, even though she was understandably confused about why this man was her messenger, she agreed to go with him anyway, not thinking there was more to it than what he told her. A taxi was waiting at the front of the office building.

Innocently and unquestioningly, Nada clambered inside. Only once the car started moving did my sister query which hospital our aunt was in and the man had a ready answer for her. 'She is in Ashrafieh.' Accepting his answer, my sister remained silent until she suddenly realised the driver was heading in the wrong direction. 'This isn't the way to the hospital!' she burst out. His reply was a curt and chilling laugh, followed by an even more chilling statement, 'You're coming with me to my parents' house in the Bekaa Valley.'

Terrified of the fate that awaited her, Nada began screaming at the top of her lungs, but her futile complaints were completely ignored by both her soon-to-be fiancé and the driver.

Undeterred in their mission, they told my sister, after about forty minutes, that they would be stopping at a payphone and she would have to call my father to inform him that she had eloped. My poor sister later told me that she was hysterical and that she couldn't stop crying—to the point of choking and almost vomiting. She was incapable of making the call herself, so the young man called my father and broke the news to him personally.

My father was furious. His usually calm and rational demeanour was replaced by shock and then fury. He shouted at the man that he had abducted his daughter. It was not long after the phone call that my poor father started to feel unwell, which was soon followed by a heart attack, which he survived. Not long after his heart attack came the onset of diabetes—all, I'm sure, due to the stress of my sister being forced to marry against her will.

Once again, I found myself in a situation where I could do little except stand back helplessly and feel tormented by my poor parents suffering and crying, their hearts breaking as they were unable to comprehend how easy it was for a man to just abduct their daughter and force her to marry him.

Back in those days, our culture dictated that if a girl was taken by somebody and asked (or forced) to marry, she was unable to return to her parents, so my sister had no choice except to marry this young man who was deeply in love with her. It didn't matter that she barely knew him and didn't share his amorous desires, she now belonged to him and that was just the way it was. Soon after they were wed, my sister and her husband moved into an apartment reasonably close to our home where she gave birth to a beautiful baby girl, Jo. Nada was now a wife and a mother to a man who—while physically attractive and humorous—was very tense due to the nature of his employment with the police and a need to carry a firearm at all times.

During my school holidays in 1968, my brother-in-law came home in the morning after working night shift. He had breakfast with his wife and four-month-old baby girl, showering them both with hugs and kisses, and then headed to the bedroom for some much-needed sleep in preparation for his next night shift.

My sister was in the kitchen making a bottle of milk for the baby, when suddenly she heard an almighty bang—the sound terrified her because it was so close and she ran to the bedroom, fearing the bang had, in fact, been a gunshot. She arrived at the bedroom to find her husband bleeding from the chest. Nada started hysterically screaming for help as she knew that her husband was critically injured and needed immediate medical attention. The neighbours next door heard the shot too and Nada's cries for help, and they rushed over immediately and called the ambulance, which arrived quickly and took my brother-in-law straight to hospital.

Given my sister's rather unusual courtship and marriage, there were some who almost instantly accused Nada of shooting her husband. Fortunately, my brother-in-law was able to dispel this terrible accusation and advise the authorities that nothing more sinister had occurred than an accidental discharge of his weapon while cleaning it—an awful and tragic accident.

Even though I was only nine-years old at the time, I recall this as if it were yesterday. Nada and my parents (who closed the shop that day) went to the hospital to support Nada's husband and be there for him. My grandma was looking after my younger brothers and me, and a group of four or five policemen came to our home and asked for someone to take them through my sister's apartment so they could collect evidence and investigate the incident. My grandmother—who was in her seventies—was unable to go up all the stairs to my sister's fifth-floor apartment, so I volunteered.

I opened the apartment door and, as the police went in, I followed them into the bedroom. They put on their gloves, pulled the blood-stained sheets off the bed, took photos and wrote notes. It was a horrific scene to watch and I was deeply shocked and traumatised and couldn't stop crying, but I peered between the police to see what I could. The mattress had blood everywhere and a hole where the bullet had travelled through. There was gun oil and a cloth resting on the right bedside table. The police should not have allowed me to be there. My innocence was being stripped away, but they were ambivalent towards violence and the protection of the innocent—a precursor to the conflict that was, in time, going to consume our beautiful country.

It was just as well for my sister that her husband was able to clarify what had happened, because fourteen days after he accidentally shot himself, he succumbed to his injuries and died. Despite the tumultuous path the union between my sister and brother-in-law followed, my family had grown to accept and embrace my sister's husband and his death was shocking news for my sister and our families. The grief of losing him turned our world upside down and was compounded by the news that Nada was pregnant again—devastating us even more that her second child would never meet their father.

The funeral took place a week later in the serene and beautiful mountain area of our homeland, in my late brother-in-law's hometown. The whole family attended and a band performed a curious mixture of melancholy music to mourn a young man's death mixed in with upbeat melodies meant to celebrate his youth. I will never forget when his coffin was being carried out towards his grave and my sister walked underneath it. Naturally curious about it, I asked why Nada walked beneath his coffin and I was told it was because my sister was pregnant by this man and the tradition of the town was for the pregnant widow to walk underneath the coffin to signify that the baby belonged to him.

It's difficult to fathom how my sister coped in those days as she had to grow up so quickly and was faced with numerous adult situations and challenges at such a young age. There she was—so young and pregnant with her second child while still caring for an infant—dressed head to toe in widow's black and forced to march under the corpse of her husband. I have no idea how she remained so strong.

After enduring this tragedy, my sister was left with no option but to move in with us and, seven months later, our number was to increase by one as my sister gave birth to a second beautiful baby girl. Nada mourned and wore widow's black for nearly six years before she was given a beautiful chance at a new life filled with real, romantic love. When her future husband, Gary, finally worked up the nerve to court her, Nada was working at an engineering firm while enjoying the blessings of raising her two beautiful daughters. She was still young and beautiful and, after all that she'd been through, was more deserving than most of a chance at a new and romantic life.

Gary managed a travel agency in the city and, as part of his work, he travelled back and forth between Lebanon and Europe on a regular basis. His family lived in our area and he had been keeping a watchful eye over my sister for years, often wondering about her suitability as a bride-to-be.

He finally asked her out for coffee and their chemistry was instantaneous and palpable. The romance was a whirlwind and three months after sharing a cup of coffee, they became engaged. Three months after that, they were married and they moved into a large three-bedroom apartment with Nada's two daughters about three blocks from our home. We were all very happy to see Nada in love and happily settled in with such a wonderful man.

By the time my sister Nada had moved in with us, my brother Walid had finished high school and decided to further his education at university with a course in law and political sciences. In my young eyes, Walid was very much like our father in his mannerisms and demeanour—often adopting appropriate etiquette for any situation. Walid, through astute observation and an innocent eagerness to follow in my father's footsteps, emulated my father's perfect table manners and elegant use of utensils. This aspect of sophistication somehow completely escaped me in my youth and I used my hands to eat almost everything, only reluctantly using cutlery when coaxed by my parents. Walid— also like my father—was popular and known for his kindness, politeness and respect for others, all traits he had learned from our parents that were reinforced by his boarding school. During his summer holidays while at university, Walid worked casual jobs to maintain his independence and I remember that he was always generous with the extra cash he made. During one such summer, he invited me to a fancy French restaurant for lunch as a treat to celebrate the end of the school term and reward me for achieving the highest mark in Maths (something that, honestly, wasn't too difficult as Maths was, by far, my favourite subject).

I was so excited by Walid's invitation, that I rushed to get ready as soon as he suggested it, wearing a baby-pink dress my mum had made for me. It was unusual for me to wear a dress as I was more comfortable in shorts or pants, but this was a special occasion and I was determined to look the part. At the time, we did not have the privilege of dining out much—most of our food was cooked at home—but on rare occasions, Mum would buy us falafel or chicken from the local takeaway shops. She used to tell us it was better and healthier to eat homemade food, but, despite the truth of it, I believe this was more due to our limited finances than anything else. We headed to the area known as Al-Hamra—an affluent area in downtown Beirut—renowned for its upmarket lifestyle, art galleries, hotels, fine restaurants, French-style cafes on footpaths, theatres and trendy boutiques. Al-Hamra was diverse and dynamic—a hub of multiculturalism with foreign diplomats, bankers and businessmen—with a trendy and vibrant atmosphere and it was always full of celebrities, media and press. I loved it there! My dad would often take me to a church in the area and we would regularly visit my dad's sister and extended family in the area.

I was extremely excited as we left our house in a taxi and drove past the museum area to arrive at the restaurant within twenty minutes. The hostess led us to our table and rushed over to my side to pull out my chair. 'Mademoiselle,' she said as she gestured for me to take a seat. She then placed a crisp white napkin on my lap and I couldn't stop smiling as Walid ordered a Pepsi for me and an orange juice for himself. I took ages to read the menu because there were so many unique dishes to choose from and I have always loved good food, so part of me secretly wished Walid would allow me to order and try the entire menu.

Finally, I decided to order a classy version of a beef burger with salad, pickles and hot chips, and Walid ordered fish. We chatted before the meals arrived. Walid has always been wise and I remember that as we chatted about school, friendships and life in general, he gave me some good advice and reminded me that nothing is impossible when we put our minds to it. He encouraged me to make the most of every opportunity, to give my absolute best when facing all challenges head on and he reminded me of the sacrifice our parents had made, so that I should always be thankful for the education gifted to me.

Little did I know that the words he spoke that day would stay with me for a lifetime, that those small echoes of encouragement would help shape my character and would stay with me through many of the tough years that were to follow.

The food arrived while we chatted and I was so hungry and excited. I drizzled ketchup on the chips and added the salad, pickles, mayonnaise and ketchup to the meat. I remember how much I wanted to impress my brother—to show him that I could use a fork and knife properly (just like he and my dad did) and that I could appear grown up and graceful. I picked up my knife and fork, but as I was cutting the burger, disaster struck when the meat suddenly slipped out from between the bun, shot across the table and onto the floor. I immediately turned purple with embarrassment and started to tear up as other patrons began staring at me. I had tried so hard to demonstrate good etiquette but had, instead, failed miserably.

But then humour saved the moment as Walid started laughing loudly and said, 'You know, you can eat a burger with your hands, silly. There's no restaurant in the world that's too fancy for that.' He then picked up the patty off the floor, called the waiter over and ordered another burger for me. It made my day! Walid's ability to make it such a non-issue made me feel completely comfortable during my first time in a sophisticated restaurant, and it made me love him even more than I already did. Ironically, to this day, when in public, I still endeavour to eat burgers with a knife and fork— perhaps as testament of my ongoing development of this skill.

5

Big Dreams

One day, while reading the paper, my father looked up at me and excitedly proclaimed, 'Chadia! There is a competition for children between the ages of seven and eleven to win a trip to Nicosia in Cyprus.' He went on to read out that the draw would be at eleven o'clock on Sunday morning, two weeks before Christmas. It was to take place on the grounds next to Saint George and Phoenicia hotels, close to Beirut Central District. What a dream it would be to win a trip to Cyprus, I thought. I had never flown before, let alone left the country, so the idea of travelling to a foreign land was incredibly mystical and enchanting. Oh, the things I would see and the people I would meet!

Even though being there in person was required to win the competition and we had no car at the time, once my dad told me about the competition, I was determined to win it. I resolved that I would find a way to get there.

Perhaps it was wishful thinking or perhaps subliminal messaging to myself, but the night before the draw I had a vivid dream—which, to this day I believe was more like a prophetic vision—assuring me that I would indeed be victorious. The Virgin Mary stood before my window wearing the most beautiful, flowing white silk gown with exquisite lace detailing around the neckline, and in her arms was baby Jesus. They both glowed, but the brightest light surrounded Jesus himself and I recall being overwhelmed with a simultaneous sense of awe and immense peace. Mary looked kindly upon me as I lay in my bed and her joyful smile told me everything. It astonished me how powerful her non-verbal communication was and how incredible this dream—or should I say vision—was.

'Chadia! Chadia...Get up!' I awoke the next morning to the deep, booming voice of my brother Antoine as he stood before me announcing, 'You must get up! You only have twenty minutes before we need to leave.' I rubbed my eyes as I sat up in bed and checked the alarm clock. I thought I must still be dreaming because Antoine was almost never up before noon on Sundays and he was not only up at 8 am, but was already dressed and ready to go.

With the world still slightly hazy and my mind spinning with excitement, I jumped out of bed and quickly chose my favourite black jeans with white stitches, a white shirt and a black hooded jumper. To complete the ensemble and without hesitation, I reached into the bottom of my closet for my glossy red shoes—a beloved gift from my sister, Nada. Not only did the shoes resemble Dorothy's in the Wizard of Oz, but I was also hopeful that they would bring me the luck I needed.

In a flash, Antoine and I raced to the street to catch a taxi. It was quite a chilly December morning as we jumped into the car and cheerfully asked the driver to take us straight to the competition venue. As we drove, Antoine assisted me with completing the form from the newspaper clipping with all my contact details and as we arrived at the competition, and Antoine paid the driver, I stepped out of the taxi and looked out at a sea of people. I could feel the excitement of the thousands of people who had gathered for the momentous announcement. It was palpable and it enveloped me, vibrating against me like an electric hug.

Antoine grabbed my hand so that we didn't lose each other as we began navigating our way through the crowd. The entire area was adorned with Christmas decorations as far as the eye could see—coloured tinsel, mistletoe, lights, bells and ornaments hanging across buildings and heritage sites. As we worked our way through the crowd, I could hear the whispers that Santa would be arriving soon.

The event was sponsored by Middle East Airlines (MEA) and the competition was good publicity and very successful marketing for the large airline. There were TV broadcasters from all Lebanese stations, including foreign broadcasters covering the spectacle and the MEA staff were dressed as elves and were collecting the clippings and placing them into large red bags. Parents and children chatted eagerly all around me and everyone was so cheerful and hopeful, as though the power of Christmas miracles was about to be bestowed on every one of us.

After a brief moment where I held my entry to my heart, said a little prayer, and visualised my success, I placed my clipping in one of the bags—a Christmas sack that was full of the hopes and dreams of thousands of children.

Parents and children alike, dressed in Christmas colours— vibrant reds, whites as pure as snow and glorious greens— surrounded us and Christmas tunes were being belted out by a big brass band. It was magical and I was thoroughly enchanted as sweets and chocolates rained from above and from every direction into the crowd. I thought briefly, *"Is this what heaven is like?"* This was one of the most memorable moments of my childhood and it was permeated by a sense of surreal and immense joy, peace and love.

Children's laughter echoing through the streets was suddenly interrupted by a loud chopping noise that drowned out the boisterous and festive crowd, leaving us all to stare upward in a silent state of awe. I looked up to see a helicopter above us and I couldn't believe my eyes when, right above us, Santa Claus began descending down a rope. With innocent, childlike wonder, I imagined if it was the very same rope Santa used to descend from his sleigh down chimneys while delivering children's Christmas gifts.

Santa, with his little group of MEA helpers stood atop a towering balcony of an elegant and beautiful heritage building, surrounded by the large red bags from which the fifty lucky children would be selected to make their Christmas dreams come true. My breath hitched and my heart beat wildly each time Santa drew a name from a sack and a roar of cheers erupted from the crowd. By the time they had reached forty-nine winners, Antoine became despondent. 'Chadia, I think we should go now. There's no chance you can win. There are thousands and thousands of entries and only one last draw left.' I had to admit that even my belief was waning. Reluctantly, I agreed with my brother but asked him to let me fix my shoe clip before we glumly headed home.

As I leaned down and reached for my shoe clip, I began one last silent prayer, but before I could even finish praying, I heard Santa's deep voice announcing my full name and then joyfully saying, 'Bravo, Chadia! Bravo!'

My name had been drawn!

I leapt up as if I had grown wings and was ready to fly to the stage. Antoine was so thrilled for me, he carried me atop his broad and sturdy shoulders, marching through the crowd and repeatedly exclaiming, 'You did it, Chadia! You won!' It was such a whirlwind as the cheering crowd separated for us to reach the building where Santa and his helpers stood.

I went up to the balcony to be congratulated by Santa himself and, as I looked down at the crowd with tears in my eyes, the joy that filled me at that moment was indescribable.

Following our names being drawn, all the winning children were rushed off for the formalities of photos for our passports (which would be ready a couple days later) and the completion of documents—including parental consent forms approving the adventure we were about to embark on.

The trip to Cyprus was scheduled for one week before Christmas and it was to be my first-ever flight, accompanied by forty-nine other children and ten flight attendants to care for us. We were to have the entire flying cylindrical sleigh to ourselves and, even more amazing, the airline's colours were, in fact, Christmas colours. The plane was white with red and green in the middle, and a Lebanese cedar was at the top of the tail with a couple of wide red lines.

Interestingly, the Lebanese flag has the same colours as the airline had with two thin red bands (symbolising the blood shed for liberation) sandwiching a thick white band (representing peace, snowy mountains and purity) with a green cedar tree, the symbol of Lebanon (representing eternity, steadiness, happiness and prosperity) in the middle of it.

We were all so excited that we sang and danced for the entire fifty-minute flight.

How stunning it was to me to visit another country as ancient and spectacular as my own. Our tour included a visit to the president's palace, to some ruins and to too many icons of historical significance to count. We dined at the best restaurants, stayed in the most luxurious of hotels and received gift packages on arrival with all the latest toys and gadgets.

Sadly, it was all over so quickly—almost before I blinked—but when we returned to Beirut the next day, I was astonished to discover that we had all been on national television and in most of the newspapers. It was all so magical and I felt like the luckiest girl in the world.

This experience really was a dream come true—the experience of a lifetime—one I believed would be always at the forefront of my memories.

But I had no idea how it would pale in significance to the experiences that still awaited me.

6

Growing Up in Beirut

Life was simple for me as a child in the sixties, growing up in our little section of the city of Beirut with so many other children.

There were no computers or electronic games back then, but we were never bored as we ran around playing together and dreaming up new games to entertain ourselves. We used what we had and our options were only as limited as our imaginations. We derived indescribably joy from simply being children playing together.

Back then our world was easy and light-hearted. We didn't stress about the worries of our parents and we didn't dwell on the cares and stresses of the world beyond our block—our playground.

I was a tomboy growing up. Most of my friends were boys and I loathed wearing dresses or skirts—preferring, instead, to wear pants or shorts because it was easier to climb trees and scale fences in them. I was sometimes endearingly called "The Monkey" because of my prowess at climbing. I often enjoyed participating in games and activities that some people considered boisterous and unbecoming of a young lady (It was the sixties, after all, and girls were expected to behave in certain ways), but I loved rough games and noisy activities. I beat the boys at playing marbles and was one of the best at fighting with wooden sticks in war games. On the flip side of that, I still enjoyed more feminine activities, such as dancing and singing, so despite my tomboy nature, there was still a feminine side to me that continued to emerge more and more as I grew older.

One of my favourite games as a child was 'Apricot Seeds Pit' which involved apricot seeds and targeting skills. We would dig a small, shallow hole in the ground and clean it of debris to make sure it was tidy, then we'd throw apricot seeds at the hole with the aim of trying to make the seeds bounce out. If we hit two seeds (an even number), we would leave the seeds in the hole, but if we hit one or three (an odd number of seeds), whoever hit them would collect the seeds. We would all take turns throwing seeds in the pit and the winner would be the person who collected the most seeds.

Sometimes my tomboyish ways made me a little too competitive and boisterous, but I didn't care. I loved apricots, but I loved our game even more, so I would beg my mum to buy them—my ulterior motive obviously to build up my store of apricot seeds! I used to collect the seeds after eating apricots at home, or after winning a round of the game, and hide them in plastic bags underneath the stairs near the water meters in our building. One day, one of the boys in the area found out where I was hiding my seeds and took two bags of seeds and started running. I ran after him, grabbed him from behind, pushed him to the floor, punched him and told him I would really hurt him the next time if he stole my seeds again.

Another time, I felt the need to fight to stand up for someone else other than myself—my friend Elaine (who lived close by and had lost her sight in one eye due to an accident when she was a toddler). Elaine and I loved to play cards and watch television together and I often invited her to come and play with me and my other friends—the rougher and rowdier ones—but she usually refused.

One day, however, Elaine finally agreed to come join us outside. I was so excited for her to come and play, but she was unaccustomed to most of our games and a little slow to pick them up, so I asked my friends to be patient with her and give her a chance. Almost everyone agreed, but one boy threatened that he would quit if Elaine continued to play. I beseeched him to give her a chance, but when he again refused, my temper got the better of me and I cursed him and called him names. I was not going to allow this injustice to occur. He was being unkind to my friend.

Angered, he threatened us with a stick and then, as I fled holding Elaine's hand, the boy started throwing marbles and stones at us. Even angrier, I stopped, picked up a stone and retaliated by hitting the boy square in the forehead. I had a good arm! He returned fire and his stone found its mark, leaving me bleeding from the forehead. I used my shirt to wipe away the blood as my other friends gathered around us to try to calm us down—both my face and the boy's were bloodied from wounds—and we were both clearly upset. But then, to my utter surprise, the entire group started holding hands. One by one, this large group of children joined in a demonstration of peace, unity and welcome and everything changed in an instant. Even the boy who had instigated the fracas proclaimed that Elaine was now part of our group and was welcome to play with us.

Ultimately, this conflict actually served to bring us closer together as friends and I still have a scar and small indentation on the right-hand side of my forehead as testament to this event, which I fondly refer to as a 'mark of friendship.'

Our little group was tight-knit and although we had a lot of fun together, we also got ourselves into a few situations that our parents would not have been happy to hear about.

There was an old lady, Em-Daher (which means Daher's Mother), who lived in a small house across from the vacant block where we used to play after school. We'd always try to be polite and respectful to her, often greeting her happily with, 'Good afternoon, Em-Daher! How's your day? Hope you're feeling well today.' Despite our efforts—we were exuberant youths and were often noisy while playing outdoors across from her home—Em-Daher did not exactly enjoy the presence of children and would often shout and throw buckets of water at us. She also threatened to tell our parents if we did not stop and leave, and it appeared that nothing would placate her and her dislike for us. However, with few spaces between the high-rise apartments and other buildings in our area, there were few options left where we could play and entertain ourselves after school. Homes were generally small and rather cramped, so we continued to frequent the vacant lot to play after school, much to Em-Daher's displeasure.

Perhaps all Em-Daher's affection was focused on her garden—which was truly beautiful—an oasis full of roses, jasmine, and lots of gorgeous white lilies. The sweet fragrance from the garden permeated the area and enchanted me.

Frustrated by Em-Daher's constant onslaught of verbal abuse and disruption of our playtime fun, three of my male friends and I decided to do something regrettable and quite out of character. One night after she had retreated for the evening, we clambered over her white picket fence, walked to her patch of flourishing lilies, cut some from their stems and stole them. We then took the lilies to a nearby cemetery and, relying on moonlight alone, scaled the high stone walls that surrounded it and carefully placed one cut white lily on each grave—paying our respects before moving on to the next. We continued to do this over a span of several nights—becoming progressively more comfortable and recklessly louder with each raid—until we had completely depleted Em-Daher's garden of all its lilies.

And although we were quite surprised that we weren't caught, once we had completed our "mission," we were loath to return to play at the vacant block and found a new area to play. While I now understand that what we did was entirely wrong, at the time, I countered and justified in my mind that we had actually done something respectful and decent in expressing our sympathy and respect for those who had passed by placing lovely flowers on their graves. As children we were brave and lacked fear; however, I now find myself afraid and nervous on the rare occasions that I visit a cemetery.

In fact, one of my favourite holidays as a child was Saint Barbara's Day, which occurs on the 4th of December every year (and is similar to Halloween, but it's religious). My friends and I would dress in costumes and go Trick or Treating from one home to the next and everyone was in truly festive spirits during those evenings. We would sing as a group while one of our friends played the derbake (the drum) and I belly danced in the middle of the circle holding a girl's straw basket with flowers on the side to collect the sweets and goodies. Afterwards, we would go back home and divide the sweets amongst us. We always did all of this without any parental supervision, even though we typically went door knocking between six and seven in the evening. It was very safe at the time, so much so that we never locked our doors, not even because we were living in the city, as everyone in our area looked out for one another and we all lived in harmony.

Despite such acts of recklessness and enjoying games and fun with my friends, I never lost sight of my sense of responsibility. I was raised with a sense of duty and took pleasure in helping with the household chores.

I loved to help in any way possible—that's what family is all about. The night before school, I would prepare what was needed for myself and my two younger brothers. I organised all the uniforms, including socks, hats and folded hankies, and would place them all on our large couch for the next day. In the mornings, I would also prepare lunches for my brothers and me to take to school. I enjoyed the responsibility as I felt it was a way to make a positive contribution in return for the wonderful life and love I had been given by my parents and siblings.

I also enjoyed helping out with the washing and, because I was so short, I used a stool to reach the top of the washing machine to load the laundry. Then I would make up fun games and sing while took the clean laundry to the top of the terrace to peg it out onto the line. Often while I pegging it out, I would see our neighbour's son, Kamil, and we would chat about this and that, as I happily continued my chores. Kamil was a bit of a jokester and I remember he once convinced me that his older brother, who lived in the United States, had bought a red car that could fly. My vivid imagination and innocent curiosity made me very gullible, and I believed everything he said. I couldn't wait to dash to school the next day and tell every one of my friends about the flying car. I discovered later that week that he was joking and he never let me forget how easy I was to fool.

In October, my mother would leave to go south and supervise workers harvesting olives on our lands, which still held plenty of olive trees. It would take approximately one month for the olives to be harvested and then pressed for products such as olive oil and soap that we regularly sold to our clients. At the end of the season, my mum would bring home a whole year's supply of olives, oil and soap. It was a necessity for her to be away and during that time, most of the responsibility for the household fell to me as my father was working all day in the shop.

While my mum was preparing to leave for the South, I somehow decided that I wanted to take on more responsibility by helping with the cooking, so I told my mum that I would like to cook three meals that week while she helped Dad in the convenience store. Mum bought all the ingredients for me and asked if I needed any help, but being supremely confident, I, of course, declined her offer.

On the first day I decided to cook spaghetti. I cooked the meat and made the sauce from tomatoes and tomato paste, then I broke the spaghetti in half and added it to the Bolognese sauce and mixed it all in. I could hardly contain my excitement as I served it up for dinner, but no one else seemed to share my excitement. Turned out, the spaghetti remained raw and as hard and crunchy as wood.

On the second day I made *kibbeh bilaban*, which is made with fine burghul, meatballs and garlic yoghurt sauce. I soaked the burghul for an hour then mixed it with the minced lamb to make the outer kibbeh shells. I shaped them into hollow balls and then stuffed them with the meat, onions and pine nuts, closed up the balls and placed them in the cooked yoghurt sauce. Again, I was so excited to serve everyone, but it was another disaster—the meat inside the kibbeh was completely raw!

On the third day I fried fish. I thought that, surely, this was a foolproof method. I washed the numerous small fish and heated the oil in a large frying pan on the gas stove. The oil was very hot and the fish were very wet so the moment I placed the fish in the pan, the boiling oil splashed me like an active volcano. I ended up running around the house screaming like a banshee from the burning pain.

In my life, I have always given myself the opportunity to do things three times—in Lebanon we say, 'The third time is the fixed or final time.' The fish incident sealed the deal for me—that was my last attempt at cooking for a long time.

7

Loss of Innocence

I was only eleven years old when my father was in his late sixties and I was sometimes teased by other children who said he was really my grandfather and not my father. Although I shrugged off these taunts, they did hurt. Despite being so young, I would often come home from school and help my father in the convenience store just so I would be able to spend time with him. I always admired my father—he was a strong and wise character who was loyal, kind and enormously generous—and I took every opportunity I could to learn more about our little convenience store business, if only to be closer to the man whom I loved so dearly.

A family man at heart—his was pure gold. Whenever I (or my siblings) would ask my father for money, he would not give us the amount we had asked for, but would always give us a little extra 'just in case'. Those afternoons with my dad in his shop were some of the best and most memorable of my life. I simply adored him and took any opportunity I could to be around him and soak up his love, which was abundant and always made me so happy.

I also helped him in the shop on weekends and public holidays. During special holidays in Lebanon—New Year's Eve, God's Day, The Cross Day and so forth—the entire city would celebrate with fireworks. We would always organise a table overflowing with firecrackers in front of the convenience store and I would wear long jeans, a white shirt or white jacket and an apron with big pockets to collect the money from customers. My father taught me that I should be strong but kind to the clientele so I, therefore, offered no special favours to anyone. This quickly earned me a reputation as, 'The Little Entrepreneur' in town. At the time, I didn't really understand what the nickname meant, but wore it proudly and it amused my father.

Although I loved my father more than anything else and even though I was young, I also always worried about his health because he had been suffering from the aftermath of a heart attack and the onset of diabetes for a few years. Even at such a young age, I understood the complications that came with diabetes. My father loved life and clearly preferred to live it short (and sweet) and fulfilled rather than long and tedious. He enjoyed his big bars of President's chocolate and, unfortunately in his condition, he consumed them on a daily basis, often hiding the wrappers in his desk drawer. I used to make his coffee, tea and lemonade, but sneakily put in sweetener instead of sugar, hoping he would never notice. As is common with so many diabetics, he also suffered with complications in his feet—feet that I willingly bathed frequently to reduce the swelling.

But despite my innocent efforts to aid my father with his health struggles, it wasn't enough. In late 1971, our tight little clan was devastated by another tragedy when, at some point between two and three in the morning of that dark and fateful day, my beloved father took his last breath and moved into the eternal life that awaits us all.

Little did I know, the winter soon approaching would be one of the saddest and coldest of my life.

My father's body was displayed on a bed in our lounge area for two days surrounded by flowers, so everyone could come to show their respects and say their goodbyes. I couldn't help feeling that it was horribly wrong to be forced to witness the remains of one who had been so vibrant and full of life looking so cold and empty. I knew it was time for me to say goodbye, but I couldn't bring myself to accept the terrible loss that had befallen us. I was only twelve years old and, although part of me behaved like a responsible adult, a larger part was still an innocent and dependent child. The man I adored so very much was gone and it was devastating.

I loved my father so much and had never considered the prospect of his passing—even as adults we seldom imagine our loved ones will not always be here. The reality of my loss and his untimely departure was something my young mind couldn't grasp. My dad, who would comfort and hold me during the hard times, was no longer there to hold me during the most distressing time of my young life.

When my father died, my mother was in her forties, but she continued to sacrifice the whole of her life for us—as she always had—never looking for solace in another man. She was loyal and faithful to my father until the day she died—determined to raise us the way she and my father believed to be the correct upbringing. She was, without doubt, the best mother in the whole world; a soul I likened to a candle bright enough to light our way but, in doing so, slowly burning away the fabric of her own existence.

Nothing was the same after my dad died. At times we would cry as we missed him so much, while at other times we would smile, remembering his jokes and sense of humour.

It was almost too painful for us to go to his convenience store, but despite the heavy weight on our hearts, we all continued to help and kept the store open for another four years after he died. I greatly missed his guidance and assurance. He had always believed in me and told me I was strong—strong enough to withstand any storms that came in life—and his strength of character and commitment to our family was something none of us have ever forgotten. I cherished the moments we had together and I was, and continue to be, determined to make him proud.

I imagine now, as he looks down on me and the rest of our family, that he is proud and he is happy and filled with love to know that we all survived his death and so much more.

When I was sixteen, I finally left behind some of my tomboy ways and developed into a more feminine version of myself. I began to enjoy wearing dresses, loved my pink lipstick and took great care of my long brown hair.

I was also sweet on a young man—Tom—who lived in an adjacent building. It was an innocent affair—just looking at each other and the occasional satisfying kiss. Tom was nineteen and he would call me often and would frequently deliver my favourite chocolate bars, placed inside a basket, from the second floor of the adjoining building down to my eagerly awaiting hands. Adorably, he would buy the chocolate from our store, then he would whistle a unique tune (sort of code that only the two of us understood) to advise me that the chocolate was ready for collection. It was sweet, quite amusing, and certainly flattering and I really enjoyed his company and attention.

On one particular occasion, when I hadn't heard from him for a while, I became anxious when people in our area began gossiping about how he was about to marry some French girl. I wasn't sure what had happened, but the rumour was that he had met this girl at a friend's party, had been drinking and, ultimately, the French girl had become pregnant. She had also assured Tom that the child was his and he was in no position to dispute the fact.

Around the time these rumours started circulating, I received a letter from Tom, delivered by his sister. It was an urgent plea for me to meet with him and to bring my passport. With all the rumours floating around, I was instantly suspicious and it turned out that my intuitive misgivings weren't entirely uncalled for. A million thoughts tumbled through my troubled mind as I wondered what, on earth, he could possibly wish to speak to me about and why bringing my passport along would have any relevance to anything he had to say. I decided that I would accept the invitation to meet, but I would bring a friend along, just in case he was up to something.

The moment I laid eyes on Tom, I could see how deeply troubled he was. His eyes were red and his body language spoke volumes to me before he even uttered a single word. He hugged me tightly and kissed me. My friend sat on a nearby wooden bench and watched vigilantly.

Tom was weeping as he explained his predicament. Already aware of the rumoured pregnancy, I explained—perhaps quite curtly—that we were old enough to understand full well how such a thing could come to be. 'But she doesn't love me and I don't love her,' he persisted. 'I can't be trapped into a loveless marriage and one where I'll become a father before my time'.

Despite feeling betrayed, even though our relationship was quite innocent, my heart did ache for him—the fact was that my now ex-boyfriend would soon become a father and he had to step up to the responsibilities that went along with that.

Tom didn't quite see it the same way, though.

'But if we apply as a couple, we can go to an interview and move to Australia,' he insisted, finally spilling the beans on his plan. I couldn't believe what I was hearing!

'There's no way on earth I'm going with you,' I replied firmly.

'You have responsibility now and a baby on the way, not to mention you've cheated on me'. I wished him all the very best, but for my sake as well as his own, I insisted this should be the last I heard or saw of him again. The consequences of his rash and selfish actions hurt me deeply, but the outcome was out of my hands and my resolve was absolute. While sympathetic for the life he was about to begin living, I was also losing a deeply-valued friend and my heart was aching at the loss. It was my first taste of the heartache of love and, again, I lost a bit more of my innocence that day.

I turned and walked away, never to see him again. Ironically, even though I chose not to acquiesce to his ridiculous plan to move to Australia, I had no idea that fate would ultimately make me a permanent resident there many years later.

8

It Begins

Years later, a hole in my heart—created by the passing of my father—still remained and I knew it would never be filled, but life went on and everything in Lebanon began to change. In general, Lebanese people are usually beautiful, warm, generous, united and supportive, but there was a religious edict in our culture, and when sides were divided, sadly, bloodshed was inevitable.

I was seventeen and in my last year of school at a Christian College. One day in my final year, the deputy principal asked me to stay behind after school to assist him in organising an upcoming school play. I didn't see his request as anything unusual as I was always involved in school plays. The deputy was an incredibly tall man with dark hair and a thin moustache, olive skin and dark, penetrating eyes. I remained on the premises perhaps an hour after everybody else had gone, continuing to work on the script for the play, still thinking nothing of it. When the deputy returned from whatever had been occupying him, he offered to drive me home to save me the walk, but it was a relatively short walk home, only around 3 km, and it was a beautiful day, so I declined. 'No, no. It's okay,' I assured him. 'I'm only about a twenty-minute walk from school.' He persisted, insisting it was a just reward for the extra hours I had put in and I easily accepted his gesture of goodwill. He was the deputy principal, after all, and I trusted him as he was also a close friend to a neighbour in our building. As we drove along the road that led from the school, I became extremely alarmed when, instead of going in the direction of my home, he took me in the opposite direction, up to the hills. He pulled up in a bushy area just as dusk started to descend.

'What are you doing?' I asked him, trying to keep my wits about me. His reply was to attempt to plant his lips over mine as he grabbed my breast and proceeded to lower his hands to other parts of my body. I pushed him away, shouting, 'Please! Please, no! Get off me! Let me walk!' As I turned my body to reach for the car door, he grabbed me by my long hair, pulling my ponytail towards him. He was hurting me, but my fear was overriding all of my other senses and the pain only registered distantly. I thought I was going to die, but was even more terrified of the prospect of being raped. He continued to grasp my hair in one hand while his other hand touched my breast. My body was facing the door and my back was to him, so I used my legs to push against the door with all my strength, trying to get close enough for my elbows to hit his head because I was unable to reach back to scratch his face. Given that he was in the driver's seat, his large body was restricted by the size of the car's interior and he was further impeded by the steering wheel. While both his hands were busy, I pushed the door with all my strength and screamed and screamed as loud as I could. He put his hand on my mouth to stop me from screaming—worried that people would hear, especially as my window was open—but I pushed against him with all my might and managed to wriggle out of his clutches before clambering out of the car.

'You get back in here!' he yelled.

'No way!' I yelled back as I ran as fast as I could towards the main road.

God must have been watching over me that day because, just at that moment, another car appeared, driving in the opposite direction. I jumped up and down, frantically waving and gesturing for them to stop. I was still in my school uniform and, luckily, the other car was being driven by a middle-aged couple who were willing to help. They stopped and picked me up without question or pause and, thankfully, safely returned me to my home.

That day marked a significantly further loss of my childhood innocence and trust in humanity. This person whom I had trusted and previously respected, was indeed a horrible and sinister monster, lacking integrity and honour.

I knew it would be useless to expose this brute for what he was, so I remained close-mouthed until much later in my adult life. When I saw him the next day at school, he glared at me as though I was the one who had exhibited absolutely abhorrent behaviour. Undoubtedly, I had been extremely lucky to escape the clutches of this sick brute. As a result of this attempted molestation, I have always encouraged my children and family to be aware and alert and to avoid being placed in a vulnerable situation.

That year, more and more incidents like that one began to occur throughout the country and tensions were running high.

Another terrifying experience happened one sunny Sunday morning when my sister Nada and her two friends and I set out for Tripoli with my brother Antoine. Tripoli is famous for its fine food (and arguably the best sweets in Lebanon) and our intention was to have lunch in a renowned restaurant. Our Mum had volunteered to look after my two nieces so we would all be free to enjoy all the delights the ancient town of Tripoli had to offer.

Even though it was an hour's drive and we found out that the restaurant where we wanted to eat had closed down, we made the best of it and had some delicious charcoal chicken at another restaurant—knowing that company and family were more important than the repast itself.

On the way home, Antoine stopped to fill up at a petrol station. I offered to go and buy some ice cream for us all, not even thinking about the fact that I was wearing one of the shortest skirts I had ever worn—a navy blue micro skirt and not the kind of garment I usually wore. I had skinny legs, I was young and, perhaps, I was emboldened by the fact that I no longer had a father telling me such outfits were inappropriate to wear.

As I was walking across the parking lot, four men appeared and began wolf-whistling and making lurid comments. Seeing and hearing what was happening, Antoine began cursing and telling them off for their unsavoury comments. I'm sure my eyes must have bugged out of my head and my jaw must have dropped to the ground as I heard my brother so uncharacteristically swearing. I started yelling, 'I'm sorry. I'm sorry. It's all my fault because of the skirt. Please, stop! Please, stop!' However, the young men were walking behind me and intent on taunting me.

At that time, in Lebanon, women were much more liberated than in other areas of the Middle East and were free to wear what we wanted. In fact, Lebanese women were renowned for their freedom and western ways across the Middle East, but the growing tensions of a country divided brought conservatism and extreme caution to all women.

I rushed to the car and asked Antoine to drive away, but before he could start the car, the men were already upon us. One of them suddenly lunged at Antoine's open window brandishing an enormous knife and pushing it painfully against my brother's throat. Without the slightest sign that he would not be true to his word, the man announced chillingly, 'I'm going to kill you now.' He started dragging the knife across my brother's throat, to the point where, horrifyingly, I noticed some blood trickle out. All four of us girls in the car were screaming, begging him to stop.

I threw open the car door and marched towards the guy who could so easily end my brother's life in a heartbeat. 'He's my brother,' I pleaded. 'He's protecting me, as any good brother would.' I begged him, 'Please! Please leave him alone!' As tears welled in my eyes, this brazen, angry man and I held each other's gaze for a moment and I don't know why or what struck a chord with this would-be murderer, but he withdrew the knife.

Perhaps he had a sister of his own or perhaps he felt my simultaneous love and terror for my brother and it moved him. Whatever it was, I considered it nothing short of a miracle that my pleading did not fall on deaf ears. We drove off, terrified but unhurt.

Unfortunately, as these terrifying incidences—violence, threats, rape, murder—began to escalate, stripping away the last of my innocence as I watched the people around me consumed by fear, stress, and uncertainty, I was forced to grow up. Gone were the carefree days of leaving our doors unlocked, speaking our minds, and women feeling safe in the streets where rape was now all too common. Our society was quickly destabilizing and, where strict rules of conduct and the inherent knowledge of right and wrong previously existed, people were behaving erratically and without regard—ignoring their beliefs and morals.

We all had to face the reality that the civil war in Lebanon had begun.

9

A Day at the Beach

I was never an ordinary girl and I always believed that my visions and ambitions outstripped those of my peers. I wanted to be a lawyer and advocate for human rights, to assist people in need. However, circumstances—and perhaps God's will—ultimately determined a different path for me. Undoubtedly, the traits of planning, goal setting, assertiveness and decisiveness have helped me throughout my journey to date, but I maintain that the greatest strength in my life has always been my love for and closeness to my family, as well as the joy I feel when helping others. Indeed, my mother always used to express her belief of my intrinsic significance to the family and its progress through both smooth and turbulent times by declaring, 'The boat will not sail without Chadia'.

Many of those who have known me throughout my life may have perhaps formed the impression that I am a rock—steadfast and unwavering in my determination—and while I accept this perception as a compliment, few know the torment and trauma that I have experienced and the vulnerability closely hidden beneath my resilient demeanour. This guise helped me in my youth, especially during the perils and dark periods of my life's journey, to show the sort of courage and strength of character required to survive and flourish. This resilience amidst adversity further cements my connection to my favourite plant—the cyclamen—and is a true-to-life metaphor of my life story. Exactly like this beautiful plant—I have survived in many inhospitable elements and wilted under the heat of oppression only to still rise up boldly and bloom, showing the world that beauty and diversity can still flower in harsh conditions.

My mother was a very wise woman and, once the war erupted, she started planning things in advance—buying and storing many non-perishable food items in the pantry and under our beds—so we would always have food available if it became scarce. Her fears went much deeper than merely sustaining us during this period as we all lived with the imminent fear of being killed or our neighbourhood being attacked. Her aim was to protect us, and she put a plan in place in case we needed to escape the war by sea or plane, as a group or individually. Knowing that children under eighteen would not be able to travel alone and without parental consent, my mother arranged to have my age and my brother Jalil's changed on our documentation, so we would appear over eighteen. To this day, I still do not know how she was able to achieve this, but we had our altered passports valid and ready. To this day, my identification still reflects this modified age.

Two months after the civil war started, my nephew Lawrence was born. My sister, Nada, now had three beautiful children, but it was never an easy task for her and her husband to protect and safeguard the little ones while living in a war zone. But, as family does, we all did our part to ensure that we all remained safe—at least as much as was in our control—during the years of conflict that followed and to keep things as "normal" as we could for the little ones.

I always adored my two nieces, but with the birth of their baby brother, we became even closer. On one particularly hot day, I decided I would take Bila, my seven-year-old niece, to Jounieh Beach for a swim and to get a bit of a suntan.

My family had gifted me with a hip orange Audi car (that my loving mother and considerate older brothers and sister had contributed to), so I was able to drive Bila and myself the twenty minutes to Jounieh. I paid entry to one of the beach resorts, which afforded us access to multiple dining options, pools and the beach. Initially, we basked in the crystal waters of one of the pools under the pounding rays of a fiery sun, before relaxing over a pleasant light lunch in one of the restaurants. It was only after lunch that we decided to cross to the beach and have an afternoon relaxing on the silky sands to sunbake and take a dip in the Mediterranean Sea. The beach was a lot quieter than the pool had been and there was a beautiful yet strong breeze that day, which led to numerous games of catch with our hats! We were lying on our towels, chatting—my sunglasses on to shield my eyes from the sun—but the warm sun and breeze lulled me into a nap. I don't think I was asleep for long, but while I was dozing off, little Bila couldn't resist the pull of the sea.

When I woke and looked around, I realised she was no longer with me. Not overly concerned, at first, I walked towards the water searching for her when—to my instant horror—I saw her hands waving frantically in the air and her head just above the water. She was only about fifty metres from me, but what neither of us had known was that there was a strong riptide at that section of beach.

Of course, now that I live in Australia, I am well aware of the behaviours and dangers of rips and I know that if everybody was educated to swim with a rip rather than against it, countless drownings could be avoided. To try to swim directly to shore through a rip is often an exercise in futility for even the strongest swimmers.

Without even considering the consequences, I charged into the sea, my heart pounding and my adrenaline spiking at the realisation that my beloved niece was drowning. I tried to pull her out, but the rip also captured me in its merciless grasp. While I had some physical strength and was not a bad swimmer, my niece was weak and it took every ounce of fortitude I could muster to keep us both afloat. I began screaming for help, but nobody could hear me over the roar of the sea and the waves crashing on the shore.

Was this the end, I wondered?

Without intervention, there is no doubt we both would have died that day. Fortunately, two young men in a small boat saw us and came to our rescue. Our knights in shining armour pulled us to the safety of their little vessel.

When we arrived back at the beach, Bila was unconscious and her stomach resembled a balloon. I had also swallowed some water, but it was nothing in comparison.

Being at a resort, there were lifeguards who only looked after the swimming pool areas; however, they were familiar with the process of resuscitation and our rescuers immediately ran to enlist their help. With my hands clasped to my mouth and tears stinging in my eyes, I watched as our saviours did what they had been trained to do, praying and hoping that life-giving breath would swiftly re-enter Bila's body. 'Come on, come on! Breathe!' I quietly prayed. She had been unconscious for what seemed a lifetime, so I desperately hoped she would pull through and, thankfully, my prayers were answered when she suddenly coughed up a lungful of the salty water and regained full consciousness. When she recovered, she couldn't stop thanking me and the others who had saved her life. The incident became etched in my mind forever and, to this day, I am still frightened of swimming in deep water.

10

Escaping the Killing Fields

It was 1976—a year after the civil war had begun—and Beirut had become known as 'The Killing Fields' by local and international media outlets. Rightly so. We were constantly under the threat of bombs falling on us, being shot in a hail of bullets, kidnapped or raped.

I was living at home with my mother and two younger brothers, Jalil and John. My brother Antoine was working as an electrical engineer for ARAMCO, an American company in Saudi Arabia, while Walid had completed his master's degree and travelled to Cyprus to teach at The Grammar School, so both were safely away from the war zone.

Our area was bombed on a regular basis.

It was now commonplace to see streets crammed with multi-storey buildings peppered with holes from bullets and mortar shells, cars abandoned as burnt out shells with flat tyres and riddled with bullets. Trash and rubbish were strewn everywhere and everything was covered with ash and soot, making the neighbourhood look squalid. We hadn't had power for six months but, luckily, our oven and stove operated on gas so at least we could still cook. But who had the time or enthusiasm to bake a cake or bread? When you are surrounded by such devastation and destruction, other priorities take precedence, such as being alert and keeping ourselves alive, not just physically but also in spirit. Despite witnessing devastation and chaos on a daily basis, we tried to remain positive. We would spend time together telling stories, playing cards and distracting ourselves from the reality of the world outside our home.

Nights became a routine of mortars and snipers, and everybody understood that young girls were at risk of being kidnapped and raped. Fighters on both sides were brutal, unfeeling and amoral. East and West Beirut were at war with each other and nobody was safe from the other side. Those in the West would kidnap those from the East and vice versa. Spies and informants were used to feed information across the Green Line—the line that divided the two sides of the country—identifying the names of fighters and potential targets. Bodies of opponents who had been killed (or captured and then killed) would be paraded on the streets or tied to cars and driven around the area. It was barbaric and I witnessed it regularly—the horror bombarded my senses daily until I reached a point of numbness and felt anaesthetised to these living, real-life nightmares.

The loving people of Lebanon were loving no more.

A few of the fighters in the area—previously good, kind, well-adjusted people—who lost loved ones even became addicted to drugs in an effort to quell the horror of the carnage that had become a part of their lives.

I suppose it was inevitable that one of the bombs that regularly rained down on East Beirut would land in our area or even hit our home, but there was no option except to continue life as we knew it, hoping for the best, yet fearing the worst.

One morning, early in 1976, our fears were realised when a huge bomb exploded at the intersection at the end of our block, frighteningly close to our home. People were screaming, running outside, watching from their balconies and helping the injured.

Body parts lay scattered like gory movie props amongst burning vehicles and scores of people were lying in the river of blood and debris that flooded our street. It was a scene from a real-life horror movie and it was happening on my doorstep.

Unknown to me, the explosion had coincided with my mother's return home from the fruit-and-vegetable shop and she'd been thrown back with the impact like a mere feather in the wind. At the sound of the explosion, I ran outside, panicked and unprepared to witness such utter devastation. As I surveyed the scene of carnage, I was horrified to recognise my unconscious mother lying among the wounded. She lay sprawled in the street, unmoving. Instinctively, I ran to her side, with no regard for my own safety, and shook her shoulders, crying, 'Mum! Mum! Please wake up!' She was unresponsive and her eyes remained closed. I was overwhelmed by fear.

She had sustained injuries to her head and legs in the blast and they looked severe and she lay in a pool of blood and shrapnel. Etched into my mind forever is the unforgettable vision of an open vein on her right shin spouting blood like a fountain. I wept and prayed. 'God! Please, God! Save my mum'. With my ears still ringing, I fell to my knees, crossed my hands in supplication and wailed again, 'God! God! Please! Please! Please save my mother'.

There was so much blood everywhere that even the welcome mat on our front step was soaked red. The street was, literally, stained with the blood of those I knew and loved. As I knelt in the street, I looked at the four pretty little windows at the front of our unit (now crisscrossed with bars and the sandbags that lay in front of them, as instructed by the local militia) and it suddenly hit home that we were living in the heart of a war zone. While we had tried to feign normalcy, none of us could escape the devastation blasting apart our country.

The shock of the situation hit me and I just sat there, numbly, with my mother's head resting in my lap. I remember thinking about how I loved nothing more than laying my head in my mother's lap and having her play with my hair, telling me stories, challenging me to dream of greater things. I thought about how precious time spent with her was—simply enjoying each other's company, laughing uncontrollably and feeling so much joy in each other.

And here I was, immersed in an unfathomable reality, with my loving mother wounded and unconscious, bleeding in my lap. I continued to pray, pleading with God to save her. Her journey could not be cut short like this. She didn't deserve to die in such a way and so young.

A barrage of ambulances arrived amidst a sea of intense screaming and wailing and medics began running through the crowds to help the wounded, but despite the noise and chaos, I felt as though time were standing still. My sole focus was on my mother as she lay in my arms, but I felt completely helpless and rooted to the ground, weeping and praying to God repeatedly was all I could muster the strength to do. I watched as ambulance personnel placed one white sheet after another on victim after victim and I became resolute that my mother would not be on one of those having a white sheet placed over her. Finally, one of those ambulance personnel swiftly scooped up my mother's limp body, still oozing blood, to take her to hospital.

I gathered the family to break the most awful news to them and then we all quickly made the pilgrimage to the Roum Hospital in Ashrafieh, where we hoped our mother's life would be spared. Waiting to know the outcome of whether a loved one will survive is a torturous experience, emotions bounce all over the place—one moment you are confident they will pull through and survive, the next you're preparing yourself for the absolute worst and mourning them before they're even gone. Once again, we were blessed with God's mercy and within a couple hours those warm and loving eyes that had bathed me in their light since I took my own first breath, opened, giving us hope anew. The doctors advised us that there was shrapnel from the explosion embedded in her cranium and informed us they were unable to remove these foreign objects because they were so close to her brain. If they attempted to remove them, she would surely die. They could treat her leg wounds and stop the bleeding, but the shrapnel would also remain indefinitely.

After ten days of treatment and recuperation, my mother was released from hospital, but she would be plagued with headaches for the rest of her life. An awful reminder of the ordeal she endured that day.

On one occasion, I, too, almost ended up with a white sheet over me. Against the pressure of constantly falling bombs, I was walking to the woodfire bakery—a mere kilometre from our home—to buy some bread when the mortars erupted in the area. My bread was thrown into the air from the force of the explosions, but that was the least of my worries as it felt as though the flesh would be torn from my body. I started running between the buildings, but the pressure was so great from the explosions that everything—human and beast—was flying as though it had grown wings after each explosion. As I was running, I saw a mother lying in a pool of blood, holding a child. Again, bodies were strewn across the landscape like broken and discarded dolls, lifeless and destitute. It felt like an eternity before I arrived home and, when I finally got there, I felt and looked miserable—covered in blood, dust and dirt. My long brown hair was grey and full of ash and when I saw my mum, I burst into tears, upset about having also dropped the bread in my flight, which had been the whole purpose of my venture out. I only received a few minor cuts and scratches to my body and minor shrapnel wounds to my right hand—one piece of shrapnel still remains imbedded under my skin—and my poor mother never forgave herself for sending me into such danger.

From then on, we made our own bread on the saj oven in our backyard.

With the ever-escalating violence, we were advised by our local intelligence officers that it would be a good idea to literally 'head for the hills' as they felt our area was likely to be the target of a direct assault that would put the entire family and neighbourhood at risk. Members from the local militia knocked on residents' doors, advising everyone to go to the shelters or the mountains and to vacate the area immediately.

During a previous bombardment, we had stayed in one of the underground shelters, trapped belowground in a cramped, dark and squalid cavern dug deep enough to withstand the bombs and missiles. I was still traumatised by memories of the darkness, the rancid smell of fear and human excrement—partly as a result of the fear and partly because the shelters had very limited sanitary provisions. Being trapped in a hole below ground that reverberated with the sound of explosions above and shook violently with every impact was, for me, infinitely worse than facing the onslaught above ground. At one point during our stint in the shelter, when I had finally found solace in sleep, I was awakened by a rat crawling up my tummy and moving towards my face. I jumped and let out a loud, hysterical scream, which was met with disdain and retorts of 'shut up' from the other weary residents in the shelter.

This time around, when we were advised to evacuate again, I insisted to my mum, 'No shelter this time.' I could not endure the awful experience again. Understanding my acute reluctance, my mother agreed that we would leave the area and take refuge in the mountains.

My mother and my two younger brothers drove to the mountains in my little orange Audi, because my brother Jalil could only drive an automatic. They followed my sister and her family in their van to a rental property which had been arranged by my brother-in-law, Gary. My task was to collect my aunt Ratiba from her home in Ashrafieh in our family's Maroon Mercedes, packed with our belongings. The drive to the mountains would take thirty to forty minutes, through narrow and curved roads.

Prior to the war, we had frequently taken this same route to the mountains for day trips. The views were breathtaking and we enjoyed the scenic drive very much. This time was different. We had no interest in looking back towards the city, nor gave any thought to nature's beauty that surrounded us. This time, we were fleeing for our lives. Similar to the countless refugees who fled their homes during the First and Second World Wars, our heavy hearts and concerns for our future were very sobering and we barely spoke as I drove. As we approached the halfway mark of our journey, the silence was abruptly shattered as bombs seemed to descend from the heavens like acidic rain drops and, once again, we found ourselves in the centre of carnage. The deathly explosions were indiscriminate in their murderous intent— children, the elderly—no one was safe.

Cars on the streets burst into flames and my aunt screamed, expecting that any moment may be our last. I steeled myself to be brave and to navigate through the blast zone. Our car had been peppered with shrapnel and received extensive damage and the roads were pitted with potholes. Explosions erupted all around us and the Mercedes' tyres popped like balloons, so I ended up driving on bare metal rims, but still driving as fast as was possible. I felt sick and shaken to my core and my heart was pounding in my chest, yet I maintained a façade of control and assured Aunt Ratiba that we would be safe.

The car was severely damaged by the time we arrived at our destination, with smoke plumes coming from the engine. I helped my aunty to retrieve our belongings from the boot and ran towards the house that would become our temporary home. We had barely made it to the front door when the car engine burst into flames and we all realised that divine providence had handed us another chance at life.

For a brief respite in time, this quaint house on a hill with magnificent views of the sea and hinterland became our home, deluding us into pretending that war couldn't come within a thousand miles of this place.

From our forest home at night, the reign of terror in Beirut sounded and looked more like fireworks, reminding us of better days when Beirut was known as 'The Paris of the Middle East' with frequently celebrated festivals and occasions with dazzling fireworks displays.

Thinking about it this way helped us cope with the terror of the civil war, though reality was only a short drive away.

The cyclamen, even when it appears dead, remains dormant as a bulb, waiting to revive itself at the end of winter to blossom in spring. Similarly, so would I survive, and through the hand of God which protected us, would get past this.

11

Soldier Girl

Our respite in the mountains couldn't last forever. We ended up staying there for ten days, until a ceasefire was declared and we were told it was safe to return home. With hope in our hearts that a ceasefire would be prolonged, we returned home. My sister and her family returned in their van and I drove the Audi, along with my aunty, my mother and my two brothers.

No sooner had we arrived than our hopes of some peace were shattered when we saw how bombing in the area had impacted our humble unit. Glass was shattered everywhere and pieces of metal were embedded in the walls. Worst of all, the glass jars containing the olive oil that my mother had worked so hard to produce were also smashed and strewn all over the floor. There was oil everywhere—covering what was left of the windows, the walls and, of course, the floor was a slippery mess. Our hearts sank when we saw what was left of our humble home, but we took solace that we were still alive and together.

While we were cleaning the floor, we discovered an oil-soaked note that read, 'If you are really with us, you must join us and fight our enemies.' Troubling as that was, even more troubling was the fact that we didn't know which organisation had sent the note. Antoine and Walid were overseas, Jalil and John were too young to join the fighters and, frankly, we couldn't agree with anyone in this civil war—not on either side. We just wanted peace and for Lebanon to return to its former glory, but we didn't doubt the threat was real and now understood all too well that the ceasefire wouldn't last long.

To prevent our family from becoming a target, I opted to join one of the local Christian militias.

One early rainy morning, I drove to a nearby militia headquarters. One of the militiamen—named Fady—met me at the entrance and walked me to the main office, a huge room on the second floor adorned with the Lebanese and the militia's flags, separated by a bulky Christian cross. Photos of the party's leaders were also displayed on the walls, as well as an enormous blackboard and maps.

The room was a hive of activity, with men and women talking on short-wave radios, on the phone, and on walkie-talkies. Fady escorted me through this control room to an adjoining office to meet his leader who introduced himself while shaking my hand, and asked me to sit down. 'Sir, I'd like to join the militia and assist. I'm a local. I'm healthy and fit,' I told him. He was appreciative of my offer to volunteer and instructed me to be there at 6 am on the following Monday to commence my training.

On Monday morning, I arrived with more than twenty other volunteers, a mixture of men and women. We were escorted by five experienced fighters who drove us by jeeps to a training camp about a twenty-five-minutes from the main facility, in the foothills above Beirut. On arrival, we were ordered to go to a huge shed and change our civilian clothes into military camouflage outfits. There were hundreds of uniforms, boots, caps and bulletproof vests, so it was relatively easy to find suitably sized apparel. We were also asked to complete forms with our personal details and emergency contacts.

The first day consisted of an orientation for all new recruits, and when we returned on the second, we were issued dog tags— tin pendants, engraved with our name and blood type.

The training was intense and gruelling. I soon became proficient in more weapons than I knew existed—the M16, AK-47, hand grenades, submachine guns, and a myriad of other weapons. I also was shown how to effectively apply camouflage paint.

I was taught to scale slopes and crawl through holes, and to endure barren environments when we camped in rocky outcrops devoid of my precious cyclamen. We were instructed to endeavour to avoid conflict, but to follow orders without question and to defend ourselves and our community when required.

I became a regular Lebanese Private Benjamin, but without any of the comic elements.

As a volunteer in the militia, I was required to attend five days per week, as at the time they needed all the help they could get. We were provided with a roster of shifts throughout the day and night.

My role was principally to undertake shifts on radio communications or administrative work in the office. Between my shifts with the militia, I volunteered with the Red Cross and other humanitarian organisations in our area.

One of my duties as a volunteer was to drive—often through the night—to take blood supplies from hospitals to other places to assist those who had been injured and required urgent blood transfusions. For these missions, we drove a black Chevrolet El Camino, owned by the militia that was often used for multiple tasks. It was sturdy enough to drive, so I felt confident driving on our roads, which were ravaged with potholes and often littered with the debris from bombardments.

On one such occasion, while transporting four bags of blood from one hospital to another with Pierre—another volunteer—we had to drive very close to the Green Line (the dividing line between the two warring sides) while a barrage of rocket-propelled grenades exploded in our vicinity. Suddenly, the barrage stopped and there was a deathly silence before a sniper's bullets rang out. To avoid being detected, we had turned off our headlights and proceeded to zig-zag through the narrow streets. Terrified, as we saw the bright trails from tracer rounds trying to determine our location, I panicked and pulled over close to a building for shelter. 'I can't breathe. I'm scared we're going to die here,' I cried. In response, Pierre took out a smoke grenade and threw it behind us before making me change places with him and he took over driving.

The bombardment began again and in the chaos of the onslaught, three bags of the precious cargo of blood were broken by flying debris. I sat there, frantically clinging to the one remaining bag, which was not only covered in blood from the burst bags, but also covered in my blood from the numerous small wounds I'd sustained from the shrapnel. I was extremely relieved when we arrived at the hospital with the remaining bag of blood, but both Pierre and I felt awful that we had not completed our objective. The following day we both gave blood to make recompense in our minds for this failing.

On another occasion, a young man was brought into the hospital with only a few hours to live if the correct blood type didn't arrive on time. Driven by desperation, we searched high and low and made numerous phone calls to find a match. None of his family in Lebanon had the right blood type except his brother, who was in Cyprus at the time. The only option to prevent another young man from becoming a statistic of this brutal war was to make hurried arrangements for his brother to return on a hydrofoil boat. It would take a few hours, but if everybody moved like they had a purpose, it could be achieved. His brother didn't hesitate. Leaping onto the aquatic lifesaver, he sped back to his homeland, where his blood successfully saved his brother's life. It was heroic acts like this one that kept my hope alive and made me see that there was still courage and humanity in my people, despite the horrific circumstances we were all immersed in.

My younger brothers became insistent that they wanted to assist me in the militia office. Although they were much too young to join the militia, I occasionally took them to the office and allowed them to help by making sandwiches. This small task helped them to feel they had become part of the war effort on the righteous side…not that any of us knew what the right side was.

No one wins in a war.

One day, when my brothers were with me in the office and I believed we were in relative safety, a bullet sped through the office window, singeing the hair on the right side of my face before exploding like a little bomb in the wall behind me. It made a hole about the size of a rockmelon. God was once again protecting me and my brothers. Perhaps too, our protection was enhanced, not only by my mum's constant blessings for us to always live a peaceful, safe and happy life, but also by the soul of cyclamen—never far from my subconscious and reminding me that there is always a way and life will go on. After the bullet incident, I told my brothers that it was the last time they were to come to the office.

So now I had become 'Chadia the Soldier Girl', and while mostly this afforded me respect, there were some who would seek to make me uncomfortable simply because I was a young woman. There was, as expected, a disproportionate ratio of males to females and it didn't take long before I was being bombarded with amorous advances. Fortunately, the declaration that service came first was taken seriously and most members of the militia were respectful as it was decreed by the leader that men were required to be polite and respectful of their female counterparts, and swearing and lewd behaviour was prohibited. Getting involved with the opposite sex was the last thing on my mind. My focus was on doing what was necessary to survive and protect my family.

However, one of the male fighters in the headquarters—a fit and strong individual named Tanios—would often sit with a newspaper, pretending to read it while obviously watching me through a hole he'd cut in the paper. Even though I was inwardly seething, I knew it would be perilous to openly confront him, but he was acutely aware from my indifferent body language that I was never going to succumb to his desires. I believe it was because of his frustration at being thwarted that made him announce one day, 'Chadia, you have a scar on your ankle. I will always find you wherever you go because you're marked.'

He reminded me of the darker side of the prince who found Cinderella through the glass slipper that only fit her tiny foot. This was no prince and his intentions were far from pure and I despised him and the fact that I was in this situation, but most of all, I despised that my country was embroiled in this bitter war.

12

April Fool's

My sister, Nada—whom I love like a second mother and will do so forever—was always very dedicated to caring for her children and keeping them safe. She tried to be everything at once—career woman, mother, wife, sister and daughter—and I recall her transitioning between roles with grace and ease. She was and still remains a woman of many talents who is also graceful, loyal and strong. Nada was also fortunate that the firm she worked for kept paying her salary during the conflict because it had many overseas projects that allowed it to keep operating.

As an aside, many people weren't so lucky during the war and numerous families became destitute, unable to even get food. This was quite common in our area, so people pitched in to help those desperate families. I remember people doing their best to give bread and other such items to families who were really impoverished; another testament to the generous spirit of my people, despite all the terrible goings-on. And, of course, the church stepped in with food aid and other items where possible.

During an uncharacteristically and mercifully peaceful time, Nada came to visit one sunny afternoon before collecting her ten-month-old son from his paternal grandmother's just down the way from us. Another ceasefire had been temporarily declared that day and there had been no shootings and no snipers anywhere that we were aware of. When the snipers were deployed, it was not at all uncommon for them to shoot pregnant women in the stomach and men in the head, such was the brutality of this conflict.

So, for a brief moment in time, people were able to breathe easier and cross the streets without fear.

While we were standing out front of our home, visiting with Nada, I noticed a friend across the street and called, 'Hi.' Smiling in reply, she called back, 'Come and visit.' Such times of casualness were rare, so I left Nada chatting with my mother and happily trotted to my friend's home only a couple of buildings away. I hadn't been there very long when we heard a single shot ring out. The sound rang out through the quiet afternoon and, honestly, nobody thought much of it—a single shot was nothing in the barrage of regular gunfire that had become so familiar to us in Beirut.

Moments later, we heard the screaming and we rushed outside to see a large group of people gathered. This day is forever etched in my mind because, as I joined the group, glancing around to see who was the unfortunate recipient of this bullet, one of the bystanders called out, 'Chadia! Chadia! Your sister. She's been shot.' Remembering the date, I loudly called back, 'You must be joking. It's an April fool's joke,' but the joke was maliciously on us.

I was in a nightmare.

A tracer bullet—a projectile with a small magnesium charge in its base that burns brightly to help a sniper aim more easily without using the sights on the weapon—had hit my sister. The impact was so powerful that after passing through my sister's left leg and inflicting horrendous damage, it hit a metal electrical pole on the other side of the road and exploded. I did my best to comfort both Nada—in physical agony—and my mother who was, understandably, in hysterics. However, deep down, I feared my sister wouldn't live. Nada's flesh was torn and hanging, the internal contents of her leg exposed. We knew many who had died as a result of such wounds, especially with the amount of blood Nada had lost.

Nada wailed as the pain intensified, yet despite her suffering, she screamed for people to stay away as she crawled to move out of the firing line so that others would not be shot while trying to help her. That is Nada, always thinking of others first, and she was incredibly brave during the entire experience.

I shared a glance with her and tried to communicate that all would be okay; well, at least that was what I prayed. One of the neighbours, thankfully, was quick to rush back to his apartment and call for an ambulance, which arrived within twenty minutes of the call. They instantly applied pressure to the wound and endeavoured to minimise blood loss. Nada was rushed to hospital for immediate medical attention, and I found myself once again heading to hospital with a family member whose life was hanging in the balance.

Later, we learned that the sniper was a foreign mercenary. Mercenaries were frequently hired by one side or the other to undertake the more unsavoury tasks in this war and to drive fear and doubt into the civilian population. My sister had been in the street just across from our unit. A normal street crammed with buildings, cars parked uniformly on either side of the road, with power and telephone wires overhead. A normal street on a 'normal' day that forever changed what my sister considered normal in her life. She was an innocent victim, targeted in the most brutal way, on her way to collect her son after having a coffee with her mother.

This is the reality of war.

The doctors advised my brother-in-law, Gary, that it was not good news and they were going to have to amputate Nada's leg. The bullet was toxic and large and it had travelled straight through the flesh and bone under her knee. Gary was far from convinced that amputation was necessary, never mind acceptable. He felt that it might perhaps be the easiest and quickest way to treat her, but it was not going to be the future for his wife. Gary loved Nada too much to see her doomed in this way. (At that time, there were few options for people with disabilities.) Fixing his steely gaze firmly on the doctor, Gary told him, 'Fix her leg or I'll shoot you.' I watched the look on the doctor's face as he realised my brother-in-law was deadly serious, and that dissenting was not an option.

My sister had lost about 8.5 centimetres of her leg bone and her leg was hanging by skin on one side, but the leg was miraculously saved. However, while saving the limb was successful, the doctor had not underestimated the risk that came along with such a procedure. Toxins had spread through my sister's body from the wound. Her leg was limp and her pallid complexion was testament to her body's struggle.

We visited her on a daily basis, but watching her suffer was barely tolerable. A junior Syrian nurse, Jamil, attended to her regularly. I listened to my sister's interaction with this nurse. 'I don't want you changing my dressing. You hurt me,' she told him. 'When I hurt you, it's because I have to dig to get the poison out,' he explained. 'When the executive nurse or the doctor who would have amputated your limb change the dressing, they don't even look at it. The stench and the sight of it is too much for them. When I do it, the infection is removed. You must trust me,' he assured her.

From then on, when the nurse in charge came to change her dressings, Nada insisted that Jamil do it. For the weeks following, she allowed only Jamil to change her dressings. It was putrid, it was painful and the entire situation was wretched, but when—finally—clean fluid started showing, we knew the efforts had been worth it.

There was no doubt in anyone's mind that this junior nurse had performed nothing short of a miracle, and had he not intervened, the original prognosis of amputation would certainly have become a reality. The poison in her blood would have commenced its deadly journey through Nada's blood vessels and to her brain, killing her.

During this uncomfortable and excruciating process, Nada was kept on a drip and under heavy medication for extreme pain management and antibiotics all working collectively to both save her leg and her life. The family all pitched in to help with the children, and on rare occasions during her recovery, Nada was allowed to return home for half a day to regain some sense of normality. Even on these return visits, she was forced to remain in a brace to prevent her knee from moving. It was physical and emotional agony both for her and for the family.

Despite the harsh reality of this war and the heavy toll that we as a country and as a family were paying, I retained something of a distant ethereal quality and spiritual belief.

One late afternoon, I sat on the balcony of the hospital while visiting Nada. I gazed up at the sky, reading the clouds—something I have done since childhood, since I saw my beloved cyclamen flowers growing as if they were intent on reaching the clouds.

I turned to my sister and asked, 'Can you read them?' She looked at me quizzically. 'Can you read the clouds?' I insisted.

'What are you talking about, Chadia?'

'I'm telling you I can see something in the clouds.'

Not quite sure what to believe, my sister pushed the hospital buzzer to call the nurses. 'My sister saw something in the sky,' she told them.

'Look. Look! Can't you see the writing in the sky?' I asked them all.

Arabic letters had been formed by the clouds to proclaim that a certain political leader in Lebanon would die the following day. Astonishingly, the other people in the room, including the nurses, believed they could see the same wording as I did, and they called other people to see it as well. Eerily, the next day that leader was killed.

Almost a year after Nada had been shot, she remained in hospital. Her recovery had been tediously slow until, one day, we heard of an experienced surgeon who had studied in Paris and whose clinic was in Ashrafieh—the same suburb of Nada's hospital. This doctor had techniques which were not accessible to the 'saw-bone surgeons' we had become accustomed to during wartime. If my sister was to ever stand a chance of walking again, he was her only hope.

There was no medical insurance during the war, so all bills had to be paid for by her husband and the family, but the cost of the operation was too expensive for us to be able to cover. When relatives and people in our neighbourhood found out, they all pitched in to help cover the cost of her surgery and it was a truly wonderful and life-saving generosity.

'Nada,' the doctor began meaningfully. 'Do you want to walk again?'

'Of course, I do,' she replied firmly.

'Then come back here on Monday morning,' he ordered.

On Monday morning, my sister was admitted to Rizk Hospital in Ashrafieh. We all prayed. I also looked for messages in the clouds.

The procedure involved removing a piece of bone from her right hip that we humans can live without. It's incredible that God supplies us with stocks of our own spare parts. The surgeon transplanted this piece of bone into the eight-and-a-half-centimetre gap in Nada's leg with a metal support to give it strength. It was a precarious and skilled procedure, but I believed without a doubt that it was going to work; it had to.

Within weeks, my sister was walking again and she was finally able to pick up her son, who was now twenty months old. Even so, by the time she was released from hospital, this young mother of three children was thin and pale—a ghostly shadow of her former self.

Just as my mother was forced to endure headaches for the rest of her life from the shrapnel imbedded in her cranium, so, too, was my sister left with a permanent disability. She was left with gruesome scars and her left leg would always be shorter than her right, but at least she would never be denied free movement.

It was yet another scar on our family from this war which was to continue for many years to come.

13

The Sixth Commandment

During the civil war, having multiple armies and militias with conflicting agendas in such close proximity was a powder keg ready to explode and, as in most wars, things became much worse before they got better. Being out in the streets was no longer even relatively safe anymore.

On both sides of the Green Line (the divider between East and West Beirut), people were being pulled from cars or taxis and taken as hostages where they were often beaten or killed and then paraded through the streets. The rest of Lebanon—outside of Beirut—was pure chaos with no clear lines for the battle. Multiple conflicts occurred simultaneously in the South, the North, the Bekaa Valley and across all regions of the country.

In Beirut, battles raged in the hotel district and became known as 'Battle of The Hotels' (which included the area of the newly-built Holiday Inn and adjacent hotels), and resulted in many thousands of deaths. To this day, what's left of the Holiday Inn stands empty as a reminder of Beirut's brutal civil war.

During this time of extreme turmoil, there was no clear distinction of who the enemy was and battles between factions were unrelenting: Christian versus Palestinian, Muslim versus Christian, Muslim versus Muslim, and Christian versus Christian.

It seemed that everybody was fighting everybody.

There was no 'right' in any of it—it was all wrong. People who had lost their loved ones retaliated by taking hostages and killing innocent people. It was a savage and devastating time for the whole of Lebanon. Mothers lost their sons and daughters; wives lost their husbands; husbands lost their wives; parents lost their children and children lost their parents. I thank God that in every year of such a bloody war, I was never put in a position where I had to kill anyone. I had the training, I had the skills and I had the weapons, but as God is my witness, I vowed only to use them for defence.

However, that doesn't mean I survived unscathed.

One day in 1978, while I was helping at the humanitarian aid organisation's centre in our area, I met a family of three—a mother and her two children—who were waiting for a social worker to arrange accommodation for them. My understanding from the social worker was that this family had fled to safety after the massacre at Damour in 1976. A Christian town, about 22 kilometres south of Beirut, Damour was attacked by militants and foreign mercenaries, and many of the town's inhabitants were killed, either defending their town or in the massacre that followed. The rest were forced to flee. Initially, arrangements were made for the mother and her children to stay in a vacant two-bedroom apartment in our area, as the owners of this apartment had fled to France to escape the war. However, the owners were now returning. The social worker explained that it could take up to two weeks to source alternative accommodation for this displaced family and, sympathetic to their circumstances, I approached my mother to ask if we could help out by accommodating Rose and her two children until a suitable alternative could be found. My mother was more than happy to assist, and she came with me to the centre to meet them. Rose and her children were grateful but subdued; as so many others who had seen and been through so much trauma were somewhat ambivalent to the world around them.

At first, Rose said very little and they all declined our offer of food and drink. They looked miserable, distraught and withdrawn.

It was only on the second day of her stay with us that Rose broke down and wept as she started to tell us of her family's ordeal. Tears streamed down her face as she described how her husband had been executed in front of her and her innocent children because he had endeavoured to defend his family and home. Her grief overcame her and she began choking, battling to breathe. Mum gave Rose a glass of water, and after she had composed herself, Rose continued recounting how she and her son had been blindfolded and their hands and feet tied. They were forced to sit on the couch helpless while Rose's daughter was raped. They were unable to do anything but listen to the cries and screams of an eleven-year-old child being brutalised. Rose took a deep breath and continued, 'The evil rapist told us that we were so lucky as he was going to spare us. He untied the ropes and shouted, "Leave right now!" Rose explained how she and her children fled—Rose having to almost carry her distraught daughter—not looking back until they were far enough away to be out of danger, their home ablaze behind them. Their hometown, once a place full of love and happy memories, had been transformed into a place of loss, pain and revulsion. The family walked all night to traverse the twenty-two kilometres to reach the relative safety of East Beirut, always cautious and looking over their shoulders in fear. While two years had passed since this terrible ordeal, it was evident that the trauma remained and the horrible and awful memory would remain with their tortured souls forever.

I thought, *"This family's only 'crime' was that they were Christians"*. This is not Lebanon—the one that we once knew and loved. In the past, Christians, Muslims, Druze and Jews had lived together in harmony; they had cared for and looked after each other. This was an unbelievable and shocking change—a new twist on our already warped new reality.

That very same morning we received very sad news that my cousin, who had been in the Lebanese Army, had been killed—

shot in the head by a sniper while endeavouring to hoist the Lebanese flag on the top of a building.

Outraged, I drove to the militia centre. Arriving at the centre, I found that my sombre mood was shared by the many forlorn faces of my comrades, and when I entered the commander's office, he was stooped in his chair, hands covering his head. When he realised I was there, he straightened and tried to disguise his obvious anguish. He described how overnight they had been relentlessly attacked, sustaining numerous casualties, several dead and even some captured, while also having lost valuable equipment and ordinance in the assault. My anger continued to rise.

I no longer wanted to feel vulnerable.

I had lost control of reason and had transcended back to a more primitive state, wanting my pound of flesh for all the injustices bestowed upon my family and my people.

I implored the commander to allow me to join the fray to go on missions, assuring him of my resolve and capability. I wanted to avenge my cousin's death, destroy the evil ones who had killed Rose's husband and raped her daughter, and exact retribution for all the losses and for everything that had occurred since the onset of this repulsive and senseless war. In a deep and assertive voice, the commander inquired, 'So many of our fighters are now on the front line, as well as in other parts of Beirut and in the mountain areas. Are you sure?' I assured him that I was ready.

Later that afternoon, an order was issued from the commander for three people from the militia to go to the basement of a bombed building (located a few blocks away from the centre) to execute twelve men from the opposition. My heart sank when I was the first to be chosen. The twelve were accused of planting explosives in our area and killing more than 100 people. With my mind in overdrive, I grasped for a way that I—a mere nineteen-year-old—could avoid taking lives.

But I had asked for this and here I was.

To make matters even more uncomfortable, Tanios—the 'dark prince' who enjoyed watching me through his newspaper—was to accompany me on the mission, and the third member assigned to this group was a teenager. I was wearing my camouflage militia uniform and a wide canvas belt that housed a sheath for a large knife. We all put on webbing to house magazines of extra rounds, grenades and other essential supplies and then grabbed three automatic rifles from a metal cupboard.

It was a five-minute walk to the building where we found the twelve men, bleeding, cut and bruised, with their hands tied behind their backs. The expressions of desolation on their faces showed they knew all too well what their fate was. Their feet were chained together, and they were crying, begging us to save them, proclaiming their innocence and assuring us they were nothing more than in the wrong place at the wrong time. The men who had beaten them to a bloody pulp had themselves lost loved ones and had left these men to die. With just the three of us present, Tanios decided to be even more cruel and cut off the thumb of one of the captives who, bloody and beaten, cursed Tanios in a soft, weak voice. Tanios told the man he would cut him to pieces if he said one more word. He seemed to take a perverse pleasure in inflicting unnecessary pain on these men whom, my gut told me, were innocent. However, in hindsight, I believe perhaps Tanios was stalling for time because he really didn't want to murder the men.

Nevertheless, Tanios aimed his automatic rifle and was about to start shooting without pause or hesitation, when I knew I had to interfere.

The teenage fighter who had come with us was so sickened at what was about to unfold before his young eyes that he turned and emptied his guts across the basement floor.

None of us wanted to do this. How could anyone feel justified in taking another's life? Even my amorous admirer so eagerly readying his rifle didn't really want to take the lives of men who, in our hearts, we all knew to be innocent. I couldn't handle it any longer. I begged him not to fire, but he snapped back at me, in a strained and taught voice, 'I'm only following orders.'

Knowing I had to do something drastic and unexpected to save these men, I turned to face Tanios, gently positioning the weapon out of harm's way. For a moment, our eyes locked in tense anticipation before I reached up and folded my lips over his. I kissed him with all the emotion I had inside of me, using my tongue to probe the moisture of his willing mouth, until he returned the kiss and began exploring mine.

I felt disgusted to the pit of my soul and I wanted to echo the actions of the teenager and vomit, but I held it in with every ounce of my willpower. I knew this was the only way I could convince him to change his mind. If he had any feelings for me, and he had shown me that he did—even though they repulsed me—he would listen to what I was asking of him and if I had to use my sexuality to save lives, I would do it without hesitation.

Finally, and grudgingly, Tanios pulled away from me, a slightly softened expression in his sparkling eyes, but he nonetheless insisted, 'Chadia, it's an order. I have to shoot these men.'

I took a step back and planted my feet firmly. 'If that's your intention, I'm going to leave now, and if I walk out that door, I won't be speaking to you again for the rest of my life.' I shouted, 'These people are innocent! Cut the ropes and let them go home to their families.'

We all knew none of these men had been given the luxury of a proper investigation, given the earlier chaos, confusion, disruption and madness inflicted upon the militia centre. Indeed, later we discovered that each of them had been in our area for a completely valid and benign reason. One had been delivering fruits and vegetables; another's daughter lived in the area and he had come to collect her and her baby; another was visiting his sister who was terminally ill. Each one of those men had a reason to live and we had no reason to deprive them of their lives.

Tense moments of silence passed between us as the twelve men gawked at the unfolding drama, I'm sure in silent prayer that my actions would spare their lives. It was as though, for a moment, time stood still and we all stopped breathing. The decision whether these men would live or die hung on Tanios's decision. The tension was palpable.

'Cut the ropes,' he finally ordered and my heart was overwhelmed with joy. Despite how horrendous the situation was, we had done something good and just. We had spared them. The teenager and I eagerly moved to release the men from a fate they didn't deserve, to allow them to return to their homes. Again, I thought, *"Their only 'crime' was that they were Muslims"*.

Even then, nothing was that simple. They had been sentenced to death, and if they were spotted, they would be killed. And so, perhaps, would we. So, Tanios and the teenager gave their shirts to two of the hostages. To ensure their safe escape and our own freedom from the wrath of our senior officers, we bundled them into our vehicles—eight in a van with Tanios and the teenager and the remaining four in a jeep with me—and hurried them to a safe haven close to the same bridge where my life had nearly been taken years before. It was getting dark and, luckily, some construction and work had been done to raise the bridge so it provided good cover from sight. Ironically, where once cars and bodies alike were sent to their doom by this bridge, these men were spared such a fate by camouflaging themselves underneath it. From there, one by one, so as not to be spotted in a group of twelve, they began the long journey home to safety and continued on with the rest of their lives.

To this day, I cannot believe we succeeded in defying orders and deceiving our commanding officers. No one asked us to show proof of the dead bodies because they assumed that we'd dumped them with the others piled under that Low Bridge.

Of course, Tanios was emboldened by the long and lingering kiss I had bestowed upon him in that dungeon of doom, but from that day until the day I gratefully saw him no more, I was always able to come up with an excuse to avoid any further physical contact.

My anger and lust for vengeance had led me to this point, and it was only when I saw how vulnerable, scared, broken and innocent those accused men were, that my anger subsided and I comprehended how anger can lead us to wrong, irrational and awful conclusions and actions.

Despite this inner revelation, the beatings and brutality continued; it was the way of life in Lebanon at the time. In fact, on one occasion, my brother Antoine, visiting us from the Gulf, was dragged from a taxi leaving Beirut airport in the West side. He received no less of a thrashing than the twelve men whose lives had nearly ended in the basement. Mercifully, he was given the privilege of some investigation resulting in proof of his innocence and, after two days, he was released. A heavy toll was being exacted on us for nothing more than having been born into this beautiful and once peaceful country.

Our two weeks with Rose and her family went by very quickly and soon the charity organisation found alternative accommodation for them. It was very emotional saying our goodbyes. We all hugged and kissed and, as they left, we burst into tears because they had touched our hearts and souls. The suffering Rose and her family had endured was indescribable, but their story was not unique in this cruel and indiscriminate civil war.

Rose's experience, the men in the basement, and my brother's vicious beating raised disquiet in my decision to continue to be part of this complicated and confused conflict, so I reduced my commitment with the militia down to three days and did not volunteer for any further missions.

14

Spies

It was late 1979 and every breath we took, every turn we made was still fraught with peril, so I suppose I should have expected trouble when my brother Walid rang us at home asking if we could obtain a copy of his master's certificate from the Lebanese University.

At that time, there was no such thing as privacy laws to deter us from collecting documents from the university on Walid's behalf. There was, however, the very real and terrifying obstacle of dodging bombs and bullets while we drove the twenty minutes into West Beirut where the university was located—in the territory of the opposition. Walid needed a copy sent to Cyprus as soon as possible—for very important reasons—and the only way to obtain the certificate was in person.

I volunteered to retrieve the document and asked my friend, Annette, to join me for the journey. Annette was a slip of a girl—almost painfully thin—but very tall, with lush brown hair cascading down her shoulders and framing her porcelain complexion and beautiful face. There was a ceasefire at the time, so we were cautious, but not overly alarmed about the journey or potential risks. It was the way life went on in Lebanon: when there was a ceasefire or there weren't any regular bombings taking place, people went to school, went to work, and generally tried to have normal lives.

We took a taxi from our home to the Green Line area and then caught another taxi straight to the university. It was a simple matter to obtain my brother's degree, so we paid a fee at the administration office and left.

We shared a taxi with three other passengers—strangers to us, but fellow countrymen—from the university to the border. We'd been driving for about ten minutes when we came across a bold orange sign declaring a detour. Dutifully, the taxi driver complied with the directions, not that he had much of a choice. We followed one sign after another until we found ourselves winding through narrow roads flanked by tall, thin buildings before we emerged into a vegetable, meat and fish market. I glanced at Annette—whose face clearly showed her fear, as did that of the old man to Annette's right and the couple in their forties in the bench seat at the front. We soon discovered, that it had been no accident that the detour had directed us to last sign and I thought I heard a collective gulp in the car when we all read the words, 'PLO STOP'.

Founded in the early 1960s, The Palestine Liberation Organisation (PLO) was developed to liberate Palestine through armed means. In the early 1970s, the PLO had moved its primary base of operations to Beirut. Needless to say, the PLO was made up of strong and tough people who believed wholeheartedly in their cause and this combination of strength and passionate belief could be deadly. It was enough to cause others to be wary of them and steer clear if possible, so even though our trip to the other side was innocent, being stopped by the PLO sounded alarm bells inside my head and I knew we were in grave danger.

At the PLO checkpoint, there were four men wearing army fatigues, brandishing Kaláshnikov assault rifles (common in that era) and the all-too-familiar Russian stick grenades. They ordered us to open the windows and demanded our IDs. All of us, including the driver handed our ID documents out of the car. One of them was holding a notebook, checking if any of the passengers' names were on the list. It was a great relief when none of us appeared to be on the list and everything was in order, but this didn't appear to please them. They proceeded to search the car, checking us all for weapons, documents or anything they could use to incriminate us. This process took about thirty minutes, while they bombarded us with questions. Finally—after some extremely tense minutes ticked by agonisingly slowly—they reached the conclusion that our fellow passengers and the driver were free to go. Annette and I, however, were not so fortunate as they decided we warranted further questioning. I froze, hardly breathing, I thought to myself, 'I'm in grave danger. I'm a member of a Christian militia.'

In a blur of shoving and constant chaotic movement, blindfolds were roughly dragged across our eyes and our hands were tied behind our backs before we were jostled around, shoved into another vehicle and driven to a remote location. We didn't know where we were heading, but noticed that the road was rough and unsealed. I guessed it was about ten minutes later when the vehicle stopped and we heard a gate creak open for us to drive through. We stopped again within seconds and the uniformed men removed our blindfolds, ordering us to walk in front of them and towards the building ahead, which was very busy and noisy, with cars, jeeps and other vehicles coming and going.

The building was an old, large one-level structure and there appeared to be significant damage to its left side. Palestinian flags were at the entrance and flying high from the roof. In the distance, I saw many small tin sheds, and a few larger structures which looked like warehouses or shelters. The ground underfoot was muddy and spongy, most likely from the rain that had fallen the night before. The men flanked us as we entered a huge room filled with other fighters who looked like they were waiting for more captives. Propaganda posters lined the walls. There were rusted metal tables and chairs and large metal cupboards overflowing with every conceivable weapon. Boxes of ammunition and additional weapons lay strewn across the floor.

I had stayed calm for the most part—despite my abject terror at finding myself in a PLO camp—but poor Annette could not stop weeping and all my attempts to calm her remained futile. The fighters unbound us and ordered us to sit so the interrogation could begin.

'Why did you come to West Beirut today?' the lead man asked with a loud and rough voice.

'I was here to collect my brother's university degree,' I explained.

'Are you spies?' he demanded.

'Of course, we're not spies,' I blustered back, shaking my head at the ridiculousness of such a comment.

'Are you with the Phalanges?' he probed further. 'Of course, we're not,' I repeated.

'Your friend is wearing a large wooden cross, which means she's definitely with the Phalanges.'

The Lebanese Phalanges Party is a Christian Democratic political party founded in 1936, mainly supported by Lebanese Maronite Catholics. As a symbol of their faith, many Maronite Christians would wear a wooden cross, and as such these PLO men assumed that we were aligned to the political group.

I glanced towards Annette, inwardly annoyed that she had been so ignorant in wearing such a symbol when knowingly travelling through the opposition's territory, and returned my gaze to the man interrogating us. As calmly as I could I said, 'As you can see, she's crying like a baby. If she were a member of the Phalanges or any other organisation, don't you think she would be braver?'

But my attempts at reasoning with him were disregarded. The man stepped closer. His gaze was piercing so he could judge whether I would flinch or lose eye contact out of fear, or more importantly, to determine whether I was lying.

'How many of you are there?' he persisted. 'Which organisation are you with? Who sent you to spy on us?'

It seemed no answer would be acceptable except for the one he wanted, which would almost certainly lead to our rape, brutalisation and, ultimately, death. I was inwardly terrified, yet I remained calm and somewhat assertive.

'I'm a Christian girl from the East of Beirut. I came to collect my brother's document from the university. I assure you I'm not a spy.' I knew I had to be firm as they were savagely violent, lacking any compassion or heart.

He ordered us to take off our coats and shoes. It was freezing that day, so we were soon shivering.

'Turn your face towards the wall and put your hands up. Both of you!' he demanded. With no option but to comply, we acquiesced to his orders.

Two hours later, we were standing like that, exhausted, shivering from both fear and the cold, and our arms were numb. Each time we tried to lower and rest our arms we were promptly ordered at gun point to maintain them above our heads. Our lives were in their hands.

'They're going to kill us,' Annette whispered to me. 'I can feel it, Chadia. I'm not going to see my mother, my sisters and my brother ever again,' she sobbed.

'Annette, stop it,' I hissed back. 'Please be strong. God will help us to survive. Please, my friend, just start praying quietly.'

Two of the fighters approached from behind and started fondling our bodies. Annette started to hyperventilate and, reaching my limit—whether it would mean my death or not—I kicked one of them and turned my face towards him. His rifle was roughly shoved up my nose and even though my heart was pounding so hard I thought it would explode, I held my preservation for life above my own fear. Then one of the men said loudly, 'We're going to enjoy raping you both and cutting your beautiful bodies into pieces to send back to the Phalanges.'

I looked into his eyes and in an unflinching voice the words came, 'I'm not scared of you.' I spat at him. 'Kill us if you wish. We're proud of who we are. Don't mess with our honour. Go ahead and kill us. Kill us and see what happens to all of you,' I challenged. 'I demand to see your leader, now! The general. Because you don't know who we are or what will happen if you hurt us!'

The fire in his eyes made it clear that he was not used to being spoken to in such a manner and certainly not by a young woman.

I showed no fear. This was it.

'Can you not see? We've been held for hours! We're exhausted. We're innocent and we need to sit down, please.' I spoke with assertion and somehow grace, not wavering or giving in to the sheer fear and dread I was experiencing internally.

Incredibly, the man brought us two chairs, but our hands were then tied and our feet were bound to the legs of the chairs after we sat down. Without warning, one of the men struck Annette across the face. I couldn't take it, I tried to get up from the chair, but it was attached to me. I was praying and praying from deep within my heart that someone—anyone—would intervene and save us from the fate that surely awaited us.

The truth is that, yes, I was terrified, but my militia training had taught me to diffuse fear by feigning courage. Such defiance was my only weapon to try to safeguard my friend and myself. My thought was that such men may respect courage and this might buy us more time. Underneath this thin veneer of boldness, I was nearly paralysed by the thought that our lives could end at any moment.

As this intimidation and chaos was ensuing, a tall man also wearing army fatigues entered the room. He was wearing a cap, which barely disguised the fact that his dark hair was greying. 'Who are these girls?' he asked the fighters.

'We think they're spies,' one of the men replied.

'Really?' the tall man mused. 'Untie their hands and legs at once.'

Clearly this was the man in charge, so some of the PLO operatives immediately obeyed his commands, to our immense relief.

The moment I was unbound, I bent to my knees in supplication before their leader and pleaded, 'Sir please! We're not spies. We're innocent. We simply came to West Beirut because I needed to collect my brother's degree from the university. In honour of your wife, your mother, your sister and your daughter, please save us. We are innocent.'

This was the first time I had allowed my emotions to come to the surface and my eyes welled with tears of desperation.

The tall man took a moment. He looked me in the eyes, then up and down, then turned his attention to Annette. I knew he was making a decision about our fate. Did he believe us? Could he sense our innocence and honesty? His face flushed beetroot as he then snapped at the PLO men, who were clearly his juniors. He barked, 'You're dogs! You're animals! You're bad! We trained you to judge the good from the bad. These girls are clearly innocent and good people. Release them at once, arrange and pay for a taxi to take them to the border.'

I couldn't believe our good fortune. 'Thank you! Thank you!'

I wept, finally showing the true extent of my vulnerability and the weakness I had been holding in until that point. I don't doubt if he hadn't intervened at that moment, we may well have been raped and killed. Two more victims of this insane war.

Annette and I were extremely fortunate that day.

The reality was, though, that too many girls in Lebanon were not as fortunate. The rotting corpses of rape victims—often found in buildings, on the streets and in elevators—had become a frequent and horrifically commonplace sight in both the East and the West of Beirut.

The reality and brutality of war is that evil often takes control and people lose their humanity by inflicting torture on other young and innocent victims. They allow their hatred for lost loved ones to take over and infect them, causing them to take drugs to numb the pain or hurt others to avenge their lost loved ones. There are no winners in war, only victims who will never break free of the pain and loss and helplessness.

Seeing my dishevelled state when I returned home and having been worried sick by my nine-hour absence, my mother ran straight to me and gave me the biggest hug. As she held me, she wept into my shoulder, 'I thought I'd lost you forever, my baby.'

I hugged her back, trying to swallow my own tears. 'Mum, you taught us all the good things in life. With your blessings I'm saved and wasn't harmed. I love you so much.'

Later, I was able to put to words the true nature of what we had experienced, but for that moment, I was completely overcome by immense gratitude and joy and so paused to embrace it.

15

Josephine

The reality of war tears at the essence of our beings and at the very fabric of society.

No one remains untouched.

Early in April of 1980, something happened that made me simultaneously realise that I could no longer tolerate the effects of the war while also giving me hope that good will always prevail over evil.

Our neighbour, Ghassan, was away in the country for a few days and his wife was violently ill. Their youngest son, Samir, who was ten at the time, suddenly came running from their unit on the second level of our building, crying. His sister, Josephine, had been kidnapped right in front of him, two hours before and had not returned. He didn't want to worry his ailing mother with his fears, so he came to me for guidance and help.

Trying to calm him down, I took him aside and asked him to tell me exactly what had happened.

Samir described how he and his sister had been walking in the area when a man in a red sports car had approached them and asked if they would like to go for a drive. They both politely declined and continued walking. The man persisted, creeping ever closer to the brother and sister until finally opening his door and forcing Josephine into the car. Before speeding off, he warned Samir not to say anything to anyone and he drove away. Samir waited innocently for some time for his sister to return, but to no avail.

Samir provided a surprisingly detailed description of both the man and the vehicle—sufficient enough for me to take at least some action. I instructed him to wait in our home while I drove to the Phalanges militia centre two kilometres away. There was a young man there I knew from the neighbourhood—Nikola—who was honest and kind, so I believed he could help me locate our missing neighbour. 'Whatever I can do for you, Chadia,' he had assured me. 'You just let me know.'

When I explained the situation, his expression became grim and his willingness to assist seemed to evaporate like a morning mist. 'Oh, I'm sorry. I can't help you with that,' he almost whispered. I insisted that the man who had abducted our neighbour was one of his militia group. 'Please! Please! I don't believe there's any hope if you don't at least make a couple of calls. She's so young. Her father is away, her mother is ill and her little brother is devastated. You can't just leave the family like this without at least picking up the phone,' I pleaded.

He studied me thoughtfully. 'Maybe we may know where the girl is,' he conceded, 'but if we go there, it will mean a big battle. There'll be shooting and bloodshed. Is that what you want, Chadia?' he asked me sternly, his eyes searching mine for an answer.

'She's only fourteen years old,' I explained, half in tears and half determined.

He sighed heavily, considering the implications of the decision he was about to make, but appeared to have empathised with the necessity to take action. 'Alright, Chadia. Let's go.' I closed my eyes, releasing the breath I had been unaware I was holding, knowing that at least now there was hope.

Nikola arranged an escort with two jeeps of fighters, to flank my little orange car while we drove to the place where Josephine was being held.

It was about seven in the evening when we arrived in the area via a very narrow and rough road. Everything was quiet and night was falling. The buildings hung in ruins, which was a *familiar* sight across a city whose buildings had been eaten up by bombs—abandoned shops and empty streets, remnants of homes that were once filled with happy laughter.

On a stealth mission, we extinguished our car lights and proceeded slowly to where we believed Josephine was being held. Finally, Nikola stopped his jeep, got out and approached my car. 'This is as far as we can go without risking bullets and bloodshed,' he told me. 'From here, you must go alone, but my men and I will be here to protect you if it does go wrong. Just call out for help and we'll be at your side.'

The idea was that a lone woman would have a much better chance at rescuing the young girl, as opposed to armed militia storming in, which certainly would have resulted in the opening of hostilities, injuries and fatalities on both sides. Although they were from the same organisation, they couldn't confront one of their own without it ending in bloodshed as it would have been considered traitorous.

They'd pointed out a whitewashed building, open to the elements from bomb blasts and militia attacks. There was rubble everywhere, and before me stood a large stairwell, which twisted to each level. As I started my ascent up the staircase, I noticed that the street was in view through the numerous holes on the adjacent wall. It seemed extraordinary that the building was even still standing as its supports had long been destroyed—the exposed beams broken in half. The staircase was precarious and with any misstep, I could have fallen straight through. Where there were once intact windows, there were now only shards of glass still attached to the window frames. The whole place was a testament to the devastation that had ravaged our land and our lives.

My heart beat a drum-like bass in my throat and ears and goosebumps erupted all over my body with every step I took up the rickety stairs, while bats screeched overhead and rats scurried underfoot. I prayed I wouldn't lose my footing and accidentally make a sound loud enough to reveal my position. The stench of something burning and the smell of rancid food wafted from a distance, mixing with the sweat of my fear and causing me to suppress a wretch as I snuck up the bombed-out stairs.

Without the moon to illuminate the interior of the building, I was worried I could easily fall into a crevice created by the blasts. I kept going up and holding on to the rickety and sticky balustrade in this abandoned, brutalised building. When I reached the second level, I realised I couldn't go any further as there was a pile of fallen concrete blocking my way. I would have to go around it.

'Josephine? Josephine? Are you there?' I whispered.

There was nothing; silence was my only reply. I attempted to navigate the unsteady floor beneath me. There were numerous holes and a wrong step could have led to the floor breaking beneath me to the level below. I was walking through a living nightmare. I looked around, hoping my senses would assist me in locating my young neighbour.

'Josephine? Josephine? Are you there?' I called again. My voice quietened as I spoke.

Straining my ears, I convinced myself I heard a soft cry. 'Josephine? Are you there?' I persisted, and held my breath, hoping for a response.

And then I heard it. The unmistakable, disgusting sound of a man forcing himself on a woman and her piteous, small cries of protest.

Everything after that happened in a flash and I had no time to think. I was overcome with revulsion at the thought of what this man was obviously doing to Josephine and I wanted to hurt him—to kill him—for his lecherous and despicable behaviour. I felt as though I stepped outside myself and became someone who I swore I would never become. I wanted vengeance for this young girl who was being used and abused by this nasty man.

But it was so dark and I was relying on the moonlight, so I couldn't see clearly enough to find them. I dared not turn on my torch for fear I would make myself a target and, to this day I can still see the tiny lights coming through the holes on the walls and the broken windows.

I believe I was standing in what was left of two rooms, but it was hard to tell in the dark because the damage was so severe that there wasn't much left of the apartment's internal walls. And then I vaguely saw the shadow of a man walking from a distance before he ducked behind a little wall. I thought he must be reaching for his gun, so without hesitation, I pulled my gun from inside my coat and yelled, "Stop! Stop! I'm going to shoot you." When he showed no sign of stopping, I shot at him—unsure of where or even if I'd hit him—until he started screaming loudly. The echo of his voice filled me with fear and loathing. Before I could turn on my torch to find him and shoot him again, he jumped from the large opening or a window and disappeared.

Finally turning on my torch, I easily located Josephine and made my way to her. It was such an awful feeling and I was sickened to see the rapist's clothes, shoes and weapons laying discarded on the broken and dirty floor. There was blood, too—his blood—and I believe he was trying to put his clothes back on when I actually thought he was reaching for a gun. For the first time during the war, I was sorry I hadn't killed someone.

'Oh, my goodness! Josephine!' I gasped.

She had sunk into a dank corner, covering her mouth so her sobs weren't too audible.

'Josephine, it's going to be alright,' I whispered softly. 'Come with me, please.'

The poor girl was too terrified to move. She looked shocked, then started crying. The walls and floors were damaged severely, making every move life-threatening as we could have easily fallen through one of the cracks or holes. I had to grasp her long-plaited hair gently but firmly to encourage her to move in my direction. We both knew she was lucky to be alive, but I will never forget the haunted look in her eyes as my torch found her face. I steadied her hand as we carefully negotiated the unstable stairs, through the rubble that shrouded the entrance and the street, towards the vehicles, where Nikola and the other fighters were waiting. I thanked him and his team, then went to my car to drive Josephine home.

I remember all this as clearly as if it were yesterday. Driving home that night, my hands felt like they'd been glued to the steering wheel. It was only when I got home that I noticed they were soaked with blood and my clothes were full of dirt, dust and blood too.

Back at home, I tidied Josephine up before I returned her to the safe and loving arms of her mother and brother. The mission was a success and Josephine was saved, but she had not survived unscathed and neither had I.

The next day, I took Josephine to a doctor in a different area from ours for a full check-up. I may not have saved her innocence, but I did save her life, and I suppose if there is a point to be made here, it is that while there were many evil fighters who committed evil acts during that infernal war, there were also many good men—like Nikola. If not for good men like him, our neighbour would have suffered a worse fate than the horror of the rape she had endured. She would have almost certainly lost her life.

I was later completely disgusted to hear that Josephine's rapist had lied and told everyone he was shot in a skirmish with the other side. He was hailed as a hero and I was helpless to tell the real story of what happened to him without endangering Josephine, myself, and my friend who had helped me find her. It was such an awful feeling, knowing what he had done and not being able to tell the world the truth of it.

Years later, I learned two things that gave me great joy.

Josephine, still living in Lebanon, was happily married to a doctor and had three children of her own. She had studied and become a social worker, helping victims of sexual abuse. Imparting new life and hope to people she could truly empathise with. God protected her that day and blessed me with the strength required to intervene.

And the man who had kidnapped and raped Josephine had later been killed in a confrontation while trying to steal items from the port of Beirut.

16

Time to Go

Although I was truly elated that I'd found the courage and resilience to rescue Josephine, her ordeal made me realise how deeply troubled I had become during the constant conflict of the war and my years in the militia.

War and hard times can mould and transfigure people to become both better—stronger, more assertive, and worse—angry, vengeful. Up until Josephine's rescue, I had believed that I had escaped the worst of it, but my emotions and thoughts while shooting her rapist told me that some of that anger and vengeance was seeping in through the cracks in my carefully constructed walls of hope.

But it was more than just my occasionally angry and vengeful thoughts that made me realise that I was ready for a change.

It is true that outwardly I was strong and that I had—when necessary—displayed resilience and bravery beyond my years. However—after five or so years of losing my relatives and friends, seeing my family injured, walking through streets strewn with bodies and watching my once beautiful country being ravaged by an insatiable bloodlust—the weight of this trauma began to take its toll. I'd lost so much weight that I was barely more than skin on bone. I began experiencing panic attacks. I would shiver anytime I heard an explosion or gunshot, which was frequently. I was constantly on edge, worrying about what could happen next. I'm sure, now, that I had developed PTSD, along with most of the other militia volunteers and citizens after spending so long in a war zone, but back then such things weren't yet recognised.

I resigned my volunteer post with the militia and tried to return to a 'normal' civilian life. I began a part-time clerical job in an engineering firm just across from the Low Bridge. The Syrian army had set up a checkpoint just before the bridge and commandeered an old building adjacent to it. Shortly after the implementation of this new checkpoint, I was stopped before driving across the bridge and was asked to present my car registration. At the time, I didn't have it on me. The Syrian guards insisted that I leave the car at the checkpoint and walk home to bring the required document. While I was talking to the two soldiers, and promising them that I would make sure I brought this document with me the next time, their commander came out from his office and, after introducing himself as Haitham, took over the conversation. He started bombarding me with all sorts of questions, including some rather personal questions about whether I was studying or working, married or engaged. I answered all his questions quickly, as I was in a hurry to leave to get to work, though was purposely friendly towards him as I wanted his favour in allowing me to drive across the bridge without any further delay. This was obviously successful and he instructed his troops to let me go. I gave him a big smile and left.

Thereafter when crossing this checkpoint and The Low Bridge, Haitham would come out of his office to greet me with boxes of Syrian sweets. The gesture may have been benign, but it made me feel extremely uncomfortable. These people were already trying to control every facet of our lives, so it didn't take me long to decide that the prudent course of action would be to drive the extra miles to avoid incurring either their attention or their wrath.

It was exhausting, always having to avoid conflict and proactively protect myself from the evil surrounding me.

While I had effectively been trained to kill, I had always refused to do it. In contrast to the brutality in Beirut, Lebanon still maintained a rich, ancient and diverse culture that was joyous and full of life. I knew in my heart that if I remained much longer, there was a chance that even my determined soul would be corrupted or tainted by the death and destruction surrounding us, as it had been, briefly, when I rescued Josephine and had felt justified in trying to kill her rapist. I never wanted to go back to that dark place.

It was time for me to go.

Josephine's rescue was an isolated happy ending in a seemingly never-ending tidal wave of unspeakable and atrocious acts that flooded our country on a daily basis.

Both sides were killing innocent people, raping young girls and looting stores. There was no honour or sanity in this conflict. And rapidly there was no honour or sanity in those it left behind. Through my parents' and grandparents' generations, it was rare to have signed contracts in Lebanon. People shook hands or men would put their hand on their moustache (as a sign of honour) to finalise a deal. Once the deal was made, nobody could change it. However, during the war, poverty and hardship sadly fostered evil and corruption, causing people to ignore time-honoured customs and treat each other without honour or respect.

I think the thing that kept us all going—despite the horrors of rape, torture, killings, revenge, and the breakdown of our civilized customs—was that, at our core, in our hearts and our souls, the Lebanese are a happy people. We are generous and we love our families and friends. We love life. We love entertainment. We love our food and we love Lebanon.

We used to joke that 'Lebanon' is a male name and all the countries around it have female names, so we were the only rooster in the hen house with all of the ladies surrounding us wanting a piece of us. Humour is a great leveller in any situation, and love, they say, conquers all. So, we used both to cope, to survive.

I believe that nobody is purely bad. There is good and bad in everything and everybody. It is how we decide to react to situations that ultimately determines whether we will be judged as good or bad. I maintain that the Lebanese people as a whole are good, joyous, loving people; it was only the tragedy of circumstances that sent a few good souls in a very bad direction, Lebanon is and will always be my homeland. It is a beautiful country and I am proud to be of Lebanese origin. It is arguably the best geographic point in the Middle East. Before the war, it was even dubbed the 'Switzerland of the Middle East' due to its fabulous four seasons. You could swim and water ski on the beach and ski in the snowy mountains, sometimes even in the same season. For a small country, 10,452 square kilometres in size, it is full of life, and for me, despite all the horror I witnessed, it is truly full of happy memories. People from all religions were friendly, whether rich or poor, so it was easy to become fluent in the customs and etiquettes of several cultures. Greetings in Lebanon are a mix of French and Middle Eastern cultures. With a warm and welcoming smile accompanied by a handshake while saying, 'Marhaba', it is a greeting that can be given to all without causing any offence. When greeting close friends, three kisses on alternating cheeks are commonplace in the French style. Taking an arm when greeting a person and being sure to ask about the health of their family, is equivalent to the Australian saying, 'G'day, mate. How are you going?'

There are many beautiful etiquettes and customs from my country which I uphold to this day as treasured traditions and memories.

When the war began, many people threw these customs and etiquettes out with yesterday's rubbish as they began to realise today could be their last day.

I admit now that I, too, fell victim to this syndrome, even if I didn't admit to it then. There were dark moments when I would huddle in the corner of a room wondering if I would live to see another sunrise, if I would ever run through those glorious cyclamen fields again, away from death and disaster and towards who knew what.

I had the most beautiful childhood. Even though we weren't wealthy in financial terms, we were rich in so many other ways—with love, family, friends, joy and the simple treasures that make life worthwhile.

Even amidst the darkness, there were frequent sparks of miraculous light.

17

Leaving Lebanon

In early May of 1980, I received a letter from Tony—an old school friend who was studying to be an orthodontist at a university in Boston, Massachusetts.

The letter read:

Dearest Chadia,

Hope you and your family are well. I don't know what to call you; my school friend only, or my sweetheart?

I wish you could come to the United States to continue your studies. You could come to any state or city. Please leave the war. I am very worried about you, my friend.

In the United States, people have better opportunities.

I know you love Lebanon and you want to stay close to your family. I also miss my family so much. As you know, I am the only man in the family, I only have a sister and my mum. My mum cries all the time, on a daily basis for me to come back home. As you know, I lost my father when I was a baby. We all get attached to our family and our country, and of course we do not forget the fine traditions, but please think about this letter seriously. I hope you will come to America to be safe and to have a brighter future.

With love,
Tony

I tossed and turned as I pondered the possibilities. It was impossible for me to continue my studies in Lebanon. My university was in West Beirut, but due to the war I hadn't been able to regularly attend classes for my business and law degree, so I quit. I'd only completed a year and a half of study.

I had also resigned from my part-time job at the engineering firm—the one close to the Low Bridge—and started another clerical job at another office. Everything seemed to be going well, but I remained anxious—plagued by thoughts of how vulnerable we all were and how I could be killed at any time or something might happen to my loved ones. This uncertainty and insecurity weighed heavily on my mind and emotions.

I loved to help others, always trying to be there for family members and friends, and I wanted everyone to be happy. My sense of duty and responsibility was paramount, but I was beginning to realise that if I couldn't help myself, I couldn't help anybody else. Tony's letter played on my mind and, admittedly, I found the prospect of living in America enticing. I started considering the possibilities more seriously as each day passed.

By the end of July, I decided that enough was enough.

Summoning my courage, I broached the subject with my mother, explaining to her that I wanted to go and wished to continue my studies in the United States. It came as no surprise that she didn't object at all; she could see and feel how much I needed this change. Not only did she know how responsible I was, but she knew a move to America would mean a new life for me—a life with no more suffering from the war and new opportunities for me to discover.

We approached the American Embassy in West Beirut, and after waiting in line for several hours, inquired as to the process and how long it would take to get a student visa. To my shock and disappointment, I was told six to twelve months or maybe longer. Perhaps the length of time to process an application for a student visa was, in some way, tied to the fact that during the civil war, a US ambassador, his Lebanese driver, and an economic counsellor from the embassy were kidnapped and assassinated. In response to these killings and given the deteriorating security conditions during Lebanon's civil war, there had been a gradual reduction of US Embassy staffing and functions.

But now that my mind was made up, that was simply too long to wait. There had to be another way.

My half-brother, Lex (from my father's first marriage), had always been in friendly contact with us, especially during my dad's illness and during our tragic bonding experience over his untimely death. Lex owned a company called AHB in West Beirut and his business acumen was matched only by his worldly wisdom. When I explained the situation, he told me it was easy to get a business visa to the United States and it would be a simple matter for him to arrange.

Without further fanfare, he crafted a letter to the American Embassy which went as follows:

Embassy of the United States of America,
Beirut 27 August 1980

Dear Sirs,

We would be most grateful if you could kindly grant a visa to Miss Chadia whom we are delegating to visit the United States for the purpose of initiating contacts with American firms in the business machines field.

Our firm has been established since May 1972 and we are currently handling Japanese and German business machines, but would like to market products manufactured by reputable American firms. We would therefore appreciate any assistance you can give to Miss Chadia in this connection.

Miss Chadia's expenses during her US visit will be borne by our firm.

Yours very truly,
AHB SRL

With the letter, they enclosed a newspaper clipping showing some of the business machines they handled. I completed my application and set out for the American Embassy with the letter, incredibly thankful for Lex's assistance. However, Mum and I were delayed by many Syrian checkpoints and never-ending lines that when we finally arrived at the embassy, I wondered if God was trying to send me a sign that I shouldn't go. Deep down, though, I knew I needed to leave.

I was certain that my time in my homeland was coming to an end. Every fibre of my being told me this was the correct decision. Patiently, although admittedly without much choice, I waited and waited for my turn. From there, it was smooth sailing and my business visa to visit America and Canada was granted on the spot. There was just one drawback: My visa was only valid for three months.

There was so much to organise: bags had to be packed, tickets to be bought and a long line of teary farewells to be made.

Not long before I was to leave for America, my mother decided that we should visit family in the Bekaa Valley, so we set out up the steep hill in a traffic jam. I was never one to refuse my mother anything, but while waiting to creep up this hill at a snail's pace, I was suddenly swamped with a sense of foreboding.

'I'm telling you, Mama, something is wrong,' I insisted.

Having learned to trust my intuition over the years, my mother decided to leave the choice up to me. I didn't need to be told twice. I made a U-turn and headed back down the mountain. Within minutes, there was a fireball in the distance, in the direction we had been driving. A petrol truck had exploded and several vehicles on both sides of the highway had burned with it, killing their occupants. Had we remained there we would have been among them.

Clearly, my time was not up but it was time for the move to America. I was looking forward to a second chance at life and the opportunity to leave the misery that surrounded us behind. Once I thought I had thick skin, but that skin was starting to melt. I was both burdened by the knowledge that I was leaving those I loved in this environment and relieved that I'd soon be saying farewell. Still, it was a surreal sensation knowing I had made a decision to say farewell to my family and my homeland.

A week before my flight to the United States, I resigned from my job. I also asked my two younger brothers to help me fix and re-paint our window shutters that had been damaged by shrapnel and bullet holes. We patched, sanded and painted them in jade green. They didn't look great as the damage was severe, but at least they were clean and green. We also painted the walls, doors and frames of both of our units. I'm not sure why I did this as we were in a war zone and it was crazy of me to do so, but maybe my mind was telling me that I wouldn't be coming back and this was a gesture of hope for my family who remained. Perhaps these green shutters could brighten their days and take away some of the traumatic memories from the past.

Two days before I was scheduled to leave, Mum and Nada organised a small farewell party for me with my friends and then all that was left to do was pack and say my goodbyes. My large white Samsonite suitcase was pristine, and I had it filled with as many clothes as I could fit.

And then, early one autumn morning, my adventure to a new life began. Wearing black jeans and a red shirt, carrying my black handbag and a brown Samsonite makeup case Antoine had bought for me, I climbed into one of the two cars that my family had readied to take me on my journey to the airport.

The weather was storybook perfect. Not too hot and not too cold. My brother Jalil took my suitcase to the MEA (Middle East Airlines) counter, where I waited to check in behind the few people ahead of me. Once that was accomplished, I passed the point of no return and it was time to have a final coffee with my family before they started paging the passengers to board the flight to New York from Terminal 7.

I hugged and kissed all the family members purposefully, leaving my mother until last to give her the biggest hug of all. While I was hugging her, she said, 'Chadia, trust God! Be patient and never give up.'

Instead of showing sadness, I threw them a big, sunny smile and vowed, 'I will see you soon.' I knew from the bottom of my heart that after a goodbye, there will always be a hello, and home is where my heart is.

I knew if I made the most of my opportunities in America, received a good education and gained profitable employment, that one day I might return to Lebanon and help my family— also hoping by then that the grace of God would allow peace in our land.

There were two transit stops en route—one in Amman and the other in Amsterdam—but the time literally flew as I befriended people on the flight. I enjoyed a game of backgammon with a young man travelling to the United States to continue his studies. He was travelling with his mother and father, who were taking a vacation. Before I knew it, the captain announced, 'Please fasten your seatbelts. We will be landing in New York in twenty minutes' time. Please adjust your watches, the local time is 9 pm.'

I gazed out of the window and was stunned by how shiny and inviting New York City was. A feeling of belonging and excitement swept over me like a great tidal wave. There was no doubt in my mind that there was nowhere in the world like New York.

As the wheels smoothly made contact with the tarmac, passengers began applauding their arrival in the *home of the brave and the land of the free*. None of the applause was louder than my own.

PART II

18

Coming to America

It was 9:20 pm on the eve of Halloween when I landed at JFK airport. Having come from Lebanon where there was a war, US Customs wanted to know every detail about me. Was I involved in the fighting? Was I a spy? Why was I coming to America? How long would I be there? Their questions felt like an interrogation. They ransacked my suitcase; everything in it was viewed with suspicion and my personal belongings were tossed around with no regard for how this might be affecting me.

I was so flustered by the end of the experience, that in closing my sturdy white suitcase, I caught my thumb in the clasp and blood poured over the smooth white exterior of the case. For a moment, I gazed upon it thinking it looked like a wounded dove, forgetting it was me that was bleeding. The officials kindly gave me some dressings to bind my wound, but I didn't feel especially grateful after their questions and the rough treatment of my belongings; all I wanted to do was escape and set foot on American soil. It was long after 11 pm when I was finally allowed to leave Customs. From the terminal, I went to the first pay phone I spotted and called the friends (neighbours from back home who had lived in our building) who I intended to stay with to let them know I was on my way. Their son, Kamil, had been one of my close childhood friends and had migrated to the United States in 1974—the year before the civil war in Lebanon began—to join his two brothers in New Jersey. His parents had followed in 1977 and they'd all settled in New Jersey, joining the rest of their family.

To my surprise, the phone number I had been given had been disconnected. Growing increasingly anxious, questions tumbled haphazardly through my mind. Had they not been able to pay their phone bill? Were the lines down due to the weather? I had no way of getting any answers, so there was no option but to seek a taxi and to head to the nearest hotel for the night.

Fortuitously, I spotted the family I had befriended on the plane. Taxis were in short supply and the demand excessive due to the holiday, so they offered to share their taxi with me, saying they would drop me wherever I wished.

Seeing a friendly face was so welcome and calming that I readily agreed. 'Have you made a hotel booking?' the mother asked me.

'No, I was supposed to stay with my friends,' I explained. 'We have a booking at the Sheraton in New York,' she told me. 'Why don't you come with us and see if we can get you a room there as well?' It seemed like a reasonable suggestion and I didn't have a better idea, so off we went.

Approaching the receptionist at this shiny hotel in the city that never sleeps, I asked how much it would be for a night for their least expensive room. 'Eighty dollars, plus tax,' she replied and I tried not to audibly gasp. I had the princely sum of 2000 US dollars to my name. Eighty dollars, plus tax was a sizeable chunk of the funds I had at my disposal. Nonetheless, at that hour of the night I really didn't have much choice, so I handed over the money for this expensive but welcome refuge that would give me four walls, a ceiling and a comfortable bed where I could consider my next move.

The next morning, I met the family from the plane in the lobby and, to my delighted surprise and gratitude, they happily paid for my breakfast. From there I intended to climb aboard my second American taxi and head from New York to Paterson, New Jersey, to find my friends.

I stepped outside and gasped in shock as the bitter cold pierced my bones. It was clear I was going to have to part with some more of my funds to purchase a much-needed winter jacket or I was simply going to freeze. An ironic and wistful smile crossed my lips as I wondered, *Who* comes all this way, after all I've been through, only to freeze to death? I immediately went to the nearest retail outlet and sourced the warmest coat at the best value, once again parting with some more of my rapidly dwindling American currency. I also realized that taking a bus to Paterson was a more economically prudent decision than taking another taxi.

Clasping the piece of paper with my friends' address, I took a bus as far as I could to my intended destination, but was dismayed—again—when I had to flag down another taxi because the remaining distance was still too far to walk.

The taxi driver dropped me in front of the house which matched the address on my tiny piece of paper. I breathed a sigh of relief, thinking I would finally see a familiar and friendly face. Eagerly, I knocked on the front door expecting to see the lady I had come to affectionately call Aunty Rosette (despite no blood relation). A young lady—who was clearly not my Aunty Rosette— opened the door and added to my woes when she informed me that she had bought the house three months prior and my friends definitely didn't live there anymore.

Walking away from her house, I felt completely lost. I was in a strange land—a foreigner who had already been eyed with suspicion by the authorities—and I had nowhere to go and knew nobody who could help me.

Clutching the small case containing all of my worldly possessions, I trudged despondently through the freezing streets. Huddled into my jacket against the biting and bitter cold—which seemed to mock me as it also sought to chill my mood—I felt small and vulnerable as it became increasingly clear to me that Paterson, New Jersey was not a safe city—at least not the particular part I was walking through.

Glancing furtively around, I could see that I was in an extremely rough area where poverty and hardship, as well as the easily-recognizable signs of people abusing drugs, were evident. Goosebumps prickled across my skin, perhaps from fear or the freezing cold. Probably both.

I was in a new country where everything felt strange and unfamiliar, I couldn't find my friends, I had nowhere to go, no idea of what to do next, and —there I was—roaming aimlessly around an unwelcoming, dangerous neighbourhood. This did nothing to ease the escalating troubled sensation that was cascading through my body. My instincts kicked in and I straightened up and adopted a positive, confident stance. My life in Lebanon had taught me that if I didn't want to be a victim, I shouldn't behave like one. With my head held high and ignoring the brutal cold seeping into my marrow, I walked on, hoping that I would soon see a third taxi to take me who knows where. Finally, a little yellow cab stopped when I called it and I gratefully asked the driver to return me to the bus station so I could head back to New York.

But then my stroke of bad luck ended as I was explaining my story to the friendly driver and he, unexpectedly, asked me my friends' last name. To my completely delighted surprise, he said, 'I know them! I believe they own a petrol station nearby.'

Sitting in the taxi, I couldn't believe my good fortune and I thanked God for sending me such a lovely stroke of luck and keeping me safe in that neighbourhood until I found a way to get out of it. I was intensely relieved when, sure enough, the driver had been right and my friends ran out to give me an enormous hug when he dropped me at their petrol station. Thanking the driver profusely for reuniting me with my friends, I breathed a great sigh of relief as I was swiftly taken from the station to my friends' home a short drive away.

Aunty Rosette was generous with apologies and said she had been certain she had written to me to advise me of their new address and phone number and had assumed that I had received the letter. It was not uncommon for letters to go astray in Lebanon, so it was only by God's grace that I happened to come across a taxi driver who was not only kind and gracious, but who knew my friends from Lebanon and was able to take me to them.

'Why did you move from your previous address?' I asked when I was settled into the family home and sipping a warm cup of coffee.

'Oh, Paterson was far too dangerous,' Aunty Rosette explained. 'Robberies occurred on our street almost daily and people were even killed because they were protecting their homes. It was just too awful to stay there. If someone was walking down the street at night time in Paterson—with a ring on their finger or something else flashy—and a passer-by decided they wanted it, it would be nothing for that passer-by to beat them up or kill them to steal the ring,' she said, clasping her hands to the side of her face in horror at the very idea of this hateful act. She went on to tell me that Paterson had one of the highest crime rates of cities in all of the United States.

My mind briefly sped back to those first trudging steps I'd taken away from their old address and I considered how lucky I'd been since I'd had all my valuables clutched in my small case in front of me. Once again, I felt so blessed that God has kept me safe.

The family wanted to know all the latest news from Lebanon and I was only too happy to tell them all about my family, even though it tugged at my heart strings to think they were so far away and I didn't know when I was to see them again. We talked and talked and talked, losing all track of time and my voice, until it felt as though there was no tomorrow and only the past to reminisce about.

Graciously, Kamil's family not only offered me the hospitality of their home, but also drove the hour to the New York Sheraton to collect my suitcase (which I'd left there for safekeeping), so I could settle in properly for the few days I would spend with them while I planned my next move. It was very clear to me that

I couldn't stay with Kamil's family in New Jersey. I was painfully thin and not equipped to ward off the cold weather of the East Coast in November and the stress and trauma of my last years in Lebanon had taken their toll on my mind, body and soul. I needed warmth and fun and a new focus.

A school friend of mine, named Rita, had also migrated to the United States with her family and was studying in Texas where, she told me, I would likely be accepted as a student due to the vast number of universities there. My intuition told me I should trust her advice, so, on the 6th of November, Aunty Rosette and family drove me from New Jersey back to JFK so I could fly to Texas.

Upon arriving at JFK, Aunty Rosette embraced me with one of her lovingly warm hugs and wished me luck as I started the next chapter of my new life adventure.

When I arrived in Texas, my friend Rita and her family were there to meet me at the airport with all of them cheekily wearing Texan hats and armed with flowers and hugs to welcome me.

I stayed with Rita and her family just long enough to source out a nice little apartment at a weekly rent of $50 and I furnished the apartment with used furniture from garage sales, making it feel—at least temporarily—like home. Rita seemed to enjoy helping me find a place for everything and making sure that everything was in its place. With my apartment now well established, I needed to think about my studies. Even though I had hoped to work toward a law degree, my qualifications were not accepted, so I applied to a local university to commence study toward a business degree and hoped I'd be accepted to begin studying in May when the summer session began. I believed that if I worked hard and earned a good wage, I'd be able to afford the university fees, but if I became stuck, I could also ask my brothers (who were working overseas) to assist me.

Since my primary consideration was to secure a qualification that would provide further opportunities (not only for me, but for my family back home), developing a social life was far from high on my list of priorities. However, moving abroad and starting over can be both a terrifying and exhilarating experience, so I knew that making friends would help ease the transition into my new home and help me to fit in.

'Your money isn't going to last long,' Rita pointed out to me once I had settled into my new abode. 'A friend of mine is looking for a place to share, maybe you'd like to meet her and this will spread out the cost for you. What do you think?' I loved this about Rita. She was always pragmatic and practical and always had my best interests at heart. What do I have to lose? I thought. Rita was clearly pleased and introduced me to her friend Mel, who soon moved in.

I was becoming a part of this new landscape. I had a comfortable home and a roommate who was helping me with the rent, as well as teaching me about the American lifestyle.

If things weren't looking peachy enough, friends of Rita's family owned a few petrol stations all over the state and offered me a job as a cashier to help me earn some extra cash. I was well and truly on my way to feeling comfortable and happy in my new surroundings in this new country.

And then I met Jerry, Mel's brother.

One night while Mel and I were having dinner in a local restaurant, Jerry came over to our table and introduced himself and even though when he sat down with us, he stared intensely at me, I didn't think much of it. However, I began to see him around more and more after that night and each encounter made it clearer that he was interested in being more than friends. Jerry seemed to appear everywhere. He even made it a habit to fill his truck with petrol at the petrol station I worked at and regularly parked his truck across the road from my apartment and my work, seemingly to watch over me. Admittedly, he was a striking figure of a man, with a tall, athletic physique, big brown eyes and a neatly trimmed moustache, but he was also in his thirties, which seemed like a far cry from my twenty-two years, so I couldn't understand why he was giving me so much obvious attention. I chose to dismiss it, though—convincing myself that this was just the "Texan way"—but regardless of how benign it seemed, I was plagued by a growing concern that his behaviour was bordering on harassment. The problem was that I didn't really know what to do about it. Mel was my roommate and Jerry was her brother, so I didn't want to start anything that would cause an issue between us.

While I did consider that it might comfort some women to have a man obviously looking out for them, my nagging intuition told me there was reason to be wary of Jerry's attentions.

19

Going to the Chapel

Time passed quickly and, because I showed that I intended to study, I was able to have an extension and renew my business visa for a further three months. I thought it was surprisingly easy, as all I had to do was send my paperwork and passport to the US passport office to be stamped and returned back to me. They also told me that I could apply for a student visa once everything was finalised with the university.

Meanwhile, the war was escalating in Lebanon. The airport had been closed and there was no way for me to return to my homeland, even if I'd needed to. On the days when my mind would drift to the conflict back home, I would feel the need to escape and let loose, to try to quiet the voices and images in my head that made me fear for my remaining family and friends still living in Beirut.

On a particularly hot spring afternoon, with the war back home heavy on my mind, I did something quite out of character and deplorable. My friends had helped me buy a Pontiac Grand Prix car—beautiful with its red leather seats and a sunroof—for a mere $500 USD (admittedly, still a small fortune to me).

The petrol station where I worked had a small convenience store licensed to sell alcohol and, with the heat of the day and the conflict in my mind, I was oddly prompted to buy a six pack of beer and take a long drive in my Pontiac. While I drove, I sipped on the soothing and cooling substance and let my worries just wash away. Drinking while driving is not only plainly stupid, but is severely frowned upon, especially while using a Lebanese driver's licence. A foreign national back then could drive with a valid foreign driver's licence for up to ninety days after moving to Texas, as long as they also had an International Driver's Permit. Not only had I passed the 90-day mark, but I also hadn't even applied for an International Driver's Permit AND I was drinking and driving.

To this day, I feel incredibly lucky that I wasn't caught and I didn't injure anyone, for who knows the severity of Texan law that would have come down on me for such stupid and reckless behaviour.

When I finally did decide to obtain an American driver's licence, I failed three times, because I couldn't answer enough of the multiple-choice questions correctly. On the fourth attempt, I managed to nail it, which was just as well because it was time for me to have my meeting with those who could rubber stamp my acceptance into a Texan university.

Again—against all odds—God was watching over me when the timing of my work shift coincided with the time of the appointment I was scheduled to attend at the university, so I asked a fellow employee if he would mind swapping shifts with me. He agreed and he took my morning shift that day.

At 10 am that morning, two men entered the petrol station and demanded that my co-worker open the safe. We didn't actually have a safe. There was a piece of rope underneath the desk and a floor mat covering a 'high-tech security vault'. Each time we made a few hundred dollars, we lulled ourselves into a false sense of security believing it was *safe* in our safe—actually just a hole in the ground accessible via a flimsy piece of twine.

Sometimes it is best not to be a hero, but in the heat of the moment, my co-worker didn't see it that way. 'Get out of here, you scum of the earth,' he screamed at the intruders, witnesses recounted.

'No chance,' they assured him. 'We want the money. Open it up.'

Stubbornly, he maintained his stance, refusing to offer them a nickel. Undeterred by his determination—in a land where carrying guns is no more unusual than putting on underpants—they pulled out a firearm and shot him square in the head. This poor man was dead before he hit the floor.

Regardless of culture and race, in human nature there is always good and evil and even though I thought I had left the war behind with all its fighting and the unnecessary suffering, here I was, seeing the same suffering inflicted on innocents, only in a different context. Human behaviour, it seemed, can be the same on all parts of the planet.

I was devastated and full of guilt that I had survived. I had so many questions for God. Why him? Why not me? God, why did you spare me from this fate?

I remembered witnessing a similar awful and terrible incident, just two months before I'd left Lebanon. There was a nice gift shop on the other side of our building owned by Rami. Jack, the man who bought our convenience store a few years before, was walking to empty his rubbish bin in a large skip— close to Rami's shop—when the wind blew some of the trash Jack was emptying and it landed in front of Rami's shop. They ended up cursing at each other and Rami reached for his gun and shot Jack in the groin. Jack dropped to the floor, bleeding while people (myself included) were screaming while we witnessed all of this. Suddenly, Jack's uncle—who was a fighter and was visiting them at the convenience store—thought his nephew was dead, so he raised his automatic rifle and shot Rami multiple times, killing him.

It was an awful, senseless scene of violence to witness and I believe this incident added to my decision to leave my beautiful, but broken country.

And now, despite my desire to be away from senseless violence, I seemed to still be surrounded by it, even in my new home in America.

Cyclamen

The next day, I was told that the owners were going to close the petrol station. They couldn't wrap their minds, or consciences, around the fact that somebody who had worked for them had lost his young life for the crime of doing nothing more than trying to protect the livelihood of the people who employed him.

To escape the despair and guilt I felt, I took my mind to that field of cyclamen and reminded myself that life is a cycle and while people die, where there is life, there is hope. I would not be thwarted or dissuaded from the path I had embarked upon—despite what life would throw at me—and I was going to find a way, whatever way possible, to make my life in America work. I sought counsel from God. I knew there was a reason why I'd been spared. I knew my performance in the play of life was not yet over. There was more to my journey. More for me to learn, to impart and to live.

A week later, I received an acceptance letter from the university, including the schedule of tuition and fees, outlining that my course would start in two weeks. Now that I had lost my job, I was worried that I would not be able to afford to pay for my tuition. I knew that my older brothers would support me and send money if I asked, but purposely did not tell them of the situation as I wanted to be independent and knew they had many challenges of their own back home.

I would just have to figure out how to make it work.

I had now been in Texas for a few months and Jerry had become more than just a casual observer in my life. As I was sharing a home with his sister, it was impossible to ignore his presence *or* his persistence, which, while it seemed somewhat intense, was nonetheless flattering. I certainly had no physical attraction to him, nor did I feel an emotional bond, but I did enjoy his company and mostly he seemed kind and caring towards me.

He was friendly and polite, but was not shy about bragging about his wealth or his successful business. Even so, it seemed convenient and comfortable to continue seeing him, although it was becoming increasingly difficult to keep an intimate relationship at bay.

'Chadia, I love you,' he told me repeatedly. 'Why can't you accept that? Who else is there here for you after all?' It sounded almost chillingly more like a threat than a declaration of love, but the fact was that I was rapidly reaching a point of no return. I wasn't able to renew my visa for a further three months, and yet, because the airport was closed, I was also unable to return to Lebanon and all the horrible things that were happening back home.

It was perhaps at this point that I should have reminded myself that caving in to fear never leads to anything good.

Using my very scant knowledge of the American legal system and hoping to retain my independence, I hired a lawyer to review my case. The decision cost me almost all of my remaining resources, but I had no alternative. Finally, I had to face facts that the only option open to me was to acquiesce to Jerry's desires and advances or I would have to return to Lebanon.

Jerry lived on a large property with separate quarters on the acreage for his mother, and I soon came to understand that the reason Mel refused to live with them in such a sumptuous state was due to the extremely hostile relationship between her and her mother. As I came to know Jerry's mother far better than I would have liked, the disdain my roommate felt towards the woman who had given her life began to make perfect sense. Jerry's mother was not a likeable woman. She was quite cruel and divisive to me and she took every opportunity to make it clear that I was not welcome in her family. Perhaps she was jealous of me in some way or believed I had taken her son from her. I never found out why she disliked me so much.

'Oh, don't worry about Mum,' Jerry would assure me when I expressed my concerns. 'Once we're married, everything will be fine. You'll see.'

Married?

I repeated it in my head, the word seeming to hang interminably in the air. How could I marry a man I didn't love? On the other hand, what other option did I have? All my attempts to legally fight my visa situation had failed, I was out of money, out of work and, clearly, out of options. The civil war back home was going from bad to worse and Beirut's airport was still opening and closing sporadically. I felt trapped by my circumstances and felt that I had no choice but to use the only avenue available to me to stay in the United States, as much as I disliked the thought of it.

Jerry's official proposal took place in a cosy restaurant under the wary gaze of a silvery full moon. 'Chadia, I love you and I can look after you. Please let me do this! We'll have a beautiful life together. I promise you.' The truth was that I was trying to like him, but something in the back of my mind was nagging me and telling me that I was making a huge mistake. We were completely different: personality, age and, perhaps most concerning, was Jerry's mother's obvious hatred and resentment toward me. For, despite how hard I tried to befriend my future mother-in-law and dispel the unnecessary tension, it was never enough.

I gazed into his imploring eyes, trying to find the courage to say the words that stuck in my throat. 'Jerry, you've been so good to me, but are you sure?' I asked, trying not to betray the conflict that was racing through my mind.

'I've never been surer of anything in my life,' he assured me. 'Will you marry me?'

I closed my eyes and held my breath while that moment in time stood still, before my heart sunk and, against all my sharpest instincts, I said the words I will never forget, 'Yes, Jerry, I will marry you.'

He crushed me in a fierce hug until I could barely breathe, which—it turned out—was excellent foreshadowing for what our life together would become. As a wedding gift, he purchased a brand new, limited-edition silver Chevrolet Camaro Z28 for me.

Neither of us wanted a big wedding, which was something of an oxymoron in Texas. There was a sense of just wanting to hurry up and get it done, which made it no less difficult to break the news to my family over the phone.

'Oh my gosh!' my mother exclaimed.

'It's okay, Mama. He's a good man who loves and cares for me. He'll be a good provider.'

'But you said you're not in love with him,' she pointed out.

'It's true,' I sighed, 'but I need to do this. It'll be okay. You'll see.'

'I don't know, Chadia,' she said. 'I don't like the idea of you settling because you think you have to. Please come home. Beirut airport should open soon.'

I blinked away a tear. 'No one is forcing me into this,' I assured her.

'Circumstances are forcing you into this,' my mother forcefully reminded me.

'Please, Mama. Trust me. Be happy for me.'

I heard her sigh before she asked, 'Are you really sure about this?'

My reply must have been less than convincing because before I knew it, my brother Antoine flew in from Saudi Arabia, where he was working, to pay me a visit. Fortunately, he was held up in New York because he did not pre-purchase an airline ticket for the New York to Houston leg of the trip, and the delay was compounded by bad weather. I say fortunately because he had flown all the way across the planet with the sole purpose of chiding me for my brashness and stopping the wedding.

Our wedding was quite small with me, Jerry, Mel and four friends. Jerry's mother did not attend, which was sort of a wedding gift in itself, and the ceremony took place in a Lutheran church— as per my request—with a Texan pastor conducting the ceremony.

Upon Antoine's arrival in Texas, Jerry and I went to the airport to meet him. We drove him to a hotel in downtown Houston and had dinner at the hotel restaurant, then we all agreed that the next day the three of us would visit the NASA Johnson Space Center. However, the next day Jerry told me that he would be unable to go due to a work meeting, so I called Antoine and asked him to pick me up. Antoine and I had a great time at NASA Center and by 2 pm we had already visited most of the centre and also had our lunch. On the way back, we saw a big sign saying 'Houston Zoo: This Exit', and, since I told Antoine that I had never visited a zoo in my life, he instantly took the exit to the zoo from the freeway.

I was ridiculously excited—it was the first time I had ever seen so many animals in one place. Houston Zoo houses more than 6000 animals—but I became even more excited as I saw a camel for the very first time! Yes, my first ever camel! One of the things people in Texas used to ask me all the time was, "Don't y'all live in the desert and ride camels and stuff?" I can say, with absolute certainty, that we definitely did not ride—or even have—any camels in Beirut. The irony of travelling all the way from the Middle East to America to see my very first camel was not lost on me! Antoine and I had an amazing day together and then he drove me back home and, when we arrived, Jerry was angry and rude to both me and my brother. Antoine—in no uncertain terms—told Jerry that he should respect me and be good to me, but Jerry retorted, 'She's my wife and you have no right to interfere.' Antoine gave me a hug and left, but he was obviously furious. After a couple of days, I phoned Antoine at his hotel and asked him to come and visit, then tried to placate him by explaining that Jerry was good to me and that his anger that day was a result of a business deal that didn't go as planned. However, it was clear that there was animosity between the two from the get go; they could not agree on much and certainly disliked each other. Antoine didn't accept my marriage to Jerry at all.

At one point during Antoine's stay in Texas, Jerry even reached for his gun, but I was able to defuse the heated encounter before any real violence took place. My brother Antoine is a rough diamond, but his heart is pure and full of love for his family. Before returning to Saudi Arabia, he secretly gave me an envelope full of travellers cheques, whispering, 'Use it when you need it.' Despite the tension, having Antoine visit meant the world to me. To see him again in person was truly wonderful. But as dreams generally are, it was short lived.

In Texas, everything has to be bigger than anywhere else, and the oversized bed which was to become our matrimonial mattress was no different. Even more disturbingly, Jerry's gun was permanently lodged underneath the feathers and springs where we would lay our heads. I had run away from everything I'd ever known in the hope that I would never see, touch or carry a gun again, and yet, here I was married to a man who had a gun on him at all times.

Despite the fact that we became husband and wife, I somehow managed to preserve my virginity until two months into our supposed wedded bliss. We would hug and we would kiss and touch and he was unbelievably patient with me and, as foreign as his manner was, he was kind to me in his way. Yet, as an unrelenting counterpoint to his kindness (at the beginning, at least), his mother was equally unpleasant and hateful.

Of course, I couldn't refuse him forever. Many nights during those first two months of our marriage, we would put on romantic music and dance in each other's arms after dinner. It was on one such occasion, on a blisteringly hot Texan night, that I finally and willingly surrendered to his advances.

'I'm here for you,' he whispered lovingly into my ear, 'I love you and support you.'

This man was my husband after all. I suppose I should have thought myself fortunate that a caring, successful man had married me and wanted to provide for me.

'I love you too,' I managed to lie convincingly. 'You're a nice person, although sometimes you're naughty,' I added cheekily in an attempt to defuse the moment.

'Oh?' he queried.

'When you try to force me to eat prawns,' I explained.

He laughed. It was a melodic, infectious laugh. Before I knew it, we were laughing with each other, holding a long embrace as somehow that laughter morphed into a long and lingering kiss.

20

A Different Kind of War

Although Jerry had been kind and patient with me both before and during the first two months after we were wed, everything changed once we crossed that final line. Overnight, as though a switch had been flicked inside him, he began to treat me as though I were not his wife, but his property. I began to feel helpless—as though the only way I could live peacefully was to keep him happy by allowing him to control my life.

It didn't take long for me to figure out that Jerry was frighteningly jealous and possessive and, finally, all that time he'd spent parked outside my work and my home made perfect and chilling sense to me. Fourteen years my senior, he would fly into a violent rage if a younger man so much as smiled a hello at me. Jerry also loved his seafood and often pressured me to join him, forcing me to eat prawns, even though he knew—all too well—my distaste for them. I was his chattel and what I wanted no longer mattered. His behaviour was abusive, but at the time I did not realise it—or perhaps, more accurately, I saw no alternative but to accept his ill treatment of me.

Like many manipulative abusers, Jerry would justify his behaviour—jealousy, possessiveness, control, violence—by claiming he was protecting me because he was afraid of losing me. In reality, though, his 'overprotection' forced me to lose contact with friends and barely ever leave our home and, when I did, it was under the constant shadow of his subliminal threats—threats that eventually became my reality.

The main reason I left Lebanon was to get away from war, to find some peace and a better life, but what I found was a different kind of war—one of manipulation and fear tactics. Just as the war in Lebanon had controlled and confined my movements, so too did my husband. My freedom to be myself, to be independent and to have dreams, was slipping away. It would enrage and embarrass him if I dared suggest I didn't share his desire in almost everything—be it food in a fine restaurant or any aspect of our personal relationship.

Jerry had also made a lot of big promises to entice me into marriage, among which he had assured me that when we were married and I was able to remain in the United States, I would be able to fulfil my dream of attending university. Of course, once I gave myself to him and he began to exert his dominance over me, I was legally at his mercy and those promises dissipated. He would neither allow me to work nor study, despite the fact that I'd been accepted to university and wanted desperately to commence my degree. My hopes and dreams of studying, of creating a better life for myself, were seemingly gone.

One particularly painful incident—that made me finally realise how violent and unbalanced my husband was and how desperately I needed to break away from our relationship—began with a trip to Vegas. Jerry knew I enjoyed going to Vegas to see shows or concerts, so he booked us in at a hotel for a few days and off we went. The first two nights were quite enjoyable—we went to a concert one night and a show the next—but the third night everything went sideways. We were walking across the lobby, after enjoying a nice dinner, when Jerry ran into one of his friends and we all went for a drink. The boys decided they wanted to go play Black Jack, but it was already late and I was tired, so Jerry told me to go back to our room and said he would be there shortly. He finally showed up at 6:00 am—drunk and looking awful—whereupon he told me he loved me and then passed out.

I was angry and upset and felt that I was being ignored since he was sleeping off the alcohol. Our flight was scheduled to leave that afternoon and I decided that I would fly home without him.

I packed my things and, since our airline tickets were in his locked briefcase, I tiptoed out of the room with my suitcase and called the airline from the lobby, letting them know I'd lost my ticket. Then I took a taxi to the airport, picked up my new ticket, and flew home, all the while with a sinking feeling in my stomach that Jerry was going to be very angry that I'd left him behind in Vegas.

My intuition was right.

Jerry arrived home not three hours after me and he was filled with rage. He started cursing at me and his fists started flying, punching me in the face—cutting my lip and causing my nose to bleed—and pulling my long hair. Cut and bleeding and terrified, I backed into a corner begging him to leave me alone and, just like that, his mood changed. He told me he was worried about me, but I didn't believe him.

I screamed at him, "You are evil. I hate you."

Jerry responded by running to our kitchen and grabbing the basket of onions off the counter. He came back and demanded that I "say sorry", but I refused so he began throwing the onions at me—one by one—until I said I was sorry.

The following day, there were cuts and bruises all over my face and bruises on my body and I was completely miserable. I knew I had to get away from him, but I didn't know how I could manage it with how closely he watched me and, of course, the near-constant presence of his mother, who I am certain cursed my very existence. The truth of it was that his mother's presence brought out a darker side of Jerry and, unfortunately, she was around far too frequently.

It wasn't long after Vegas that I became pregnant and then also had to worry about bringing a new life into such a warped and twisted relationship. I was expected to be his pretty, obedient and, now pregnant, wife.

I have no doubt that Jerry's mother did not relish the thought of becoming grandmother to the child I was carrying, but never in my wildest imagination—not even after all the horror I had witnessed back in Lebanon—could I have conceived the contemptuous lengths she was prepared to go to ensure her grandchild never took their first breath.

In the property we lived on, she had her own fully-equipped kitchen and therefore no reason to ever be in ours. One morning, barefoot and twelve weeks pregnant, I ambled towards our stove, not noticing a transparent yellowish dishwashing liquid covering the kitchen floor. I slipped, landing heavily on my back and sliding across the soap that had been deliberately placed there for the exact purpose of causing me to fall. It was as though the entire floor had been painted with clear yellow soap which immediately began to mix with the blood that had begun flowing freely from my womb. I screamed in pain and shock and Jerry— quickly by my side in robust boots that wouldn't slip—saw only his wife, splayed on the floor and bleeding. It didn't even cross his mind, not for a moment, how this could have come to be. He scooped me up and we raced to the hospital, but it was, of course, much too late.

The life that had been growing inside me was gone, another innocent soul lost to a vindictive act that would never be avenged. While I lay in hospital, mourning the loss of our unborn child, Jerry's mother paid me a visit. She said all the right things, but I will never forget the smirk on her face and the wink she gave me as she stated, 'Well, I guess it just wasn't meant to be.'

Oh, how cruel can a person be, to harm an unborn child out of hate? I was distraught and, ridiculously, also felt somewhat guilty that the reason my unborn child wasn't allowed to live was because someone hated me for being who I am.

Jerry was genuinely devastated at the loss of our child, but never once did I suggest to him that it had been deliberately perpetrated by his mother. What would be the point? It wouldn't undo the harm that had been done and would more likely result in her seeking even greater revenge.

So, I wept openly, as was expected of me, for the death of my first conceived child.

After that, my prudent silence was met with even further loss of privacy, as though the secret police were ever vigilantly watching me, waiting for me to make that one fatal mistake. Even when my family called from Lebanon, my mother-in-law would listen in on the other line, eavesdropping on every word. She made no pretence or secret about it either, showing disgusting delight when it would upset me if she repeated, 'Your mother said this and your brother said that.' My mother-in-law, who was originally from Eastern Europe, understood some of the conversation because as Lebanese, we speak one word in Arabic, two in English and three in French.

Once I lost the baby, my every move was monitored—and the accusations came thick and fast about things I never did and the reprisals were swift and merciless for crimes I never committed. They ranged from the seemingly banal, such as accusing me of stealing her jewellery—an accusation she maintained for at least a week—to the far more personal and hurtful.

'My big jewellery box has gone missing. I'm sure you took it,' she said, her eyes narrowing like a cat ready to pounce on its prey. Despite my protestations of innocence and a claim that I had never even seen the blasted jewellery box, I was in a blind panic as Jerry was increasingly taking her side over mine. I cried nearly every day that week, feeling completely hopeless and badgered.

Instigating issues like this seemed to give her perverse pleasure, but as Jerry never stood up for me and often believed her, I could only rely and trust in myself and God.

I was truly alone.

'I haven't seen it. I didn't do anything,' I insisted repeatedly, until one day she said, 'I found it. Don't worry about it,' sounding as though she'd misplaced a grocery list and her accusations had never happened. Her emotional abuse was nearly as bad as his and never ending.

I tried to be a good person. I tried to be calm, congenial and please them all, but she was constantly pushing me to the breaking point, which came one day when she announced, with complete conviction as though she would have been in a position to know, 'You weren't even a virgin when you married my son. You've been pretending all this time.'

By some standards, such an accusation would be of little consequence, but to a young girl from Lebanon (whose virginity was of utmost importance), she crossed a line. And even though we both knew she was doing it on purpose to provoke me into rash action, I still couldn't contain myself and I lashed out at her and left trailing wounds by raking her bitter face with my nails.

Back in Lebanon, where I had been trained to kill, I wouldn't have hurt a fly, but this woman pushed my buttons one too many times. And, of course, that was all the excuse she needed to call my husband and her daughter Mel to accuse me of domestic violence and assaulting a poor, harmless old lady.

The bleeding wounds on her wizening flesh were undeniable, so naturally I was told by Mel and a family friend that I should consider myself lucky that the assault wasn't reported as a felony to the local authorities. From there, things went from bad to worse. Jerry and I were drifting ever further apart—albeit I had never felt close to him in the first place—and now his mother openly flaunted young, attractive girls in our presence for Jerry's benefit, laughing when this caused me further distress. Eventually, the situation escalated to the point where Jerry made no secret of the fact that he took one of these would-be suitors away on a jaunt to Florida for an affair.

Enough was enough.

I don't know how I came to my senses or where I found the strength to take action and change the course of my life, but I finally reached a point where I could no longer bear this way of life. The constant lies, manipulation, control tactics, craziness and his mother's continual attacks—were turning me into a person I didn't even recognize. I didn't like who I was becoming. I was constantly on edge, at times jealous, and rather than seeing the good in people as I had nearly always done, I began questioning everyone's motives. I was slowly turning into one of them— through no fault of my own—and I knew it was time to break free. I had been married for nine increasingly miserable months and couldn't take it any longer.

While Texan summers are blistering with the heat shimmering over scorched earth, the winters are equally cold. There may not be snow, but the pipes freeze and, frankly, the blood in my veins had turned to ice at the prospect of remaining with that family one more moment. And so it was, that on a dark and frosty night in the depths of winter in 1982, I finally made a break for it.

I still had my old Grand Prix Pontiac stored in the garage, so feigning an excuse (as I rarely left the premises unattended), I walked out of that cursed place, got in my car and drove away, swearing to myself that I would never return.

21

Freedom

Not knowing who to turn to or where I was heading in the bitter and ever-plummeting temperatures, I drove with no particular destination in mind. As I drove, I recalled several sweet memories of my childhood, feeling the love and warmth of my family coming through, so that, for a time, I felt warmed and my heart burst with joy. Memories of the joy of Christmas and Easter celebrations with my family came to mind. As a little girl on Palm Sundays, I would wear a nice pink or white dress made by my mum, and we would go to church with the neighbours and their children, all carrying white candles decorated with olive-tree branches and white or light-coloured flowers with satin ribbons. We were all so happy. So lively. My dad would carry me and twirl me around.

Sudden emptiness replaced the joy in my heart as I wondered if I would I ever be able to celebrate Christmas or Easter with my family again? Would I ever have children of my own, with whom I could impart these family traditions and celebrate these events? At that moment, I honestly didn't know. I imagined my mum's face when she learned that I wouldn't be coming home for Christmas. I could almost sense her worry about her daughter being abroad, unsure of the next time we would meet in person again and it nearly broke me. I asked myself as I drove along a winding road, 'Where is home now? I have no home now.'

'God,' I begged, as I began to weep. 'Please, God, I know I've sinned. I know I'm not perfect, but this can't be all that you have for me in this life. Please, I beg of you, please help me. I'm so alone. And so scared. Help me. Lead me down the roads you want me to go. Let me trust you and be strong.'

After driving around for about an hour, I found my way to a deserted car park, locked the door slept there for the three more nights. I was wearing a tracksuit and a long coat that night, but it was freezing. I dared only turn on the heater for a few minutes each night so that I didn't waste petrol or suffocate myself. Had I thought things through, I might have planned my escape a little more practically, but Jerry and his mother had gaslighted my mind to the point where I could no longer think clearly.

After three nights with no shower and no change of clothes, I must have looked a picture, but slowly some semblance of sanity was returning to my mind. I survived on two bars of chocolate, which I'd purchased with a few coins I found in my glove compartment. I knew I couldn't continue in this manner, so I subtly approached a manager at a small residential complex in the area. I just needed a cheap place to stay for a little while, it didn't even have to have any furniture—I would have been happy just to sleep on the floor.

My dishevelled appearance must have pulled at his heart strings because he agreed to give me a studio apartment that he had available for one week, free of charge. He was in his sixties and reminded me of my dad, being just as generous and caring in nature.

Getting any money out of Lebanon would have been almost impossible, but fortunately, I had my hard-working brothers, Antoine in Saudi Arabia and Walid in Cyprus. I knew they would provide enough to help me get back on my feet again and escape from the clutches of the situation I had found myself in.

Nonetheless, my personal belongings remained at that cursed property; they were mine and I had every right to them. I wanted nothing of theirs—not Jerry's Z28, nor any of his other fancy cars, nor his reviled ring, nor the designer clothes he had lavished on me—certainly none of his money, but I did want what little I had brought with me from Lebanon.

I knew I needed to return, even temporarily, but it made me feel physically ill. Nevertheless, breaking my own vow never to return, I summoned my courage and returned to that accursed place to gather my things.

Of course, once again it should have come as no surprise that when I did try to re-enter, every lock had been changed. I hammered on the doors, screaming, 'Please, open up! I need my stuff. You can keep everything else. I just want what's mine.'

I knew they were in there, probably laughing at my thwarted attempts to enter, feeling it was justly deserved for daring to rebuke or challenge them on any level.

Undeterred, I moved from the door to the windows, brandishing a fist with such force that I shattered the glass of our bedroom window clear through. Shards embedded into my skin and blood spurted everywhere as a large chunk of skin came off of my pinkie, but I didn't feel it or even care—I just wanted my little Samsonite case and my personal belongings, then I could walk away for good and leave everything else behind.

Once I'd managed to break into my own matrimonial home, Jerry's mother pounced on me. 'You've been out sleeping around, haven't you?' she spat at me.

It took all my strength not to swipe her once again across her ghastly face; this time, though, I held myself together.

Wrenching the ring from my finger, I threw it on the floor. 'Take it! I don't want it. I don't want anything that has anything to do with any of you,' I spat back at her.

Surprisingly, I was monitored but not challenged. Good to my word, I collected only that which had belonged to me before my marriage and then turned and left, this time forever.

While the old man in the complex in our area had been so kind as to give me a week's free rent in a cold, unfurnished room, I now had a little of my own cash in my possession and I knew I had to get as far away from this wretched family as fast as I possibly could.

I was also pleasantly surprised and truly felt that God was with me when I realised that I'd also completely forgotten about the envelope with traveller's cheques my brother Antoine had given me when he came to Texas. Now I could afford to rent a unit on my own.

Praying to God to continue watching over me, I drove to an area that I considered suitably safe and away from any proximity to Jerry's home and I was fortunate to find a kindly couple who rented me a clean, one-bedroom apartment that would, for now, become my home.

When I tearfully explained to them what had happened, they looked upon me with sad and knowing eyes, betraying years of experiences of their own. 'My goodness. God bless you,' the man said softly.

'My mama will be praying for me,' I assured him. 'Everything will be okay.'

'Well if you need any help at all, you let us know,' the man kindly replied.

Although I didn't have a phone line in the apartment at the time, I managed to buy myself an old mattress and a small old black-and-white television from a garage sale, but that was the extent of the furniture in my new apartment.

Obviously, this wasn't a situation which could continue indefinitely. I needed to find work as income and survival were my priorities now.

Returning to the site manager who had rented me my new home—now cleaned up and a little clearer in my head and no longer tear-stained—I smiled nervously, and he smiled back. 'You look better,' he said warmly.

'You said if there was anything I needed,' I began tentatively. 'Of course,' he assured me. 'What can I do for you?'

'I wondered if there's any chance you could call a few supermarkets, hotels, department stores and others, maybe I could get some work as a receptionist, cashier or anything really.'

'For sure,' he replied tenderly.

It made me wonder for a fleeting moment if maybe he had lost a daughter of his own and understood the desperation in my heart. Whatever the reason, he made a few phone calls, and soon I was transferred to a lady called Jean in the personnel department of the Holiday Inn.

'Is there any work available at the moment?' I asked, trying to disguise my urgency.

'It's possible,' she said thoughtfully. 'Come and see me tomorrow. You can complete an application form and we'll see what we can do for you.'

The next morning, I arrived at the hotel dressed in a crisp white shirt, my favourite black jeans, and high heels. I'd straightened my long brown hair, put on lipstick and I was determined to secure gainful employment. After completing the form and participating in a polite and prospectively positive conversation, I was instructed to contact Jean at 10 am the next morning for an outcome.

The following day, the site manager watched as I telephoned Jean from his office, holding my breath and crossing my fingers, praying that there would be a job for me. I watched his face light up, mirroring the smile that spread across my own as I received the wonderful news that I had secured a job as a front office cashier and receptionist at the Holiday Inn.

I was incredibly excited to be independent and free again.

Over the ensuing weeks, most of the people who became my work mates were pleasant enough. However, Texans at that time were somewhat known for their prejudicial views and occasionally, I did hear things along the lines of, 'They kill people and then expect us to welcome them into our country.' I often bit my lip, as I realised that despite having an American Social Security number, if I was no longer married to Jerry, there was a possibility that I would become an illegal immigrant in this strange land. Jerry had told me that he'd arranged for my visa extension, but I believe he never applied for my permanent resident visa (Green Card).

I was earning four dollars an hour and working between the hours of 7 am and 3 pm, five days a week. My rent absorbed much of my weekly salary, so there really wasn't a lot left over and I had yet to get electricity and a phone line connected in my apartment. When my tiny black-and-white TV died, I bought my first brand-new coloured TV but, ironically, I couldn't yet afford to subscribe to cable television to enjoy the purchase. Nonetheless, I scraped by and for the most part got along with my co-workers. I made it my policy to be purposefully pleasant, even when I would consistently hear ignorant comments from some of the staff like, 'Where the heck is Lebanon?' And, 'I've heard Lebanese people are bad and murderous. Have you heard about Jesus?' and other ridiculous comments.

Also, on the back of two of the cash registers in the front office were the words engraved, 'Blacks are slaves and will be forever.' I was shocked when I first saw that. Colleagues who were black were always so friendly towards me, but when I first started there, I felt that Texans were racist, as I was a foreigner.

Jean, the personnel manager, was extremely kind and generous. She was so supportive that when her birthday came around, I wanted to be sure that I expressed my sincere and profound gratitude for the opportunity I had been given. Previously, she had complimented me on a pair of eighteen-carat-gold earrings I had brought with me from Lebanon. Thinking this would be the perfect gift, I cleaned them up and placed them carefully in a small box and cheerfully presented them to her as a birthday present.

'If you could please accept them,' I began. 'I'm sorry that they're used. But I haven't worn them for a long time, please put them on.' Though this might seem odd to some, for a Lebanese person, it is a common gesture to offer a gift from amongst your things, particularly when someone expresses admiration for it, even if you are poor. Culturally, it's commonplace, and it represents the generosity of our people. The Lebanese have an open heart, especially to those who open their hearts to them.

'No, no,' she insisted. 'I can't take those; they're part of your memories from Lebanon.'

I smiled understandingly but earnestly insisted, 'Please! It's the way of my family to show generosity to those who have been generous to us. It would make me sad if you refuse this gift.'

A little reluctantly and I think perhaps slightly embarrassed, she took the earrings, put them on and admired herself in the mirror. 'Well, they do suit me.' She smiled cheekily at me.

Now employed in a 400-bedroom, clean and respectable hotel, I had a way forward even though I was on probation for the first three months. During that time, I was able to procure furniture for my modest apartment from garage sales, and though it may have been mostly second-hand, my home was my own. Nobody disturbed me. Nobody accused me of anything. I could do what I wanted, when I wanted and with whom I wanted. I was thoroughly enjoying my life of relative solitude and complete freedom.

I didn't have contact with Jerry or anyone from his family for many weeks, but I knew that sooner or later I was going to have to broach the subject of divorce.

22

Blooming

I kept my head down and laid low during my three-month probation at my new job. The last thing I needed was to make any waves. This was my only chance to remain in America and maybe start the life that I had dreamed about when I first left my homeland.

The concern with my divorce, and ultimately my visa, weighed heavily on my mind since my visa had only been renewed due to my marriage to Jerry; once that ended, I wasn't sure how I would be able to remain in the United States.

Things were relatively peaceful during my probation period at the hotel and once I was through it and the financial part of my life seemed somewhat secure, I knew it was time to turn my attention to ending my marriage.

I spoke to my friend Rita (who had originally introduced me to Jerry's sister), but somehow the Chinese whispers had made their way to her ears and of course had been misconstrued, so she wasn't pleasant or kind to me any longer.

It was a still evening—more still than I can ever remember during my time in Texas—and I was chopping up a salad to go with the chicken nuggets I had cooking in the oven, when a brick came hurtling through my apartment window. Posttraumatic Stress and muscle memory from living in a war zone immediately had me diving for cover, waiting for the grenade to explode. Of course, it wasn't a grenade, but the intent was just as sinister.

I raced outside and eyewitnesses described Mel, Jerry's sister, as the brick bomber. I imagined it was her way of attempting to frighten me off petitioning for any kind of settlement in the forthcoming divorce proceedings.

Obviously, the brick incident—a ridiculous and inane act of immaturity—was intended to scare me and, although it had startled me for a moment or two, it did not, in any way, diminish my burning desire to divorce my husband.

Given that Rita remained in contact with Jerry's family, I suggested that she let them know that it might be better if Jerry petitioned for the divorce, as I would be willing to sign anything. I didn't want a cent or an item from them, all I wanted was to end the relationship and move on with my life.

Once again, I decided it was better not to make waves. I was employed, I had a social security number, I had a place to live and I was finally free again.

Once the lease was up for my apartment, I moved to another unit both closer to work and further away from the terrible memories of my awful experiences with Jerry and his mother. Little by little, I became a local in this new area—learning more of the Texan slang by frequenting the local coffee shop, shopping when items were on sale, and going to the movies and dining out with friends to better understand the language—basically, doing as the locals did and being part of the culture. It was such a wonderful feeling.

I was also able to reconnect with my family without fear of being eavesdropped on and I would call my mum and the family in Lebanon on a monthly basis (as overseas calls were very expensive in the 1980s) and, occasionally, write to them. Letters to Lebanon used to take weeks and weeks to arrive, or they would go missing because of the war so it was much easier to just call.

Life started to feel good and look promising again!

Although it hadn't been my initial choice of study, working at the Holiday Inn provided me the opportunity to study hotel management and I also secured a second job as a babysitter through an agency in the area. Babysitting reminded me of one of my favourite films, The Sound of Music. One of my babysitting jobs was for a Texan senator's three children. He had a mansion with full security and a butler and his kids always asked their parents to 'book the Lebanese girl' to babysit. We had so much fun, singing and dancing and the kids jumping on their beds. Surprisingly, word spread at how easily children could relate to me and I soon began to babysit for a few other notable families.

After an 18-month struggle and tumultuous start in the United States, I was finally finding my footing and beginning to ease into my new lifestyle. I often felt a wave of gratitude wash over me at how far I'd come since arriving at JFK and I looked forward to the promise of a bright and exciting future. Like my beloved cyclamen, I was once again coming full circle—pushing my way up through the hard and barren wasteland of the previous year—beginning to bloom again.

23

Tales of the Holiday Inn

The Holiday Inn in Texas was filled with many humorous and heart-warming memories. There were also some fairly dramatic incidents during my time there that will forever stick in my mind.

Some of these incidents were minor misunderstandings caused by a lack of understanding of the idiosyncrasies of American—and particularly Texan—slang; others were far more serious. On one occasion when I was working night shift as an auditor, a group of people arrived at the hotel at two o'clock in the morning wanting a handful of rooms to stay for six nights. They offered to pay with a cheque and provided a driver's licence as identity. This was quite a normal procedure, so I checked them in, gave them a receipt and watched as they headed off to their rooms.

Perhaps something from my training and experience in Lebanon was kicking in or perhaps it was just plain intuition, but something about that driver's licence just felt wrong. By then, I was quite familiar with the hotel and its operations, as well as its security measures. We also had a good relationship with the local police, and I felt duty bound to call one particular officer I had come to know, named John. As it happened, John was nearby and was only too happy to attend to my request. His uniform was dark blue and crisp, his buttons and badges shining brightly under the hotel lights as he smiled at me and said, 'What is it, Chadia? What is it that you think is wrong?'

'Have a look at this driver's licence,' I said, handing it over to him. 'On the face of it, it looks exactly like mine, but there's something I don't feel comfortable with. Would you mind checking it for me?'

'Sure.' He shrugged, not seeming to think much of it. He went away and made a few phone calls, and when he returned, he looked sombre.

'Chadia! How on earth could you have known this wasn't real?'

'I don't know,' I shrugged. 'It was just a feeling.'

It turned out that this group had been fraudulently operating for some time, but nobody until that night had spotted that the driver's licence was a fake. The scam was that the group would check into a hotel in the small hours of the morning, request multiple rooms and pay by cheque, which at that hour could not be verified. After two hours or so, they would return to the front desk claiming their plans had changed and requesting only a partial refund. This meant that the hotel held the original cheque and partially refunded in cash what was a considerable balance of money.

Just by going with my gut, I had managed to expose a large fraud operation that had been operating at that time in the state of Texas. Once I realised what was happening, I immediately picked up the phone to the Sofitel, the Four Seasons, the Sheraton, the Hilton and all the other major hotels in the area, to alert them to this cunning operation.

The perpetrators were apprehended by the authorities and everyone was congratulating me, which made me feel worthy and welcome in a manner I hadn't before experienced in Texas.

The warm and fuzzy feeling wasn't to last long though because a month later there would be a major court case—with little doubt that these criminals would be incarcerated for a considerable period of time—but I was going to be called as a key witness.

Of course, I wanted to do the right thing, but if I was to be a witness in a court case, I was concerned that the issue of my visa would be raised. I didn't know then (because I had been too afraid to check) and I don't know to this day if my visa was valid and current at that point in time.

From being hailed as a hero to being at risk of being seen as just as culpable as those I was acting as a witness against. The Attorney General even called many times to pressure me into being a witness.

On the day of the case, I went into work early in the morning, frantically considering what my course of action might be. None of the options that presented themselves seemed to be viable and suddenly, the girl huddled in the corner, flushed with cold sweat and having panic attacks was alive inside me once more. My breathing was laboured, my heart was racing, my mind was panicking and in a complete nervous breakdown, I literally collapsed unconscious on the floor.

The general manager revived me with the assistance of some smelling salts and assured me it was quite natural to be nervous about presenting oneself as a witness in a court of law, but that it was something I had to do.

'I can't! I can't do it,' I sobbed to him.

I was just about hysterical and clearly in no fit state to attend to my duties, never mind attend as a witness in a major trial so I was taken by ambulance to one of the local hospitals where I was advised that a full check-up and internal examination needed to be completed. Fortunately, the timing of my mini breakdown led to the unexpected discovery of a tumour in my large intestine, which was surgically removed. I didn't return to work for a full week, during which time the case was successfully heard without—ironically—any help from me. But I was still so fearful of the outcome of the tumour tests that I never asked nor accepted any further information about it from doctors.

While I lay there, recovering from surgery in my hospital room, I looked around and found myself completely desolate and alone; not one visitor, not one flower to cheer up my despondent spirit. To lift my disheartened self, I ordered a cyclamen flower pot and had it delivered to my room. It's amazing sometimes how the small things in our lives—such as a beautiful little flower that is a symbol of both strength and the *circle* of life—can give us the greatest encouragement and strength—fuel to keep us going.

Witnessing the bloom of my cyclamen, my inner spirit was re-energised once more and I knew that, just like this flower that I related to on so many levels, I too had the strength and determination to flourish again. With tenacity and an element of stubbornness, I fought my way back to health and returned to work.

24

The Dating Game

After I left Jerry and was working hard to put my life back together, potential suitors pursued me every so often, but the last thing I had any interest—especially after my experience with Jerry—was becoming involved in another relationship. To this day, I cannot fathom why they found me attractive. I've always believed I am an average-looking woman, so perhaps it was because I was different or a foreigner and, hence, stood out? Perhaps I appeared to them as a rare, delicate and exotic little flower? Little did they know or understand that, just as my beloved cyclamen whose flower appears delicate on the surface but has sturdy foundations underneath, so too, did I and I was not about to make the same mistake again.

If the Clampetts felt out of place in Beverly Hills, there were times I felt even more out of place in Texas. I remember a persistent young man named Rodney who took me out to dinner at a cozy and romantic French restaurant with an open fire. I love French onion soup and Rodney suggested that the soup tasted even better with double cheese, so I ordered mine that way. While chatting and laughing, my soup arrived and, as I couldn't wait to taste it, I dug in eagerly, digging my way through a thick layer of hot cheese. My first spoonful was excruciatingly hot and burned my mouth, but trying to be polite I kept it in my mouth, smiling and nodding until it cooled. When I finally swallowed, it had cooled into a solid block and became stuck in my throat. I began to choke and Rodney's panic was only drowned out by the waiter's screams for someone to help me. The restaurant manager took charge of the situation and performed the Heimlich manoeuvre, resulting in a piece of mozzarella flying out of my throat across the room and into the fireplace. After this, the date lost its easy momentum and Rodney barely said a word. He probably couldn't shake the picture in his mind of that chunk of cheese flying past his face in slow motion before it dropped into the fireplace to sizzle away. He dropped me off at my place and I never heard from him again. I suppose it could have been worse—I could have spat the cheese directly into his face or choked to death.

There were many incidents—although most less dramatic—like the one with Rodney and, in hindsight, I wouldn't say that I wasn't made for dating, it's more that dating wasn't made for me. I guess I have always been a little clumsy, which meant that any dates I did go on, often ended up becoming somewhat farcical.

One of my colleagues at the Holiday Inn—Demi—who was originally from Mexico, sort of set me up with her brother-in-law, José and he took me out to an upmarket Mexican restaurant—the kind of place where the valet takes your car and makes you feel like royalty. José ordered multiple dishes to introduce me to his culture, but the food was hard to make out given the romantic setting with only a few candles at the table. I was able to spot a dish that resembled tabouli—a healthy Lebanese salad made from finely chopped parsley, tomatoes, mint and fine cracked wheat—but which turned out to be finely chopped chillies, not tomatoes. Just as I took a healthy spoonful of the chillies and nearly burned my tongue out of my mouth, a band of mariachis came and started serenading us at our table. They must have thought I was overwhelmed with affection and love as tears welled in my eyes, but rather than choking up, I was quite literally choking, trying to manage the fire raging in my mouth. Unsurprisingly, José also barely spoke a word post-incident and promptly dropped me off at my place. I never heard from him again. It was probably just as well though, as my taste buds would forever cringe in horror whenever I passed a Mexican restaurant after that.

One particularly memorable admirer appeared in the hotel with his bodyguard one day. He was an extremely attractive and charming man; in fact, I was later to learn that he was a Middle Eastern prince. He stayed at the hotel for a few weeks over the holiday season and it was my job to assist interpreting for him.

At the same time, the prince was gracing us with his royal presence, I had another, even more exciting visitor: my mum! She had managed to leave Lebanon to come and stay with me for a while.

I really couldn't have been happier at that moment; I had my home, my employment, I was working towards my degree, and now my beloved mother was at my side. What a great feeling to celebrate Christmas that year with my mum.

The management of the hotel invited my mum and I to spend New Year's Eve at their suitably flamboyant Texan celebrations. The prince was also in attendance and—to add to the celebratory atmosphere—it was also his twenty-first birthday on New Year's Day. It all mattered naught to me, except that I had the chance to spend a fun evening with my mum for the first time in too long. The place was lively, cheerful, colourful and full of inebriated revellers as the countdown approached midnight.

When the countdown hit one, there was an eruption of palpable joy that filled the room as champagne corks popped and fireworks exploded. It all seemed perfectly normal, until the band decided to sing Happy Birthday to the prince. He was obviously quite intoxicated by this time and he grabbed the microphone after the final 'Hip! Hip! Hooray!'. Scanning the room, he located me and screamed, 'Chadia! Chadia!' across the hall.

My blood turned to ice water and I froze on the spot, suddenly feeling all eyes on me.

'Chadia, will you marry me?'

I think my jaw actually hit the floor; I couldn't believe what I was hearing. My mother looked at me in astonishment. 'What have you been up to in America?' she murmured.

'Nothing, Mama, I swear,' I whispered back.

Quietly wishing the world would open up and swallow me whole, I looked for the nearest escape route and let the prince's question hang in the air, unanswered. Already people were tired of waiting for my answer and began to mingle again.

'Mum, come with me,' I hissed loudly, grabbing her hand.

Quickly we made our way to the parking lot, clambered into my waiting vehicle and drove off into the darkness hoping I would never have to see him again.

I actually chose to miss another week's worth of work trying to avoid him for another few days, so he would leave before I returned and hopefully forget about that silly, impulsive proposal. Once the prince returned to his own country, I was able to return to work in this new year with new hope and after all those dating catastrophes, I decided not to date anymore and to, instead, embrace single life.

This fresh new year with my loving mother beside me in my nice comfortable home, made it easy to believe the illusion that things were normal in my life. I suppose I should have known better.

25

Deceiving the Devil

Jerry had heard that my mother was in town and one day amongst my mail, I found a little audio cassette that he had recorded and sent to me with Lionel Richie singing his hit song 'Hello'. He knew, all too well, how much music had always played a great part in my life, so Jerry knew that in sending me Lionel Richie's 'Hello', the words would resonate with the underlying current of their intended meaning. As I listened to the lyrics, I also understood that meaning all too well. This was Jerry's way of expressing how deeply he had missed me and gauging whether I had missed him much the same. The line that said, 'Tell me how to win your heart...' perhaps resonated the most. He loved me, but he'd always been clueless to my true feelings and he obviously didn't know what love was. Along with the cassette was a note demanding a meeting. I dared not refuse him, still being uncertain as to the status of my visa situation, so arrangements were made for a rendezvous in a nearby coffee shop.

'What does he want with you?' my mother asked me.

'I wish I knew,' I said in reply, already beginning to tremble.

A couple of days later, Jerry swaggered in looking tall, proud and in complete control of the situation.

'It's so good to see you,' Jerry said smarmily, politely shaking my mother's hand. 'I think we need to have a conversation,' he continued, speaking as though I weren't even present.

'What is it you want of us?' my mother asked him nervously, in English.

'I think you should look at your daughter's driver's licence,' he urged her with a self-satisfied smirk.

My mother glanced towards me. 'Chadia?' she queried.

I didn't know what he was up to, but I obediently produced my driver's licence. He snatched it from my hand and slammed it on the table and exclaimed, 'Look! Look at that!'

My mother glanced to where he had indicated.

'You see the name on her driver's licence? That's my name. She's still married to me and I want her back.'

My limbs turned to lead and I believe my heart may have stopped beating for a moment.

'Jerry, you said we were divorced,' I insisted. 'I can't come back to you after all after this time. I won't. I can't live the way we did.'

'Sweetheart,' he said, 'you may not have a choice.' 'What do you mean?' I stammered.

'Your fate and your future are in my hands,' he assured me smugly. 'If you want to stay in this country, it means staying with me.'

To my shock and chagrin, he explained to me that while the divorce paperwork had been completed and I had signed it, it had never actually been filed with the courts. So, all this time that I had believed I was single and worried about my visa were both inaccurate and moot. It was just as well I hadn't accepted the proposal from the intoxicated prince—I might have been committing bigamy!

For a few moments, I completely deflated as the realisation hit me that Jerry and I were not yet divorced. Tears welled in my eyes and a lump choked my throat. I grabbed my mother's hand under the table, hoping to find some comfort in her touch, but none was forthcoming.

He locked his gaze on the pallid expression on my face, searching for a reply. He had learned well from his mother how to press my buttons and he was not going to be embarrassed by having his foreign bride walk out on his respectable family. For a few breaths, I felt trapped, despair washing over me in waves, and I almost fell back into his controlling trap.

But then, another thought occurred to me.

This was not about love or even lust, it was about ego, possession and control. When I tried to end our relationship, he couldn't allow himself to give up control or to allow his family to be mocked or ridiculed if his wife left him. However, should he end our relationship, that would be another matter entirely! He had been happy enough to engage in dalliances with other women—on occasion provided by his mother and on occasion procured by his own activities—but he would never be able to accept that I had perhaps done the same to him.

If this was about ego and control, then what I really needed to do was not return to him, but to find a way for him to save face by making it appear that he had ended things with me.

Composing myself while quickly constructing a cleverly contrived lie, I took a deep breath and said, 'There's something I haven't told you.'

'That would hardly surprise me,' he scoffed.

'No, please listen to me,' I continued, adopting a most serious expression. 'The truth is that I never loved you and I've found someone else that I really care for.'

'Chadia!' my mother gasped.

I glanced quickly at her, squeezing her hand tightly to suggest that if she was ever going to trust me, she should trust me now and play along with the deception.

'Oh, my goodness, Chadia!' she exclaimed again.

Jerry pulled away and sat back in his chair. 'You deceiving bitch,' he spat, abruptly standing and pushing his chair back so hard it fell sideways onto the floor. 'You little piece of useless trash!' he exclaimed. 'This marriage is over, sweetheart,' he announced, turning to storm out of the café.

I watched him leave before I dared look towards the expression on my mother's face.

'Chadia?' she said.

'I had to say something, Mama; none of that is true, but if he didn't make the decision to leave me, I would have been stuck.' Mum and I embraced. 'Oh, Chadia, Chadia! You clever girl,' she praised me before pulling back and wagging a scolding finger at me. 'And don't let me ever catch you lying again.'

'Yes, Mama,' I said with a grin.

It was time we took a holiday.

26

Whirlwind

Travels with my mother were a bit of a whirlwind. Our first stop was New York. A bustling city during any time of the year, whether it be day or night, the Big Apple took on an even more intense vibrancy with the post-holiday season in January and, even though I detested the cold, I forced myself to forget it in my happiness at sharing the sights with my mum.

We visited one of my father's cousins—a prominent pathologist in New York—before rushing to hop into one of New York's famed yellow taxis to take us to where we could do a little shopping. We were determined to experience and enjoy all *New York's* best sales!

Everyone was rushing from one department store to another designer boutique, but I seemed to be attracting several smiles from the native New Yorkers. I had come to learn it was commonplace for the passing pedestrians in that city to avoid eye contact at all costs, so I didn't know if perhaps they had been sprinkled with fairy dust containing the season's spirit or if we were exuding a vibrancy that demanded attention. But it seemed that everywhere we went, people would look at me and grin or even laugh. Eventually, I turned to my mother and asked, 'Do I look okay?'

My long coat, scarf, gloves, a nice hat and lipstick were in place!

'Yes, darling,' she assured me. 'You look fine.'

We walked several more blocks unable to ignore the strange phenomenon of smiling strangers, until, finally, I passed a shop front with a mirror. It was only then that I realised that, when we jumped into our last yellow taxi, I must have settled my backside on the sticky end of a very large red gift bow which had then affixed itself to my rear end. I had been walking up and down the fashionable streets of New York looking like a giant gift. For a moment, I couldn't breathe with embarrassment, but when my mother erupted into laughter, the jovial spirit of the moment was infectious and as each one of us laughed, it only made the other laugh harder.

From New York, we travelled to New Jersey to meet the friends whom I'd originally stayed with when I arrived in America. From there, we headed to Canada to visit family and friends who had settled on the Canadian side of Niagara Falls.

Eventually, it was time to return to my American home base of Texas, where unbeknownst to us, a genuine whirlwind—aka, a tornado—was on the not-too-distant horizon. Tornados are not that uncommon in Texas, but I had never experienced one so huge before.

As there wasn't a washing machine in my apartment, I always used the laundry facilities on the other side of the complex to do my weekly washing. Mum, of course, insisted on helping me with the laundry, so while I filled two machines with a couple of loads, Mum took it upon herself to handwash some of the more delicate items and placed them in a small green bowl.

The dryer cycle was going to take around forty minutes, so in the interim, we returned to my unit, leaving the little green bowl in the laundry. Little did we know that within those forty minutes, the tornado was brewing towards its full intensity. By the time we returned to the laundry, trees were already beginning to bow to the pressure of the wind.

'Oh, my goodness!' I exclaimed to my mother, 'I think we need to run.'

I threw everything I could into one basket while my mother grabbed the compact green bowl, placed it on her head like a combat helmet, and we hot-footed it out of the utility room with the twister almost upon us.

The entire complex was comprised of identical buildings with four units each. Unable to keep our eyes open due to the pressure of the swirling elements around us, my mother began walking in the wrong direction. 'Mum! Mum, please stop!' I called to her. 'You're heading to the wrong building.'

'Leave me alone,' she called back, unable to hear me properly. 'I'm almost there. Don't stop me now.'

Of course, she arrived at a neighbour's door, not mine, and she was clearly frustrated and confused when she couldn't get the door open.

Dropping my basket at my own front door, I forced my way through the storm to my mother, grabbing her hand and dragging her towards what would be our sanctuary from this damned tornado. Once we stumbled inside and slammed the door shut, with our crumpled washing I sat on the floor and actually peed in my pants from laughing, unable to hold it in a moment longer. 'I'm glad you think it's so funny,' my mother scolded. 'Look at you! What sort of a mess are you in?'

We looked at each other again, realising that she had continued to fashion the green bucket as a helmet, and again, we were overtaken by another fit of uncontrollable laughter. It may have seemed strange for us to be laughing uproariously in the midst of a tornado, but humour is often one of the only ways to survive through harrowing and stressful situations.

Mum and I were always close, and the tornado incident only added to my fondest memories of us laughing together.

It was so wonderful having my mother with me for such a long visit. She stayed almost nine months and it was so special that it almost made me feel as though I had reunited with my whole family again. Inevitably, the time rolled around when we tearfully had to say farewell to one another once again, and all the feelings of desolation and loneliness flooded back.

During this time, my sister and her family had also left Lebanon for Australia when my sister was granted a skilled visa, and the rest of her family were fortunate to make the move without requiring sponsorship.

For the umpteenth time in my life, I found my thoughts were in turmoil. Notwithstanding I had suffered a great deal through the torment of an unhealthy marriage and a vicious mother-in-law, I now had a few friends in America, a good job and a good life where I didn't have to worry about bombs exploding around me. But I still felt out of place and despondent.

Adding to the conflict in my mind was that my younger brothers had been pressured to join the militia after I left and a sense of guilt weighed heavily upon me, as I knew precisely what it was they would be going through and witnessing, and how quickly their young minds would be forced to grow up.

The war in my homeland was still raging and continued to ravage the country and everybody in it. A large part of me was drawn to return to my family once more, but then a semblance of sanity would kick in and I would remember what the war had turned me into, and I knew I would be useless to both myself and my family should I return to that state of being.

Whenever I watched the news from back home on the television in Texas, I was incapable of witnessing the ongoing horror without bursting into tears. It was an impossible decision whether to stay or to go, until my sister orchestrated the next twist of fate, which made the decision-making process considerably easier.

27

Heading Down Under

Not only had my sister been shot and wounded back in Lebanon, leaving her with a lifelong disability, but she had witnessed too many friends and family maimed, tortured and killed. She could no longer remain in the land of our birth. With her husband's family now in Australia, the choice to emigrate was made easier.

Her son was five, her youngest daughter, one, and her two eldest daughters were eleven and twelve. They immigrated to Queensland and started a life in the capital, Brisbane, opening a takeaway shop near the Mater Hospital.

Concerned as I was for the family left in Lebanon, Nada organised affairs in such a manner that the remaining family could leave the war and move to the other side of the planet. A place where the sun shines brightly, the oceans lap the shores of a gigantic island paradise and the ravages of war hadn't scathed the landscape since the Second World War.

My mother accepted Nada's offer to move to Australia with my two younger brothers, and one after another, the elder brothers also joined with their families.

I didn't know much about Australia except for one vital fact: most of my family were going to live there. Studying up on this far-off land at a library in Texas, I was surprised to read about the particulars of this amazing country. The information was as enticing as it was intriguing, and yet at the same time disturbing in ways I had never previously considered. It was certainly a vast, diverse and beautiful land. The rich heritage of the Indigenous Australians was remarkable, the wildlife quite unique, its shores and the huge unpopulated areas quite extraordinary to comprehend. Perhaps most alarming though, was that I learned that if it swam, slithered, crawled or flew and was deadly, it seemed to live in Australia.

I began talking with friends in Texas about the possibility of me leaving the United States to move Down Under. They all appeared quite horrified at the prospect, advising that I was bound to die at the hands of one of the deadly animals. It sounded like Australia was one tough place.

Nonetheless, as much as Texas had become my new home and Lebanon always had been home, the truth was that my family was my real home—the home that never changes that I longed for daily. With most of my family residing (or on the way to residing in Australia), I made an appointment with the Australian Embassy in Texas to discuss the prospects of moving there through sponsorship by my sister and her husband.

On the day of the appointment, I once again found my heart pounding and the thoughts in my head racing. I still wasn't a hundred percent sure of the status of my American residency visa as I could not ask Jerry about it, or contact the US visa department because I was terrified it would be a signal for them to investigate me.

The receptionist greeted me in the entrance hall and I followed her, my footsteps echoing resoundingly around the chamber. I was informed that the consul was waiting for me. A grey-haired, bespectacled man with a serious demeanour was seated across the desk from where my interview would take place. Eagerly, I handed him all the information I had collected and collated, but I could hardly contain myself before I burst out saying, 'I'm sorry, but I have to tell you. I don't have an American Green Card.'

'What do we care about an American Visa?' he scoffed with a broad Australian accent. 'You're in a different country here, not in Texas anymore, Toto!' He grinned cheekily at me.

Immediately, I liked what I have come to understand is the trademark of the Australians, a completely cheeky sense of humour. Of course, now that I was in the Australian Consulate, I was legally on Australian soil. My legal status in the United States was of no interest or relevance to him whatsoever. I was intensely relieved about this!

Wading through the paperwork I provided him, the consul studied page after page and then examined my nervous expression thoughtfully. 'Well,' he finally said in his Australian drawl, 'everything is looking great here. Leave it with me and you'll receive something in the mail from us very soon. Have a great day!'

'Is that it?' I asked.

'That's it,' he confirmed. 'Don't you worry, young lady! We will rescue you from the Yanks and you'll be reunited with your family in Australia before you know it! Mark my words.' With that he offered his hand across the desk. Not knowing whether to laugh or cry, I willingly accepted his firm grip and hoped that his assertions would prove to be true.

Sure enough, early in 1986, my permanent resident visa to enter Australia was granted; my time in America had come to an end.

I shipped a few items ahead and gave what was left of my personal belongings, mainly furniture, to friends. I also sold my constant friend and companion (that I had grown to love, my car 'Ponty') and then I said my farewells to the amazing friends I had met during my time in Texas. You never realise how special the people are who come into your life until you have to say goodbye. In truth, Texans are very friendly and generous people once they get to know you. Leaving was very bittersweet. Part of me had developed a deep affection for America, while the other part of me was ready for a new chapter and a fresh start. I was stronger now. Every challenge I had experienced in the States had made me more mature, humble and even more tenacious.

I chose to make the journey on QANTAS airlines—a true Australian icon. I knew it was time for me to embrace my true country. I had learned so much from my time in America, but most importantly were the lessons I learned about myself. Regardless of the situations that life presents us, we always have a choice in how we react.

Despite all the hardship of that first year with Jerry and his mother, I now had a degree in hotel management and years of work experience under my belt and I was on my way to the land Down Under!

The staff aboard QANTAS were full of fun, with their enthusiastic tradition of cheering 'Have a nice day!' The smiles and service seemed to be delivered with a genuine, relaxed and carefree nature and I settled back and enjoyed myself during the flight, reflecting on my life up to that point.

I had been a strong child, with a firm foundation, just like my much-loved cyclamen. Like that flower, I was a sweet, happy and carefree infant, dancing as much as those delicate flowers with heart-shaped leaves in the spring breeze. Yet, I had also been forced to face hardships that no soul should ever endure—my young life was bathed in bloodshed and struggle. My leaves were wilted and crushed from the horror that surrounded me, but like that flower, I bloomed again and again, through each obstacle and struggle I was faced with.

Once in the United States, I found myself jumping over hurdle after hurdle, facing challenges I could never have imagined, but again, my foundation remained strong. I prayed for strength. I was always one who prayed and asked God for guidance, and I believe, that He provides me the strongest foundation of all. Like the cyclamen, I would bloom again as I said goodbye to my Stateside adventure to begin another.

My first experience on Australian soil, which in the tropical north of Queensland in Cairns—which appeared incredibly reminiscent of Hawaii to me—was being sprayed, like some sort of human bug, with pesticide once the plane touched down. I had no idea this was going to happen, but my fellow passengers seemed to be aware that it was about time to close their eyes and cover their noses as quarantine officials entered the aircraft and released canisters of noxious fumes. Later, I learned that because Australia has such a unique and delicate balance of flora and fauna, authorities are very cautious to prevent foreign bugs arriving on their soil. It is somewhat ironic, given how many poisonous creatures were indigenous to the land.

And so, with bug repellent imbued throughout the aircraft, we departed the humid tropics of Cairns and headed to Brisbane, where my sister, her family and extended family were waiting at the airport to greet me.

Finally, I was truly home.

PART III

28

Following Fate

Once again, I found myself arriving in a new country at the busiest possible time—in America, it had been during the Halloween festivities, and in Australia, it was Easter. On both occasions, it was a distressing ordeal to escape from the airport into the new land I was to potentially call home.

In the case of Australia, I arrived in Brisbane around ten o'clock on the morning of Easter Monday. Apparently, a big drug deal had just gone down in Melbourne, and although I couldn't for the life of me understand what relevance me coming from America had, somehow the authorities deemed that I needed a more thorough investigation than my fellow passengers.

I was smartly dressed in a black dress, red jacket and black shoes, but nonetheless, I was interrogated and, once again, officials ransacked my luggage. To make matters worse, I was desperate to go to the ladies' room, and although I was graciously permitted this luxury, a female official stood at the door the entire time in case it was discovered that I had been hiding drugs or ammunition on my person. It was not a pleasant experience and, coupled with being sprayed like some giant insect upon arrival, I was not exactly falling in love with Australia at this point.

My sister, her children and extended family were forced to wait nearly three hours before I finally emerged from my interrogation, but the welcome sight of them warmed my heart and brought tears to my eyes. It had been nearly six years since

I had last seen them and, as we all crushed each other with love-filled, heart-bursting hugs, I didn't even consider it remarkable that the armfuls of flowers they were carrying hadn't wilted while they were waiting for me.

As we left Brisbane airport, we headed to Kangaroo Point—it overlooked the river and the striking city of Brisbane—and, as my eyes soaked up the surrounding breathtaking lush and green tropical foliage, I was mesmerised by the contrast of this city and the large American cities I'd seen and lived in.

I stayed with my sister and her family to start with, in their Queenslander-style home in Camp Hill, close to Brisbane city. Despite having grown up in a busy, boisterous household filled with people, I had just come from surviving solo for a few years in a small, neat apartment (notwithstanding the extended visit from my mother), so, at first, I was quite overwhelmed to be suddenly thrust into a house overflowing with people. I was no longer accustomed to standing in line for the bathroom or worrying about covering myself for privacy, but it didn't take long for all the memories from Lebanon to start flooding back. How we had all lived and gathered together. How we'd laughed, and loved, and joked. I might have been at the end of the earth in a new and extremely foreign land, but I was surrounded by my family and embraced with unconditional love. The thought of that was enough to allow tears of joy to stream down my face and I soon readjusted to life in a busy household again. It was such a warm and wonderful experience, even though I was something of a loose cog in the well-oiled wheel of this family that had now settled in Australia.

My sister had become a shadow of her former self since her days as a vibrant youngster in Lebanon. I had brought some beautiful medium sized clothes with me from America for her, but with the stress and hard work of running a takeaway business, keeping track of a burgeoning family and caring for others—amongst other things—she had dropped to an extra small size.

Emotionally, she was powerfully strong about her situation, but her leg caused her constant pain and discomfort while she was dealing with a myriad of other life issues as well.

It saddened me to see her so very skinny, but I was sure once we were all together again and could spread the burden, we could fatten her up with some good, healthy Lebanese food and put that glow back in her cheeks.

On the Tuesday following my Easter Monday arrival, I asked my sister to bring me to work with her. I was feeling well rested and I wanted to help, but my sister still protested that I must be exhausted and jet lagged after such a long flight.

'I need to do this,' I explained to her. 'I want to do this. I can help you chop the lettuce, the onions…whatever!'

So that first working morning in Australia, I joined my sister in her takeaway shop, cutting lettuce for sandwiches that would be served to hospital staff, visitors and the general public.

Around eleven that morning, I heard the telephone ring and my sister answered it. 'Yes, Chadia. Yes, she arrived yesterday,' I heard her explaining to the caller.

My interest piqued, I wondered who she could possibly be talking to about me on my first full day in Australia and why it was pertinent to explain that I'd arrived.

'Okay. Alright. Just one second,' my sister added into the telephone before glancing towards me. 'Chadia, there's somebody I'd like you to speak with,' she explained.

'Who is it?' I wanted to know. 'Who even knows I'm in Australia?'

'Her name is Sandra and she's calling from the Holiday Inn on the Gold Coast.'

'I don't understand,' I stammered. 'What's this all about?'

'Please, just talk to her, Chadia,' my sister insisted as she gestured the phone to me.

Perplexed and puzzled, I took the receiver my sister handed to me. 'Yes?' I asked into the phone. 'This is Chadia.'

'Welcome to Australia,' the voice greeted me. 'I've received your sister's letter.'

'What letter?' I wanted to know.

'The letter that explained that you worked for the Holiday Inn chain over in America. We'd like to meet with you ASAP. You seem like a good candidate,' the voice explained.

'But I don't have a car. I've just arrived,' I stammered.

'It's okay,' Nada called to me, 'we'll drop you at the interview. What time?'

I glanced backwards and forwards between my sister and the telephone before asking the disembodied voice, 'What time would you like to see me?'

'Ten o'clock tomorrow,' Sandra replied, then gave me the hotel's address. 'Bring your passport with you.'

'Okay,' I said numbly. 'I'll see you tomorrow. Thank you so much,' and, with that, I hung up and turned back to Nada, perplexed.

'What's this all about?' I questioned my sister, my head feeling a little dizzy. Nada explained to me that when she and her family had been on a picnic to the Gold Coast a couple of weeks prior, they had seen a big sign advertising that the Holiday Inn was opening soon and staff vacancies were available. The sign said that applicants should write to PO Box such and such, so my sister had immediately decided she must write them a letter on my behalf. So, on a random piece of paper she found in her car, she wrote:

Dear Sir/Madam,

My name is Nada. This is an unusual application since it is not for me, but for my sister—Chadia—who is coming from America.

She has studied hotel management and worked for three to four years at the Holiday Inn in Texas and will be arriving in Australia on 31 March.

Please contact me on the numbers provided below.

Thanks, and regards,
Nada

Those simple few lines—written on that random piece of paper from her car—became my entire job application.

I can only surmise that the hotel was, indeed, very desperate for staff, but regardless, I have always believed that everything happens for a reason. Little did I know that the outcome of that interview would change the course of my life.

The following day, we drove about an hour from Brisbane to Surfers Paradise, an area on the Gold Coast, for my interview at the Holiday Inn. My brother-in-law, Gary, expected my interview to take about an hour, so he suggested he would have a cup of coffee in Surfers Paradise while he waited. Unfortunately for him, the interview process took two hours. First, I saw Sandra—who was the personal assistant to the human resources manager—and we went through all the paperwork together and she made sure to confirm my identity and take copies of my passport and other documents. Then I paid a visit to the financial controller before waiting patiently for the actual interview with the general manager.

At the end of it all, I still didn't know if the process had yielded a positive result. I was advised I would have to wait one more day and I would be notified of the outcome.

Due to the fact I was waiting for a phone call, we all considered it unwise for me to help out in my sister's shop the next day and I was left to my own devices, which meant pacing, waiting and wondering when I would receive the promised phone call.

Suddenly, the house that had contained people almost swinging from the rafters, was empty and devoid of life and I was watching the clock tick by in anxious silence.

When the phone finally rang, I almost leapt out of my skin and pounced on it as though I was a starving predator. 'Hello?' I said, trying to sound calm.

'Hello! This is Sandra,' she said on the other end.

'Oh yes, thank you for calling,' I offered, trying to sound nonchalant.

'Well, I'm calling with good news,' she proclaimed, 'I want you to know that you have been offered the job.'

Although I felt grateful and lucky to have a job a day after arriving in Australia, I wanted to know how much the salary was.

'You'll start at $21,000 a year,' she informed me.

'Oh,' I said apprehensively. $21,000 per year didn't seem like that good an offer and I wasn't sure I wanted to take a job so soon. 'I don't think so,' I answered. 'Thank you very much, but I'm really not in a rush to start work as I've only just arrived in Australia,' I added.

'What are you talking about?' Sandra gasped.

Thinking quickly, I suggested a number that would persuade me to fill the vacancy. In truth, I really wasn't emotionally committed to remaining in Australia at that point and in no rush to jump into a new position. Afterwards, I speculated if my lack of a plan for my future had left me in a laisses-faire type mood and perhaps boosted my courage to the point of being brashly bold enough to declare the terms and conditions I would accept. Clearly, Sandra was somewhat surprised, but said she would talk it over with senior personnel. Within five minutes she had called back, advising that my terms had been accepted and a contract would be mailed to me the very next day. That was it. It seemed I would be staying in Australia...at least for a while. I really wasn't quite sure how I felt about any of it, as it seemed I had been manoeuvred into a situation that I was in no way ready for. Part of me wanted to go back to the States, part of me wanted to go back to Lebanon and part of me wanted to see what this opportunity could lead to.

Nevertheless, I wasn't one to back away from an opportunity and accordingly, when the contract arrived, I dutifully signed it and made arrangements to attend the one-week orientation beginning on Monday, the 5th of May 1986.

I was offered the option of working day or night shift, but from experience I had already decided that should such an offer be made, I would opt for the night shift. I was given the title of senior night auditor and advised I would have four or five staff on a permanent basis to support me. This meant I would be doing the auditing—the accounting—and I would be reporting to the finance department.

Fortunately, there was going to be a time lag before I started work officially, which gave me time, with the help of my family, to search for a place of my own on the Gold Coast. First and foremost, I needed to be conveniently located close to the hotel, and to buy my first Australian car. With my family's help and through an estate agent, I found a neat little unit in Southport, but I took a bit more time deciding which Australian car would suit me. In America, I had driven extremely large vehicles, but the cars in Australia seemed tiny and gutless in comparison.

'Look,' my brother-in-law said to me, 'the largest cars we have in Australia are Holdens or Fords, so let's go look at some of those.'

Finally, I settled on a red Ford Falcon—the largest car that I had test-driven—and decided that it would probably suit me quite well.

I still had a little money saved in America and a little money I had brought with me to Australia, but I decided to start slowly, not knowing yet where this new adventure would take me. I purchased used furniture and my sister, God bless her, gave me a bed with a mattress, a bedside table and many other items.

My new place was a lovely two-bedroom unit, but I started by only furnishing one room. Not wanting to pressure myself financially, I didn't buy a fridge straight away, which was surprising given the warm weather in Queensland, but life had taught me to be prudent and inventive, so I figured out a workable solution. My brother-in-law gifted me a large Esky cooler in which I could place blocks of ice (purchased from the convenience store across the street) that made a suitable refrigerated compartment for milk, cheese and cold meat. Still not emotionally committed to staying in this country, I made do with the Esky for the first two months I lived there.

On the second day of orientation for the new job, our orientation leader addressed us on how we were to present ourselves in the hotel. At this point, none of us had received our uniforms, which we were told would be blue-and-white shirts and we women were also ordered to wear navy-blue, high-heeled shoes. The lady conducting the orientation was explaining business and office etiquette, how to talk, how to walk and how we should apply makeup, style our hair and, most importantly, how to serve customers and clients. In the middle of this orientation, she suddenly called out, 'The brunette lady in the red dress. Could you please come up to the stage?'

I had hoped that I would not be selected; however, I dutifully obeyed her request. She held up various coloured fabrics against my skin, explaining that with my natural colouring, most colour combinations would flatter me.

Next, it was time to call up one of the males in the group. 'Young man in the back there,' the lady summoned. 'Would you join me on stage, please?'

A tall, trim, taut and terribly handsome young man with healthy glowing skin and neatly trimmed dark hair strode up to the stage.

'What's your name?' the lady inquired.

'Martin,' he replied with a foreign accent I didn't immediately recognise.

'Where are you from?' she asked.

I was later to learn that he was, in fact, from Zimbabwe, but rather than try to explain where and what Zimbabwe was, he simply replied, 'I am from Southern Africa.'

That was May 6, 1986 and I had no way of knowing how our chance meeting would change the course of my entire life.

29

Holiday Inn #3

By now, I should have noted the significance of my tendency to give things three chances and the fact that the Holiday Inn had popped up for the third time in my life, but I was blissfully oblivious until much later!

The hospitality industry in Australia at that time was relatively new, so having studied and worked in the industry in dramatically different cultures—Martin in South Africa and myself in America—allowed us to bring a wealth of experience and ideas to our new positions at the Holiday Inn.

Martin worked as the night manager, so he was in the front office and I was in the finance department. Since both positions allowed us to liaise with personnel across the hotel operations, we often crossed paths while working the night shift. There was an immediate attraction between us—so much so that Martin quickly fell into the habit of singing Frank Sinatra's 'Strangers in the Night' as I would pass by his desk.

Martin had a little brown book with Jewish Bible written on it on his desk, and it always made me wonder whether he was, in fact, a devout Jewish man. It was only later that I found out that this little book was actually a calculator, given to him by a close Jewish friend and intended as a gift of Jewish wisdom to a young man too generous with his money. At the time, it was only meant as a harmless joke, but nowadays, I very much doubt he would consider having such labelling on this otherwise harmless device.

It wasn't long before we quietly started seeing each other, both of us deciding it would be best to keep our new relationship to ourselves. Our first date was, well, less than elegant and super low key—we went to McDonald's for breakfast! I'm not sure if he was just trying to play it cool or maybe he didn't want to overwhelm me and frighten me off, but in any event, McDonald's is where it all began.

Not long into our courtship, I invited him to my apartment for one of Australia's favourite meals, a good juicy T-bone steak. Martin is extremely fussy with his steak, liking it almost rare, but I like mine well done. That evening, I had made the steak so well done that it was completely burnt. Martin, being the gentleman that he is, was already determined not to set a foot wrong and he happily munched down every morsel and complimented me on my cooking, even though it must have been like chewing burnt rubber. It was years later when I realised how bad that steak must have been for a man who enjoys a steak so rare it is almost still mooing.

Our early days were also beset with some confusing moments and misinterpretations. For example, sometimes I would notice ten and twenty-cent coins affixed to his desk with tape and I would wonder if this man was a bit of a scrooge. It turned out that back then, when he purchased a pack of cigarettes from a vending machine, the change in coins was attached with a sticky tape at the back of the cellophane packet that covered the cigarette box, and eventually, he would pull them off and put them on his desk. How easily we can pull muscles jumping to the wrong conclusions about what we see. Nonetheless, years later, it still makes us laugh.

Even though Martin and I knew that we would be together forever, we managed to keep our relationship a secret from our co-workers. There were many reasons we opted to keep it quiet. Partly because we were amused by how cleverly we managed to dupe even those closest to us—especially as we both had other staff members romantically pursuing us—and partly because, in the wise words of my mother, 'Keeping your secrets, allows you to gain what you want in life.'

We spent most of our days off together, exploring the Gold Coast region and getting to know each other better, but we successfully carried out our ruse at work, to the point that people in the hotel actually thought we were enemies. We would pretend to disagree on reports and ignore each other if we happened to pass in the corridor, always quietly giggling to ourselves that our efforts were a success. We felt like secret agents on a spy mission, keeping our romance from those we worked with, which only served to intensify an already rapidly growing affection between us.

When I'd lived in Texas, I'd occasionally run into issues with my understanding of English while working at the petrol station as a cashier. I look back now and laugh about the time a nice-looking, young Texan guy—a regular customer—whispered, 'Chadia, I'd like to take you to the rodeo.' I loudly told him, 'Get out! Get out now! I do not go to these vulgar places.' It was only much later that I finally realised I had mistaken a rodeo for a bordello.

As you can imagine, the varied language backgrounds between Martin and I sometimes led to comical misunderstandings in the early days of our relationship. After all, I was a Lebanese woman used to speaking a combination of Lebanese Arabic, French and English (and fresh from learning all the American slang that Texas had to offer), and Martin was a man of English and Scottish heritage (born and raised in Zimbabwe), so communication lines were bound to get crossed here and there.

However, I have always said that 'love and music are understood by all languages', so Martin and I managed to make it through all language issues relatively unscathed.

One day, early in our relationship, I noticed a slight bulge in Martin's shirt pocket and—picking up on my curious expression—he extracted a small plastic bag filled with a reddish, powdery substance, and smiling, asked, 'Have you ever tried Peri Peri?'

'Martin! How could you? No, I don't take drugs,' I gasped in reply, somewhat shocked at this request.

His musical laughter carried on the wind as he replied, 'It's not drugs! It's a spice from South Africa and Mozambique.'

Of course, nowadays Peri Peri is a commonly used flavouring in many restaurants around the world, but back then it was extremely foreign and exotic.

In October 1986, five months after Martin and I met, we decided that we would be united forever and, even though he hadn't proposed or anything yet, we decided we would look for a house to buy together. We headed to the bank and, just like that, secured our first mortgage. We couldn't wait to get settled in a home and begin a new chapter of our lives together.

However, the house hunting would have to wait because the following day, disaster struck when Martin nearly lost his life in a car accident.

The day after we were approved for our first mortgage, Martin, exhausted after finishing his night shift, dropped his mother and a friend of hers—who had been holidaying—at the Brisbane airport and then headed home through the rain. Unfortunately, his exhaustion caught up with him and he fell asleep at the wheel, causing the car to careen out of control on the slippery road, cross the line into opposing traffic and slam into a rock face. Luckily, due to the time of day, there was minimal oncoming traffic so his car didn't run into anyone, but it was totalled anyway. Martin was rushed to hospital, where the doctors and other staff were surprised that he had survived the ordeal at all. But survive, he did and it wasn't until he was safely back in his apartment that he contacted me to simply say he didn't think he could make it into work that night. Somehow, my mind immediately wondered if he was having cold feet and maybe even second thoughts on the decision we had made. Clearly picking up on the concern and curiosity in my voice, he tentatively explained, 'Chadia, the truth is that I was in a car accident this morning.'

I think my stomach just about fell out at that news. 'Oh, my goodness, Martin!' I exclaimed. 'Are you okay?'

'I'm fine,' he assured me. 'A little cut on the lip, a fractured wrist, cuts on the chest area from the seatbelt, and some other small bruises. Nothing serious.'

Of course, I didn't believe him and I hung up and headed straight over to his apartment in Broadbeach, which was a short drive from my place. It is in moments like this that we are reminded of how precious life is and how, in an instant, everything can change. I can't imagine how I would have coped or how bleak my life would have become had Martin not survived that day.

Because of his accident and a few issues with his car insurance, our house hunting was temporarily put on hold until we were in a more secure financial place to start looking.

One gloriously sunny, tropical day—on my Birthday in November 1986—we returned to Cascade Gardens in Broadbeach and Martin took my hand, lowered himself to one knee and said, 'Chadia, I love you with all my heart and want to spend the rest of my life with you.'

Tears of indescribable joy welled in my eyes as I threw my arms around his neck and said, 'Martin, you've made me the happiest woman on earth.' Moments later, we embraced with the longest lingering kiss I can ever remember.

The next few days were like a whirlwind montage from every romance movie I have ever watched, as we shopped for rings and began talking about wedding plans.

In late 1986, we found a lovely home in Southport—conveniently close to our work in Surfers Paradise—on sale for $60,000. We even managed to secure for it for $5000 less and we were thrilled with our purchase. I had insisted that I wanted a brick-and- tile house and that we needed a minimum of three bedrooms. Our 'home sweet home' was on a good-sized block and, very quickly, it was filled with our personal belongings, our love and dreams.

And then it was time to tell our families the news about buying a home and planning to marry.

My sister, Nada, already knew about my relationship with Martin and our plans, and I had also told my mother, shortly before we moved in together, but I still hadn't told the rest of my family and Martin hadn't told his parents either. As it was considered a cardinal sin in my culture to live with a man before marriage, I was reluctant to share our news with the rest of my family.

We decided to call Martin's family in South Africa first to share our happy news. I listened as he told his parents, 'Chadia and I are in love and we're going to be together.' I really don't think I heard any other words after that, but I knew his parents were excited and happy for us. Those words hung in the air like a blessed dream— so perfect and pure that I was afraid if I pinched myself, I would wake up and once again find myself in war-torn Lebanon or stuck in the horror of my previous marriage to Jerry.

But first, Martin wanted to be respectful of my culture and my family and, since my father had died when I was young, one Saturday evening in January 1987, my fiancé-to-be and I presented ourselves at my eldest brother's house in Brisbane, so Martin could formally request my hand in marriage. After he asked for my hand, and was given my brother's blessing, Martin placed a gorgeous ring on my hand in front of my family.

Of course, all this meant he finally had the chance to meet my entire family and my lovely sister-in-law, Andrée, prepared a very nice dinner for the occasion. Martin was a little shy—fairly reserved and quiet—that night, but I knew in time he would become an integral part of the family.

Excited that she could finally celebrate my happiness openly, my sister, Nada, invited the whole family to a brunch at her place the next day.

She prepared a light lunch of cold meats, cheeses, salads and fruits. There were crackers, bread rolls and, of course, Lebanese flatbread—a staple in her household. Martin, not being familiar with Lebanese bread, decided he would make a good Australian cheese-and-tomato wrap. He put the tomatoes and cheese in the middle of the flatbread and rolled it up like a money bag, causing the entire family to erupt with laughter. A bit worried that he had erred somehow, he glanced at me with inquiring eyes, clearly wishing for me to explain, but I was laughing too hard. And so, without even trying, he broke the ice with my family.

Whereas Martin's parents had expressed pleasure in the fact that their son was to be married, my mother still wasn't sure at all. She was understandably worried after the fiasco of my marriage to Jerry and how much I'd been hurt and deceived by him.

However, despite my mother's misgivings, we were now officially engaged.

I had found real love, something that was foreign, new and incredibly exciting and everything about my life in that moment felt as though it had been destined to reach that point in time. The cyclamen was going to blossom this time with those heart-shaped leaves surviving until death did us part. My cyclamen destiny was unfolding.

In an ideal world, we would have been married before we moved into our new home, but fate and circumstances worked against us. Although we had originally planned to marry right away, we ran into a few issues that ended up delaying our wedding by two years. Firstly, when his mother had visited Australia in October

1986, Martin had put his car insurance renewal notice to one side and forgot to pay it prior to his accident. The car was a write-off and we had just secured a large mortgage, so we were not only burdened with mortgage payments, but we also had to pay off Martin's car loan that had not been covered by insurance.

Secondly, our house needed a few renovations and we opted to do them ourselves, so it took time to get the house fixed up to our standards.

Lastly, Martin's parents were unable to make it to Australia from South Africa due to business and other commitments.

All of these combined created a two-year delay in our wedding plans, but we managed to make the most of it and enjoyed our time living in and fixing up our home while we continued working and slowly making wedding plans.

30

Love Changes the Taste of Everything

Time flies when you are having fun and spending quality time with a loving, caring and amazing human being like Martin, so those two years didn't really seem very long at all.

Martin and I often enjoyed dining out at a number of different restaurants in the area we lived in, although he did seem to tire of my consistent menu choice of chicken. Chicken of every variety, but always chicken. I have always enjoyed a variety of meats (except for pork, because I've never developed a taste for it) but for one reason or another, the chicken option on the menu was the one that always called to me.

One day, my fiancé decided to take matters into his own hands and ordered an entrée for both of us. In fairness, he did ask me first if I would eat prawns, but horrible memories of Jerry forcing me to eat prawns—which I loathed—prickled goosebumps on my skin and made me feel slightly nauseated.

'Okay,' he said understandingly, 'please let me order it and if you don't eat it, I will eat both *entrées*, is that fair?' I had to concede that it was fair—what did I care if he ate two servings of prawns? Incredibly, he also ordered his own main meal of prawns, but thankfully, he also ordered me a chicken dish. Bracing myself and trying not to gag when the curved creatures arrived, sprawled in full view, I gazed at them with barely concealed contempt and reminded my husband-to-be, 'I really don't like them.'

All the while, the trauma of being force-fed prawns by my ex-husband weighed heavily on my mind, but Martin knew about my prawn ordeal and he was very patient and understanding.

'Look, I do understand, but this is a different time and place,' Martin assured me soothingly. 'Let me cut you a tiny piece, less than a quarter of a prawn. You don't even need to chew it. I'll just put it on your plate and you decide whether or not you're going to try it.'

'No, no, I'm not going to eat it,' I persistently assured him. 'Well, just dip it in the sauce,' he suggested and we began eating our dinner and chatting.

As we talked, I barely noticed Martin cutting pieces of prawn and placing them on my plate and, before I even realised what was happening, I had been absentmindedly dipping and munching down the tiny slices he had been serving me. I had consumed the whole lot and thoroughly enjoyed them.

He smiled at me with a secret, knowing grin before I became fully aware of what had just transpired. Glancing down at my plate, I completely shocked myself. 'Hey! That wasn't bad,' I muttered, almost to myself.

The prawns were a perfect symbol for how different my life with Martin was compared to life with my first husband. Martin would never force me into anything; rather, he would gently advise and guide, putting my feelings above his own needs. And from that day on, I fully understood how much better everything with Martin would be and I began eating prawns regularly.

Our wedding plans continued, slowly but surely. I never would have imagined that selecting a church could be such a tiresome exercise. It was rapidly becoming something disheartening—we just couldn't seem to find a church that felt like "us"—until we happened to stumble across an old Lutheran church in Southport. We both fell in love with the quaint little building immediately. This was a place with heart and soul and character. Without hesitation, we looked at one another and knew this was the place where we wanted to take our vows to become husband and wife for the rest of our lives.

The rest of the planning went much more smoothly!

Even though our wedding was quite humble and small, we were blessed with a beautiful mixture of international guests. The reception was planned to be a relatively modest affair of around 100 people with a simple cocktail party. It was an extremely multicultural wedding with many different nationalities attending and we just knew the occasion would be so full of love and laughter with all the diversity. Knowing that our wedding was such a mix of different ethnicities really filled up my heart and reinforced the feeling I'd always had. Love doesn't discriminate—how magical it would be with all of us, together, celebrating and enjoying each other's company.

We also planned to entertain our guests with both Western and Middle Eastern music, symbolising the union of our two cultures meeting, merging, mingling and of course marrying.

My mother and my sister have always been something of an inspiration for me, and in shopping for the wedding dress this was no different. Excitedly, Nada came to me one day detailing a dress she had seen in a shop in Brisbane, which she was convinced would be perfectly suited to my taste.

It was a full-length dress of white lace with a satin underlay. Unlined lace covered the cleavage to a scalloped neckline and long sleeves with a few pear-shaped pearls scattered over the chest area, with a slight puff on the shoulder and a long train. Nipped at the waist and with a large bow on the rear, below the waistline, it was dazzling, elegant and terribly refined and it had been tailormade to my petite figure. During my first fitting, as I was turning in the mirror, I started laughing as my memories darted back to that large red bow attached to my rear end in New York. I recalled the story to Nada and we both roared with laughter.

Two weeks before the wedding, Martin's parents arrived from South Africa and, of course, we had to introduce our families to each other. Martin was (and always has been) a bit of a jokester and, on one particular day when we were enjoying lunch in the beautiful tropical climate of Queensland, without my knowledge, Martin whispered to his mother, 'When you finish lunch, you must burp loudly.'

She looked at him, horrified. 'You're kidding me? We don't burp!' she hissed back.

'No, no it's the Lebanese tradition,' he assured her. 'People burp to express their appreciation for the food and the cook. It's an important cultural symbol.'

Naturally, this made Martin's mother feel extremely uncomfortable, and as the end of the meal approached, she started staring at me in a most unsavoury manner.

Not only was I innocent, but I was unaware of my fiancé's prank. All I knew was that my soon-to-be mother-in-law was giving me some very dark looks, reminding me chillingly of my former mother-in-law.

Finally, flustered and anxious, I demanded, 'Okay, what's going on?' Martin grinned at me, cheekily confessing his prank. 'Excuse me?' I gasped. 'Where did you get that tradition from, you son of a gun?' Son of a gun was an expression I had picked up from my time in America but, in fact, if I am going to be honest with you, what I really said was *sana-ma-ba-gun*. Somehow, I always managed to get the local idioms a little askew. The result was that everyone around the table shared a good laugh—perhaps a little at my expense and that of Martin's mother—but it definitely broke any ice that there may have been remaining and a bond was formed that day which remains until now.

To this day, I am teased by family and friends about my mispronunciation, or should I say *creation*, of a curse word.

31

Lucky Storm

As it turned out, it was unseasonably hot that January in 1989, and on the way to the church on our wedding day, a massive tropical storm knocked out all the power for the surrounding area. That old proverb about it being good luck if it rains on your wedding day clearly never considered a lady's hairstyle. The storm started as our white limousine collected the bridal party.

I managed to arrive at the ceremony unscathed by the elements; however, our beautiful and soulful Lutheran church had to be illuminated entirely by candlelight. This only served to enhance the ambience and heart of what was the most special day of my life so far. Our guests were convinced this was by design rather than accident, because all the flickering flames combined to create the most romantic atmosphere for a wedding imaginable. My brother Antoine walked me down the aisle towards Martin, who was waiting anxiously, while the organist played 'Here Comes the Bride'.

My bouquet, although not filled with my beloved cyclamen—the flower of love and hope—because of the time of year, was still elegant, comprised of all white garlands.

My hat resembled that of a refined lady at the races, with piles of white lace around the medium-sized rim and perched on an angle atop my long brown hair, which had been defined and curled beautifully for the occasion with just a wisp of a fringe across my forehead. All in all, I was the glowing image of a bride completely in love and excited about the marriage ahead.

Martin was dressed in a well-tailored grey suit which gave the effect of a slight blue sheen to it; his shirt was white and his bow tie electric blue, reflecting the colour of his eyes. His twin brother, taking the role of best man, was dressed similarly.

Nada, as maid of honour, wore a tailored two-piece suit also in electric blue. While the two little flower girls—my nieces—were dressed in sky blue and our little page boy (my nephew) wore black trousers with a white shirt, a black satin vest and a blue bow tie.

Taking our vows was incredibly special to me, as this time I truly meant each and every word. I was committed and head over heels in love with this man. Through the trials and learnings of years past, I couldn't help but feel thankful that God had blessed me and helped me to find real love. I had found the sort of love that others wrote songs about, and others have even died for. Martin was a wonderful surprise in my life journey and our marriage was just the start of blessings to come. Standing by Martin's side on those perfectly polished wooden floors against the whitewashed walls of the Lutheran church, I felt I was the luckiest girl in the world. Our guests sat in pews decorated with little bows at the end of each aisle and watched us swear that we would love, respect and cherish one another for the rest of our lives. On the one hand, it seemed so stiffly formal and on the other, so profoundly meaningful. Once it was declared we would forever be husband and wife, I kissed the man whose name I would now proudly have as my own, took his hand and walked back down the aisle as Mrs Chadia Chalmers.

The reception was at the hall next door to the church. As per tradition, speeches were presented as everyone enjoyed the cocktail-style food and drinks. My favourite speech was Martin's. After he thanked the guests for coming and thanked everybody involved, he turned towards me and said, 'Thank you, Chadia, for marrying me. I promise I will be there for you always. I do, however, believe the main reason you married me is not for my good looks, my amazing family or my career, but you married me because I'm tall and can change the light bulbs around the house.' Clearly a joke about the notable height difference between us, this was the perfect display of Martin's sense of humour, a trait I obviously valued more than his height.

Our wedding cake was three heart-shaped tiers forming a pyramid. It was decorated with the most delicate and intricate powder-blue and baby-pink flowers adorned with white trimming; a fine gold band circled each heart-shaped layer with a carefully crafted filigree figure on the top. It was such a superbly delicate and elegant creation that it seemed a crime to cut into it. As we lowered the knife, I thought back to our vows and how meaningful they were to me and my heart felt so full.

I could hardly wait for the moment when I would be swept into his arms for the bridal waltz to the tune of 'Lady' by Kenny Rogers—a song we had mutually selected. The words could truly have been written for our undying love. As the song describes, Martin was (and is) my knight in shining armour. He is my only one. As we twirled and glided across the dance floor, I knew our love was that everlasting love, the one that I had dreamed of. A love so deep and honest, so beautiful. I knew that the joining of our lives wouldn't be easy, but that we were determined to work through it, to stand side by side through the ups and downs of life. I was now his lady, and he my incredible man.

As we swirled around the dance floor in each other's embrace, gazing into one another's eyes, somehow Martin managed to stand on my dress and it temporarily dimmed the magic of the moment as it savagely tore a little way up one of the seams. I pulled it up to drape over my arm so it wouldn't tear any further, but this exposed my entire leg. So much for my modest dress, as there was now a priceless and embarrassing moment of my prim and proper wedding dress pulled up almost to my waist. I guess it all goes to show that as perfect as everyone wishes their wedding will be, we are all human, and Martin possessed that wonderful trait of clumsiness, which further endeared him to me.

While we were saying goodbye to our families and guests, suddenly Martin's mum, dad, and everyone (all the family and guests) started holding up their hands, creating a bridge for Martin and me to pass under. Then couples lowered their hands so they could capture us in a kiss, a hug and goodbyes. It was a great feeling to be surrounded by so much love.

This joyous and momentous occasion was all captured on video, so we would be able to enjoy it for many years. However, Martin—an avid rugby fan—accidentally recorded a game over our precious and priceless wedding video. I cried, stressed, but reminded myself that it's the marriage and the memories of our special day that are really important. At least I still have my wedding dress—still torn—stored in a white box in my cupboard.

32

Flourishing

Although my mother had been unsure of our relationship at the beginning, her love for Martin grew stronger with each passing year until soon he was her son just as much as I was her daughter.

It also didn't take long for Martin to learn that he was going to be immersed in Lebanese delicacies and the culture that went along with it. In the beginning, he took a distinct dislike to baklawa, my favourite Lebanese sweet, complaining it was dry and flavourless. Clearly it was an acquired taste, for these days he considers it one of his favourites as well. Meals would be accompanied by ample servings of homemade tabouli, meat-stuffed cabbage rolls, tahini of lemon and garlic and a wide array of Lebanese mezza and foods. When I met Martin, he was a mere sixty-one kilos—very thin for a man of his height—but today he is a healthy eighty-eight kilos. Let's just say an added benefit of being married to me was the Lebanese food, not only mine but my family's as well.

It was fun teaching him Lebanese traditions and etiquette. One of the first priorities being that he shouldn't put his feet on the coffee table in front of visitors—something he was all too accustomed to doing prior to being immersed in our traditions. It was also expected behaviour that when guests arrive, they were first brought juice or other cold beverages along with snacks and only later, when the host feels the guest wishes to leave, you would present the coffee, biscuits or sweets. If coffee is brought out too early, it may be considered offensive as it may suggest that you wish your visitors to leave after they have just arrived.

It was a couple of months after the wedding that I discovered I was pregnant. The seed of our love was growing inside me and soon a new life would be born to this beautiful earth, but first, I needed to share my exciting news with my husband. After dinner that evening, I approached him, holding the stick behind my back. An impish grin had spread almost from ear to ear, and he could see I was itching to impart some news.

'Guess what?' I said.

'What?' he repeated, feigning nonchalance.

'Within months we are going to be three,' I announced proudly.

Martin leapt out of his chair so fast I was worried he was going to knock the side table over and send it flying across the room. Throwing his arms around me, he hugged and kissed me as he said, 'Oh, Chadia! That's the best news I could have received.'

Soon we would become a family of three!

The beginning of the pregnancy went swimmingly; I was able to continue work, transferring to day shift.

I love my morning coffee, but the one downside of my pregnancy was the very smell of coffee turned my stomach. Normally, I would have had two or three cups before lunchtime, but it seemed for the duration of this process, it was a luxury I would have to forego. Instead, I started drinking tea—with one sugar and milk—and seemed to adapt to the new beverage rather well.

It's amazing how people's attitudes change once they discover you are carrying a child. Everyone at work was so helpful, almost to the point of being intrusive, and now knowing I was addicted to my new Ceylon tea, each morning I would be asked, 'Chadia, did you get your tea?'

I also developed cravings, especially for fresh figs and dates, which we used to buy in small quantities at a local shop that specialised in these international delicacies.

It is a common phenomenon for husbands of pregnant wives to share pregnancy symptoms—especially cravings—and Martin was no exception. I recall waking up in the middle of one night hearing a crunching sound next to me in bed. I heaved, my now whale-like body up and flipped on the bedside light, looking questioningly over at Martin.

He said, 'I've got cravings too,' almost sounding annoyed. 'I have to have my chocolate-chip cookies. You're craving dates and I'm craving cookies.'

'Are you sure it's a craving?' I questioned him. The difference being that his craving appeared to be all day and all night, whereas mine appeared to be ebbing and flowing in fits and bursts.

A week before I was due, I visited my doctor for a routine check-up. He looked me over and asked what I had planned for the next day. 'Well, I stopped working a week ago,' I told him, knowing the baby's time was near. 'But I still have to clean the house and organise a few things.'

'Oh no, no, no,' he assured me. 'You're going to have the baby early.'

'What do you mean?' I gasped.

'This baby is coming, maybe five days early. I'm going to admit you in the morning as I'm not happy with your readings. I'll be inducing you by the afternoon.'

'What's wrong with my readings?' I wanted to know.

'Your blood sugar and blood pressure are elevated and I'm concerned for you and the baby. It will be safer for all concerned if we can't stabilise these readings and induce you as quickly as possible.'

'Oh, my goodness!' I clasped my hand to my face. 'I don't want to do this.' I didn't feel ready to have the baby yet and the doctor's concern was scaring me.

'Chadia, you must be sensible,' he said soothingly but with an air of control. 'There are two lives at stake here and I'm responsible for both of them. Please take my advice.'

Pursing my lips, I nodded without answering, returning home, not at all sure that this was how things were meant to be. My mother was staying with us at the time, so it was some comfort to confide in her about the doctor's ominous warnings.

'Not a natural birth!' she exclaimed, horrified. 'Are you sure about this, Chadia?'

'No, Mama. I'm not sure about it at all, but what can I do?'

That night I went to bed, tossing and turning and fitfully wondering what the morning might bring. Luckily, I didn't have to wonder for too long. By 5 am, my baby had decided it was going to make its entrance into the world, completely on its own terms. My mother was already up having a cup of coffee outside. 'Mama! Mama, the baby's coming,' I called.

'Oh, thank God, they won't have to induce you,' she cheered, quickly adding, 'You mean it's coming now?'

'I don't know, Mama. I haven't done this before,' I said. 'My water has broken and I'm having some contractions.'

'Oh! That is good. God is great!' she said. 'You're having the baby naturally, thank God.'

While the contractions had indeed commenced, it was my mother's considered opinion having ample experience in these matters, that the baby's arrival wasn't imminent. There was time for me to sit down and have a cup of tea and a piece of toast with her before waking Martin.

About an hour later, I approached him, somewhat astonished that he was able to sleep so soundly given what was transpiring under his roof. 'Martin, wake up!' I said, pushing him with my finger.

'What?' he said blearily. 'Are you alright?'

'Yes, yes, I'm fine, but we need to go.'

Suddenly he was bolting upright. 'What! Are you sure?' 'Oh, believe me, I'm sure,' I assured him.

The check-in procedure at the hospital didn't take long and soon I was sitting in front of a television waiting for the process of delivery to unfold. Earlier, when we had arrived, the nurse told me that the pink and the blue suites were both available. 'Which one do you prefer?' she asked.

'I'd like to be in the pink suite,' I replied, as though I already knew my baby would be a girl. We didn't want to know the sex prior to the birth, but I always had a feeling that the child I was carrying was a girl. The doctor assured us the baby would not be here for some time. I told Martin he may as well go to work rather than pace uselessly up and down the hospital. My sister joined my mother at my side, waiting and watching as I endured indescribable pain throughout the day. Martin returned after work and together we welcomed the arrival of our baby girl at 8:29 that night.

The drama aside, after a full nine-month pregnancy, the most beautiful baby girl arrived weighing 3.5 kilos. We named her Samantha (Sam) and her golden hair and white, pinkish skin could not have been more perfect or pure. Finally, I was a mother and I was near bursting with pride and pleasure. Family and friends rushed to our side to congratulate us, full of helpful advice about how our lives were about to change as we stepped into the brave new world of parenthood.

I was advised to stay for three days in hospital, during which time my family was constantly around me, which was very comforting and filled me with love.

On one particular occasion—the memory of it still makes me burst out laughing to this day—my youngest brother, John, offered my mother a lift to the hospital in his red, convertible Mini Moke. A Moke is a small car, open on all sides, that looks like a large insect with bug-like eyes. When my mother walked into the hospital, I couldn't help but burst out in a belly laugh, despite the pain this caused my extremely sore abdomen.

'What on earth is wrong?' my mother wanted to know.

'Are you joking?' I spluttered. 'Have you not looked in a mirror?' All her hair was standing on end and my brother had either neglected to notice or neglected to tell her. She looked like a comedy character out of a cartoon series.

After three days we returned home and settled into our new life as parents. Initially, I had taken only three months' maternity leave from work, but when it came time to return, I couldn't bring myself to leave Samantha. The Holiday Inn was surprisingly accommodating and, ultimately, ended up extending my maternity leave for a year.

We did have a mortgage to pay and funding a family of three on one salary was certainly going to present a financial challenge—even though Martin had been promoted to Front Office Manager shortly before Samantha was born—but there was no way I was going to leave my baby and so we decided that I would become a stay-at-home mum. It was also pretty obvious that we were going to need a bigger home, so we were going to have to carefully consider what our next step would be.

In the Spring, when Martin was away on a business trip, a larger home (in need of a lot of love) just across the road came up for sale. Trying to contain my excitement, I immediately phoned Martin to let him know about it and asked if we could offer them $120,000.

'How on earth are we going to pay for a $120,000 house?' he wanted to know.

It was a reasonable question and though I had no reasonable answer, I have never been one to give up—not since birth—and

I knew we could make it work if I just thought a little creatively outside the box. Martin had been promoted again at work and we had done quite a bit of work on the house we had purchased for $55,000, so I knew I would be able to find a way to afford the house between his new, higher salary and my creativity. I decided to try my luck and put our current house on the market. As fate would have it, it didn't surprise me in the least when it sold within twenty-four hours for $110,000.

It was truly a gift from God and, just like that, we managed to buy the larger property across the road at the price we wanted. Sure, it needed some TLC, but we had time and we were excited to make our new house a home.

33

Life at Home

Life as a stay-at-home mum was both exhausting and brilliantly beautiful. Samantha—who we also called Our Sam and Sunshine—was such a busy and easy toddler, occupied playing with her toys and helping me cook, bake, clean and garden. We both loved being outside and in our beautiful front garden— full of a wide variety of so many flowers—and our backyard vegetable garden filled with cherry tomatoes, eggplants, cucumber, green beans, carrots, potatoes, herbs, lemon and mandarin trees.

Somehow, I also managed to teach myself how to sew, and I really enjoyed the simplicity and almost meditative time when I would make dresses for Sam and me. I also learned how to make curtains, lounge-suite covers, cushions and so on. While she was young, I also spent time completing some evening courses in oil and fabric painting. Of course, I painted cyclamens on canvas and on cushions.

It wasn't long before I became pregnant again and we were so excited at the prospect of another life joining our small family. Tragically, my third pregnancy ended the same way as my first— in a miscarriage—but this time, I really had nobody else to blame for this second loss of life except myself. While it could never be proven, I suspected that—due to some vigorous gardening and an attempt to dislodge an enormous and extremely well-bedded plant—I managed to bring on the miscarriage. Not only did I bleed out, but the tests that followed revealed I would never be able to conceive again.

The news was obviously devastating, but God has always been there whenever I need Him most and, miraculously, we proved medical science wrong when, approximately one year after I miscarried, we conceived again. Of course, Martin and I were perfectly happy with one child, but if it was God's will for us to have another, then nothing could bring us more joy!

This time, somewhat apprehensive about the fate of the little one I was carrying, I refused to go and see a doctor until I was three months into the pregnancy. I knew I was pregnant—a combination of missed periods, a positive pregnancy test and a woman's intuition—but I still did not visit our family doctor until I was past the first trimester. Even then, after he did all the usual testing, I was apprehensive when he called the following day to confirm my pregnancy.

When he phoned, I took a deep breath and steeled myself, but sure enough he said, 'Congratulations! I'm so sorry I was wrong. You were right, and you're going to have a second baby.' Again and again, the doctor expressed his profuse apologies for having been so wrong in his initial assessment.

Again, God's hand demonstrated that the impossible can be possible.

This pregnancy was not without incident and we had a few moments that caused some concern. At one point, I experienced back pain that was extreme—to the point where an ambulance came and rushed me to hospital—and at another, I came down with such a severe case of the flu, I thought I would lose the baby. Ironically, where I had refused to see our doctor until I was well into my second trimester, I was now so fraught with worry that five times I snuck away to the nearby hospital in the middle of the night—leaving Martin and Sam asleep in bed—to seek reassurance that all was well. I did this right up to my ninth month, just to check that nothing untoward was occurring.

As expected, and on schedule, I went into labour at the end of my term. Far from my tomboy days, I also insisted that my lipstick be perfect and, during the entire delivery process, I continued to reapply it so I would look attractive as I gave birth. Crazy, but true! When Sam had been born, Martin had cut the cord, but his hand had been shaking so badly from nerves, I'd worried he would miss and damage me or our newborn child. For Alex's birth, the doctor thought it would be more prudent for Martin to assist in pulling the head out; something he was much more capable of doing without risk of injury to any of the parties involved.

Four years and ten months after we had Sam, our handsome son, Alex—who we often call Sunny—entered the world amidst much pain, excitement, elation and periodic lipstick reapplications.

Nothing will ever surpass the unbridled joy I experienced with the delivery of my two beautiful children. Although, I must confess, those first cups of coffee after they were born came pretty close to surpassing the elation I felt at their births.

By the time Alex was born, Martin was extremely busy managing two to three hundred staff and the stress of it was clearly taking a toll as his smoking—a nasty habit that he'd had since before I met him—was getting out of hand. He would regularly have three or four cigarettes burning at work, in different offices, at any given time and it wasn't unheard of for him to drop a cigarette in the bin and start a small fire, setting off smoke alarms at work and at home. I also couldn't keep up with the burn marks everywhere—on the carpet, furniture, bedding, his clothes. I would sometimes wake in the middle of the night to see the reflection of his cigarette end burning in the mirror across from our bed.

One morning, upon finding yet another fresh burn mark, I decided that enough was enough and approached my beloved husband. We had reached a point in our lives where we had managed to save a few dollars and would soon be able to purchase our first investment property, so I thought I would appeal to both his good sense and his money sense.

'Martin, look,' I reasoned. 'We're planning to buy a small investment property and we have two children, so I think it's time you considered trying to kick the habit. It's not healthy, it's expensive and, frankly, it's causing damage both at home and at your work.'

'I promise you, one day I will stop,' he assured me, 'and I keep my promises.'

'Yes, but when is one day going to come?' I wanted to know. He pursed his lips and nodded, begrudgingly accepting that what I was saying was sound. 'Alright, Chadia,' he said reluctantly.

'I will try to stop.'

From then on, it was rare for me to see Martin with a cigarette, and shortly thereafter I foolishly believed he had actually kicked the habit for good.

We went house hunting and found a small investment property in Brisbane, which we purchased with the intention of renting out. It was not even a week after that when I noticed he'd started smoking again.

Hoping to encourage him to leave the cigarettes behind forever this time, I put booklets, brochures and flyers about quitting smoking in our bathroom, but as time passed, try as he might, he was still not able to quit the habit altogether. So, in a final act of desperation, he asked me to book him into a hypnosis centre in the area we had heard about. Thankfully, Martin kept all three appointments, and by the time he returned at the end of that week, he threw his remaining cigarettes in the bin and said he would never smoke again.

'Oh, thank God!' I cheered. 'The hypnosis worked!'

He turned around, put his firm hands on my shoulders, and fixed his gaze firmly into my eyes. 'It wasn't the hypnosis that worked,' he told me with a smile, 'it was paying him fifty dollars a session to do something I should be quite capable of doing myself.'

I chuckled under my breath. Whatever works, I thought.

34

One Big Happy Family

The most incredible time of my life, by far, was the time I spent with my young children. Watching them play, imagine and laugh, filled my heart with pure joy and the innocence they displayed was priceless. An innocence that so many children, such as those who had endured the war in Lebanon, could only dream of. I tried not to let thoughts about less fortunate children bring me down. I just enjoyed how fun our life was and how blessed we were. Some of my fondest memories include times when we would play in the pool—singing and dancing to a plethora of songs, including Frank Sinatra's 'New York, New York'—and playing with playdough, making mud pies and 'colouring in' (even though there were times that Alex's creativity led to 'colouring in' our walls rather than paper). Our house was constantly filled with laugher and, of course, the occasional scream and cry, as with all children.

My entire extended family had now settled in Australia and were residing either in Brisbane or the Gold Coast region and I was ecstatic. We had made it out! Despite all the pain and suffering we had endured as a result of the war, we were safe now—safe in a country that allowed us hope and better opportunities for our children.

Martin's parents had also moved to Australia from South Africa. They initially stayed with us for three months until they bought a property within walking distance from our house.

As such, our children were truly blessed with the opportunity to grow up and spend quality time with their grandparents, plus a large number of aunts, uncles, and cousins.

Weekends at our home were and still are filled with family and friends. Martin and I love hospitality and as such, we never miss an occasion to entertain and open our home to those we love.

As young children, Sam and Alex adored having their cousins over to play, whether it be on the Nintendo 64, in the swimming pool or playing The Tunnel Game—an all-time family favourite. The Tunnel Game was a hide-and-seek game created by the kids which involved draping my clean white sheets over furniture and converting our living area into a maze of tunnels. With lights off, whoever was 'up' would have a torch and be required to search through the maze to find the other children. Despite being concerned for the safety of my furniture and for the cleanliness of the sheets at times, I admit that the adults often wished we were small enough to join in as it was such a hit with the kids.

To say that our lives were perfect would be a lie, but this time in our lives was wonderful, and, as always, God's grace comforted us in the more difficult times.

To me, miracles are always reminders of God's grace and I truly believe we are constantly surrounded by them, but rarely notice them in the hustle and bustle of our daily lives. One such miracle—which occurred when Sam was nine years old—will stay in my mind till my last day on this earth.

Sam's tonsils had been removed and she'd stayed in the nearby hospital for two days before being discharged home. The poor thing was experiencing severe and unbearable pain and, around midnight, the pain was so terrible that she was in tears. Seeing my first-born suffering was heartbreaking, but there was little I could do. I helped her downstairs to the living room so that we could be together on the couches and not disturb the boys' sleep. I tried everything I could—painkillers, ice—but the pain didn't let up. Sam was lying on one of the couches, while I sat up and kept my eye on her until I saw her finally fall into a deep sleep. It was already early morning by that time and I was so exhausted that I also closed my eyes to get some rest. I don't think it was five minutes before I felt a hand vigorously shaking my right shoulder in an effort to rouse me from sleep. I opened my eyes to realise that there was no one next to me but, when I then turned my attention to Sam, I was horrified to realise she was struggling to breathe and choking. I jumped up quickly, pulled her up, turned her face down and, with a small hit on her back, caused a large clot of blood—as large as a pecan nut—to dislodge from her throat. We took her straight back to the hospital, along with the piece of clotted blood, and all the staff in the emergency room told us that Sam was very lucky. Later, they told me that the previous Christmas, while the nursing staff had been celebrating, a boy who'd had his tonsils removed, had also choked to death due to a similar blood clot in his throat. If it hadn't been for that hand, or should I say the intervention of what I believe was an angel, Sam may not be here today.

35

New Ventures

As the new millennium was approaching, our charming little Alex was four and attending preschool three times per week, and our beautiful Sam was nine and attending an excellent school close by in Carrara.

I was starting to think about returning to the workforce, when Alex turned five, and making a new start for myself in the new millennium. Of course, as time marches on, nothing stays the same and I was no longer who I was before having children, so I really wasn't sure what to do professionally after being off work for nine years.

I felt incredibly blessed to have had the opportunity to stay home and look after my two children until my youngest was at nearly school age. Many mothers have no such opportunity or privilege, and have to work while their children are babies. I believe those mothers are superheroes, and one such superhero was my amazing and loving sister.

I'd secretly always had a passion for real estate, but at that point in time we couldn't afford to pay the course fees of around $3000. My brother Walid, now living nearby, was aware of my passion and desire and he was equally aware that I couldn't stretch the family budget sufficiently to finance the study necessary to acquire my real estate office licence.

I remember a pristine sunny morning, with a faint breeze rustling the surrounding trees when Walid walked in and slammed down $3000 on the kitchen bench. 'Chadia,' he said, 'I really want you to do the course you've been telling me about.'

I can't stress strongly enough what a close and loving family I have, or how I appreciate and value each and every member of my family, but perhaps the incredibly generous gesture made by my brother is a very clear indication of our unshakeable bond.

I looked at the money and teared up as I embraced my loving brother, who had given me the opportunity to take the first step in making my next dream come true. This was the same brother who had once told me, 'Nothing is impossible when you put your mind to it!' and had encouraged me to give everything in life my absolute best. And Walid was proof of this! He has always been successful at chasing his dreams. He had once been a general manager for 10 years for a big American company overseas—with staff exceeding 4000—and, at the time he loaned me the money, he was working as a senior interpreter in Australia. He was married with three sons and a lovely English wife and, knowing that he had his own mouths to feed and bills to pay, I—at first—refused to take the money. In true Walid character, he insisted I take it, explaining I could pay him back in instalments once I started working. The temptation and the gesture were too sensational to refuse, so right there and then, I wrote a note and put it on the fridge that I owed $3000 to Walid and, and the moment I started working, I would subtract payments to him until I had fully repaid the debt.

Immediately, I booked myself into a course with the Real Estate Institute of Queensland and, within months, I was a fully graduated and licensed real estate agent. There were long nights of study and it was extremely difficult sometimes with two children to care for, but my ever-loving mother—even though her own health was beginning to fail—was always there to lend a hand. Martin was the same and, even though it was sometimes midnight or 1 am by the time I finished assignments and was blissfully able to rest in the land of nod, he continued to support me every step of the way.

One of the instructors during the course was a wonderful woman by the name of Maria, who was working as a sales manager for a real estate company in the area. Seeing my natural aptitude for the subject, she asked whether, once I qualified, I would like to come and work for her as a sales consultant. I could commence employment in the new year. Everything seemed to be coming up roses, or perhaps I should say cyclamens. I was thrilled at the offer and only too grateful to accept it.

I graduated just prior to Christmas in 1999 and applied for my official licence from the Office of Fair Trading and in January 2000—starting out as the new kid on the block—I started work as a real estate agent in another adventure in this extraordinary life of mine.

For the first couple of weeks, it was all in-house training about protocols, legalities and the mechanics, but come the third week I had secured my first listings and by the end of that month I had three sale contracts.

I was so happy and, to make matters even better, I was able to work flexible hours between 10 am and 2 pm, so I was still able to take my children to and from school.

I also worked on Saturdays and on one of those first working Saturdays, I experienced a particularly embarrassing episode that made me realise how long I had been out of the workforce! One of the sellers I was dealing with was located in Sydney and I needed to fax him the contract for approval and signature. I had never seen, much less used a fax before, but never one to be dissuaded, I approached a couple of female sales consultants in the office and asked them if they could show me how to operate this foreign device. To my embarrassment and annoyance, they both started laughing at me. 'I'm sorry,' I spluttered, 'I've never used a fax machine. When the fax machine was invented, I was a stay-at-home mum.' Of course, that wasn't true and the fax machine had, in fact, been invented long before, but hadn't been deployed in office use the last time I had been gainfully employed.

'Chadia,' one of them smiled at me, 'it really couldn't be simpler. You dial the number, put in the paper and press that button. That's it.'

'That's all there is to it?' I asked, raising an eyebrow.

'That's all there is to it!' they assured me. Even now, I must admit, my children always tease me that I am one step behind with technology.

From then on it was smooth sailing...well, for the most part. During one of my first property viewings as a real estate consultant, I was nearly swept away by wind and heavy rain. I parked my car across the street and gathered my items to take to the appointment, but I ended up frolicking through the rain when my open umbrella was hoisted by the wind and scattered me, my phone, brochures, folder and car keys down the street. The family, who had just arrived from Spain, must have taken pity at my ungraceful waltz through the rain because they ran to help me collect my things off the wet ground. Looking back, the memory is quite comical, but at the time I was flustered and embarrassed. However, if I claimed that this was the least awkward and clumsy moment in my career, I would be a short woman telling tall tales; let's just say that this episode is actually one of the most embarrassing moments of ungainliness I've had professionally.

Despite being married with children and working with a group of young, childless professionals, I took to my new profession like the proverbial duck to water and I did quite well.

Irrespective of my success and enjoyment of being a realtor, something told me I could still do better. Once word got around that I was doing well in the market and was also fluent in Arabic, one of the larger real estate firms in the area contacted me and made an offer I couldn't refuse. They saw my worth in dealing with clients from the Middle East and, within a surprisingly short period of time, I found myself working in the international market operating from an office in Surfers Paradise.

In early 2002, I decided to go solo and start my own company and I learned that I was able to display my office licence from my home. Fortuitously, our property was divided into three levels with separate entrances—the ground level contained a granny flat with a large living area, a kitchenette, bedroom, and a bathroom. We decided to convert most of it into an office and, in March 2002, CCR (Chadia Chalmers Realty) was established. To say I was excited about my new venture is an understatement; this was going to be the beginning of my boutique real estate office and our motto was, *"When Excellence Matters"*. As usual, I had help from family to get off the ground with my amazing niece and nephew, Jo and Lawrence, creating both the logo (with my favourite colours, black, white and red) and the motto.

Of course, in that first month of setting up my own business from home, I made the princely sum of six dollars, but I was known and becoming well-respected in the industry, so it wasn't long before I built up my rent roll and also began selling properties. At first, I couldn't afford a photocopier, but the new fax machine I had now become so adept at using, was an equally efficient copying machine. Ironically, this little machine that I had originally struggled to understand and use, was a modern marvel that allowed my new business to begin blooming. This was a time of big changes for our family as well because, at the same time I started my business, Martin transferred to another renowned hotel, Royal Pines Resort, owned by the same Japanese business group as the previous hotel with the same executive title.

I quickly adapted to becoming an extremely skilled time manager. I had a business to run, Sam and Alex were still small, my mother was a constant part of my life, and—as a married couple—Martin and I needed to share our love and affection. Of course, it seems as though God will give you the time and energy if you are willing to put in the effort, so I spent an hour here, two hours there and three hours somewhere else and that's just the way it was. It worked, but sometimes it was a constant, hectic dance.

Frequently, I would hear the fax machine tone and would have to run downstairs in the middle of the night to push a button on the fax machine to receive sale contracts from overseas. It seemed as though overnight there were suddenly multiple phones in the building, a pile of new office equipment and so many balls to juggle at one time that I am really not quite sure how I managed it. I think this is a magical superpower mothers develop. Like so many working mums around the world, juggling the same demands, I also somehow managed to do it all.

36

Legacy

By March 2004, as all this happy chaos was unfolding in our lives, my mother, who was in her seventies, was also living with us as her health was deteriorating. Of course, accommodating and caring for her needs was always at the forefront of my mind, but eventually it became too much for me to handle on my own.

We hired a nurse to come in three times a week to assist mum and, at first, it was enough, but the inevitable day arrived when even the nurse and I were no longer able to care for my mother. When my mum—ever one to put others before herself—insisted on moving to an aged care facility, it broke my heart. My loving and caring mother had always been the rock of our family and my best friend. I wanted to be there for her, to help her, to take away all her pain, tell her everything would be okay and that tomorrow would be better.

The decision to relocate her into a home was excruciating. One evening, I poured a glass of wine and gazed into the pristine petals of a beautiful cyclamen plant I now had growing at home. I searched for inspiration and answers, even though I knew what had to be done. I prayed that some divine intervention would offer me an alternative I had not considered. However, as I gazed into those petals and reality settled into my heart, forming an uncomfortable lump in my throat and bringing stinging tears to my eyes, I knew there was no alternative. I had no choice but to accept that the time had arrived when my mother was not only demanding, but also needing to move to an aged care facility. It took all my courage not only to cope with and quell the inner conflict and pain I was experiencing from reaching this decision, but to discuss the subject with my mother, husband, siblings and the rest of the family.

Ultimately, we all agreed that finding a facility as close to our home as possible would be best and we found a home close by where we could take a simple stroll to see her whenever we wished. Every morning and afternoon somebody in the family would visit. She was given a room on the second level with a balcony and there were nurses on duty 24/7 to take care of every other situation that might arise, or so I thought.

With Mum visiting our home on a weekly basis and so many visitors to the aged care facility, not a day went by when she either did not receive a visitor in her room or a sojourn in the garden. Unfortunately, despite our large, caring and loving family all pitching in to do as much as we could to make sure that she maintained her sense of normality, as well as the knowledge that she had not been deserted, as mum's time in the home went on, we realised that she and the other residents were being mistreated by some of the staff. The retirement home had many good staff, but there were also some awful, cruel, and abusive staff.

We realised this by piecing together evidence of things we had seen directly and by chilling accounts Mum and other residents provided us with about inhumane treatment. Unfortunately, we discovered this all a little too late and we were too scared to take any significant action as our mother was in their hands. It was killing me inside that Mum was not with us twenty-four hours a day and she was being mistreated. I was barely coping, physically, but the emotional pain was ever escalating in my mind, knowing I was unable to do more.

We did discuss issues with the staff who we trusted and our concerns were also presented appropriately to management, but afraid to speak up, most of the good nurses were unable to stomach what they knew was going on behind closed doors and ended up leaving, one by one. However, a new manager, Anne, arrived, and with her assistance, there were some improvements made, although there was still a long way to go.

Sometime in early 2006, I was extremely stressed and busy and I suggested to Martin that I should close down CCR. I simply wasn't able to keep up with everything I had to do, especially with Mum's Parkinson's continuing to progress and the conditions in her care home. The load was too much and Martin could see how it was affecting me, so he asked, 'What would you like me to do? Do you want me to quit my job?'

Within an instant, as if it would be the solution to everything, I replied, 'Yes, please.' Martin was an executive at a hotel where he managed multiple departments, but knowing the desperate situation I was in and feeling that he could use the change, he resigned.

Martin sent me an email on the last day of his job at the hotel:

Hello Chad,

> Coming together is a beginning
> Staying together is progress
> And working together is success – Henry Ford

Love, Mart xxx

In mid-June 2006, Mum experienced a nasty fall which resulted in her breaking some ribs and she was taken to the hospital where, thankfully, she was cared for by good nurses.

My husband was an angel and so supportive during this time. All the family took shifts visiting her, but things descended into a state where she was unable to open her eyes, even when her beloved grandchildren were visiting. I knew this was the ultimate sign of her deterioration because she loved nothing better than being with her grandkids.

Whether due to neglect or design and desire on my mother's part, her time on this earth was nearing its end. She suffered from a fever due to a chest infection.

On Friday, June 30th, I picked up the kids from school and went straight to the hospital to see Mum. She was very frail and struggling to open her eyes, but regardless of this, she used what little strength she had left to smile and turn her face to Samantha. I asked, 'Mum, can you see Alex?' He was on the window side of the room. She tried valiantly to turn her head towards him, you could see her strain, and it was incredible that she could even hear us or feel us. That was the last time I saw her moving.

That evening, the entire family was down from Brisbane. Sam and I remained at her side until about 10 pm, when exhaustion and desolation caused us to trudge back home where Martin had dinner waiting for us. As wiped out as I was, I only took a bite of a morsel before announcing I had to return to my mother's side.

By 11.30 pm that cold night, I struggled to even see her breathing, but I vainly held on to a faint glimmer of hope that, by tomorrow, there might be an improvement. I left the hospital in the early hours of the morning, kissing my mother and telling her that I would see her soon, as I always did.

At 8.30 am on Saturday, July 1st, I received the call that no daughter or son wants to receive, informing me that my beloved mother had died.

In a private corner of my bedroom, I sank to my knees, buried my head in my hands and wept like I had never wept before. The person who had given me life, who had inspired me, who had been such a guiding light through everything I had experienced and endured in both joy and turmoil in my life, was gone. I would never see her smile, hear her laugh or feel the warmth of her embrace ever again. I know that she awaits me in heaven, but to lose her from this earth was heartbreaking.

37

Saying Goodbye

My memories ebbed and flowed like the coming and going of the endless ocean tide.

When I thought of my mum, I remembered her getting up in the early mornings, making her Lebanese coffee with cardamom—our home was always filled with the rich *aroma* of boiling coffee. I remembered her baking the 'Maamoul'—Easter or Christmas cookies filled with dates, walnuts or pistachios—a *smell* of that woke us all and woke our appetites. I can still smell them now.

Martin had been amazing when my mother used to visit us. He would carry her to the car and put on her warm shoes, covering her in a fluffy jumper. She had loved her ice cream and he never failed to make sure that she had all her favourite flavours to enjoy. On more than one occasion, my mother had told me she considered my husband to be her fifth son. He was such a loving and caring son-in-law. It hurt my heart that I would never get to see her spending time with Martin or my children again either.

As a family—despite our vast experience with it—we don't deal with bad news well. Upon receiving the news that my mother had passed, I burst into screaming tears in our bedroom, prompting both Martin and the children to join me in the ensuing flood. It was a gut-wrenching, soul-deep experience for all four of us.

Martin called the rest of the family and, together with my brother Jalil, we went to the hospital. To my dismay, disgust and amazement, I found my mother lying deceased in her bed in a room with three living patients. People were eating and drinking coffee around her, while I fell into hysterical sobs, hugging her lifeless corpse. It is a scene that never should have been allowed and I believe there should be a special room for families to pay their final respects to their deceased loved ones in hospitals.

Her wedding ring and earrings had been placed in an envelope for me and I clasped them to my chest as Martin suggested I step outside to get some air.

My youngest brother, John, and his lovely wife arranged to open their home in Brisbane (in a tradition we still follow to this day), so people could visit and pay their final respects before the funeral and offer condolences to the family. For three days, their home overflowed with family, friends and members of the community visiting us.

My niece, Nadine, arranged the funeral and also contacted the Greek Orthodox pastor—because my mum was Greek Orthodox and would have wanted a Greek Orthodox service—while we were left to endure the wait leading up to her final internment in Brisbane.

On the day we laid my mum to rest, friends and relatives and people I didn't even know overflowed the church's brick-and-mortar bounds. It meant the world to me to see so many people shower the departure of my mother's soul in such an ocean of genuine love. One person I did know, however, was Anne—the manager at the retirement home—who hugged me after I saw her signing the attendance book.

As was tradition, the priest also left the coffin open for a few minutes for people to say a very last farewell. It was cyclamen season in Australia and, clasping a white and mauve posy of this blessed and treasured flower that was always present to remind me of the circular nature of life, I took the final steps to gaze upon my mother for the last time. I placed the cyclamen posy in my white scarf and laid them in my mother's hands and remembered all the years when those loving arms had embraced me with their warmth. It seemed so unnatural that now those hands were cold. I remember quietly muttering, 'Mum, your hands are so cold.'

The flowers on the coffin were incredibly beautiful and the altar was full of different flower arrangements. The photo of my mum standing in the middle of a field of beautiful wild flowers (including cyclamens)—in spring in Lebanon—was displayed in the middle of a small table, adjacent to the coffin.

As we sat through her service, a lasting memory of my mother's wisdom popped into my mind. 'You may have been born tall, short, thin, fat, black, white, rich, poor, male or female, but there is one thing we all have in common: we all have a brain, so use it wisely. To make the right decisions is the best thing you can do in life.' This was a philosophy of my mother's that I have honoured and will continue to honour until the day I meet her on the other side.

It wasn't long after she passed that I was in our lounge full of people and a shape emerged in the condensation on the window pane. It depicted a defined shape of a dove and it was clear enough for everyone to see. A dove, of course, symbolises peace, which had been so desperately sought after in our beloved homeland and in our lives. From there on, there has always been a dove in some way, shape or form making its presence known around me. A clear message to me that my mother will always be with me.

On Valentine's Day in 2007, Martin's parents (who lived close by) asked if they could have Sam and Alex for a sleepover. I was still not coping well since mum had died the previous seven months before, so Martin decided to prepare a nice, romantic dinner for the two of us. After dinner, he served dessert and then excused himself from the room for a few minutes. I assumed he had gone to the bathroom, but when he came back, he had a giant, red bow wrapped around his waist. This instantly reminded me of the red bow I'd sat on in New York City and I started laughing and couldn't stop. Despite my sadness and struggling so hard with the grief of losing my mother, Martin was always finding ways to make me laugh, make me feel loved, and cheer me up.

Each year on the anniversary of my mother's passing, everyone in our family—except me—would go to the cemetery to visit her. I just didn't have the strength. The last time I saw her grave was on the day I put the pristinely pure white cyclamens in her cold hands and said goodbye. Each year I tried to summon the courage to go, but I had not managed to succeed.

Before she'd passed, we had all made a promise—especially me—that we would keep having family gatherings as long as we had the strength, and God always gives me the strength. Anytime I am not feeling well, if the family are going to be around, suddenly I am imbued with a surge of strength and calm. I have an incredible husband who loves me and also loved my mother, and as such he also loves our family to be around. As Mum always said to me, 'The boat wouldn't sail without you, Chadia.'

In keeping with my mother's wishes, our family still gathers on every major occasion. This past Easter, Martin ordered a lamb to cook on a spit, along with every accompaniment imaginable. The night before, we hardboiled five to six dozen eggs and painted them before placing them in a big basket. On Easter Sunday, the family enjoyed lamb and the other dishes at our vast buffet, and then we all chose an egg. We then proceeded to have an egg competition, a typical Lebanese Easter tradition where we hit each other's decorated eggs and the winner was the person whose egg remained unbroken.

On Christmas and other celebrations, it is likewise a thinly disguised excuse for an excess of food and an overindulgence of love and joy. It is quite common for us also to entertain the gathered throngs with western and belly dancing. I used to cut quite a dashing figure wiggling my firm abdomen, but these days I am determined to firm my wiggling abdomen and to continue to dance. I'm also determined to continue to spread the joy and laughter that my mother imbued into our lives—something we so desperately needed in our youth to survive war and now need to celebrate being on the other side of it.

This life of mine has been full of both misadventures and beautiful, joy-filled years.

38

A Visit from Royalty

If there is one truth in life, it is that life does indeed go on. After the dust settled, I returned to running my business and juggling my time between personal and professional life once more. My business grew and became stronger as my reputation spread by word of mouth—without the need for big, flashy, expensive advertising—to bring clients to my door.

I believe part of the secret to my success was the ability to put myself in another person's shoes, or perhaps more accurately, to walk a mile in them. Whether people had one dollar or were millionaires, they received the same treatment from me.

I remember receiving a call from the Queensland Government advising me that a young prince and his entourage would be arriving to the Gold Coast via Sydney, and as I was well known as an Arabic-speaking professional who dealt a lot with Middle Eastern clientele, my presence was requested to meet and assist them as they deemed I was trustworthy. Accommodation had already been arranged at the Palazzo Versace—a six-star hotel— and I was advised that he would arrive at eleven o'clock in the morning, with his wife and no less than fourteen pieces of luggage. Martin organised a stretch black limousine to meet me at the airport for the prince's arrival. After I finalised what was necessary in the office, Martin, his father and another staff member took the reins while I headed to the Gold Coast airport, arriving just prior to 11 am.

As my footsteps echoed on the cold hard floor of this regional airport, I noticed a big sign being held by a limousine driver wearing a black suit and hat, with my name and the prince's name on it. Immediately approaching him, I asked him not to put up any sign or advertise who was arriving, as the last thing we needed was to be surrounded by paparazzi.

Naturally, I assumed the prince would arrive looking…well, like a prince, wearing robes and so forth. I was wearing a smart navy-blue suit, white shirt and high heels and I just looked… well, Chadia. Scanning the arriving guests, I returned to the limousine driver to ask if he had spotted anyone. By now it was about 11:45 am and it appeared that all the guests from Sydney had left the terminal.

At that very moment, I received a call from the consulate in Canberra asking where I was as the prince and his family had been looking for me. The prince, his wife, baby, housekeeper and nanny had apparently been wandering up and down the airport terminal aimlessly, unable to locate me because I had insisted on no signs.

I had noticed two ladies, one of whom was carrying a baby, but didn't pay them any attention. Suddenly, a tall young man in his early twenties loomed behind me and in a controlled voice asked, 'Are you Chadia?'

I spun around to see a man wearing a white baggy Nike top and blue jeans. His wife was wearing a sky-blue tracksuit with a zip open slightly from her neckline. It was really not surprising that I hadn't identified them as the royal couple.

'Yes, I am Chadia,' I replied with a sigh of relief. 'Lovely to meet you. The limousine is waiting for you,' I gestured, trying to sound dignified.

The limousine, as large as it was, was ill-equipped to convey so many people, let alone the most ridiculous amount of luggage I had ever seen. The professionally calm limousine driver stacked as much as possible in the trunk of the vehicle and I suggested the rest be put in my boot and back seat so we could follow in tandem. Once the royal family and entourage were safely inside the stretch limousine, I pulled up behind it, giggling to myself about how much the scene reminded me of Eddie Murphy's movie Coming to America.

By one o'clock, we were all ensconced in the luxurious surroundings of the Palazzo Versace, although we weren't able to check the royal family into their two suites quite yet, as the hotel hadn't finished preparing them.

I told the prince and princess that I was there to help and that they could call me if they needed anything. I wrote my mobile number on a small piece of paper and, while handing it to them, the prince asked, 'Chadia, can I have your business card?'

I said, 'I'm here just to help you. I'm not here on a business level.'

The prince replied, 'You have been checked from top to bottom and passed all tests. You are trusted and have an excellent record. Please, Chadia, I would like to have your business card.'

How could I possibly refuse? I smiled and gave him my business card. At the beginning, I was hesitant to do this because I didn't want him to think I had come to meet them as a business opportunity for me, I was only there to assist because I understood their language.

After our shaky start at the airport, the ice was broken and we began forming a friendship which blossomed as the days unfolded. They remained on the Gold Coast for about three months, one month at Palazzo Versace before moving to a penthouse in Surfers Paradise and we have remained in contact ever since, becoming firm friends with this beautiful couple and their lovely family.

On another occasion, Martin and I were flying around in a helicopter, showing two Middle Eastern princes (brothers) some properties. At lunch, after the flight, I suddenly realised it was time for us to pick up the kids from school, so I asked the princes if they would mind if I cut our meeting short. When they heard my reason, they insisted on accompanying us to the school to meet our children. It was a beautiful experience to watch two very wealthy and influential princes—who certainly didn't have to take time out of their busy day to accommodate my schedule— greet our children with friendly, down-to-earth smiles and casual questions about how their days had been. For me, caring about people has always been a *habit*, so it warmed my heart to know that others out there also made it habitual.

39

My Pride & Joy

As with most mothers, my children are truly the sunshine of my life—hence why I call Sam my Sunshine and Alex my Sunny. I have watched them grow from infants into two stunningly beautiful, high-achieving adults.

I hold in my mind and my heart a colourful image of three-year-old Samantha blowing out the candles of her heart-shaped birthday cake, wearing a pretty pale-blue skirt scattered with multicoloured dots and a baby-pink short-sleeved top with a collar of stripes in the same coloured dots as the skirt. Her shining pigtails were crowned by a pointy party hat covered in dots and circles of all sizes.

Alex was always a curious, active, and cheeky wide-eyed child, with eyes that sparkled with wonder. Even at the age of two, the sparkle in those eyes betrayed a seemingly innocent infant's smile with shades of mischievousness. One of my favourite images of him as a toddler is one where he was wearing a formal outfit for my brother John's wedding. His bow tie was the same vivid cobalt-blue of those clear bright-blue eyes of his. His shirt was adorable, with Mickey Mouse motifs all along the panel where it buttoned together. His smart, tailor-fitted black vest completed the image of a fresh-faced youth bursting with eagerness to run headlong into all that life had to offer him.

These images morph into the two sophisticated adults my children have grown into, sitting side by side at the dinner table.

Samantha, with her dazzling smile, beautifully styled hair, and striking green eyes, wears an elegant sleeveless black dress adorned with a simple necklace. Alex, his smile sparkling in his eyes as brightly as on his well-curved lips, wears an electric-blue suit and matching tie over a subtly checked white and light-blue shirt.

Nothing I could imagine could make me prouder of my children.

Samantha is bright, beautiful and deeply caring. Alex is strong, charming, loyal and hilarious. We always knew Samantha would be able to sing with bell-like clarity in the voice of angel—mostly because, as a toddler, she would cry and scream at least one octave higher than the average child.

Alex, on the other hand, enjoyed and developed skills with a range of musical instruments. His favourite, however, was and still is the guitar. He had the patience and persistence to be selftaught—a skill I am not sure where he got, as both Martin and I are neither musical nor have the patience to do something like that. During high school, both kids were actively involved in helping the community. They offered their time to attend mission camps, help in nursing homes and local schools and with farmers struggling with the floods in Queensland. Both were also part of the leadership program at school. The school was truly wonderful, imparting wisdom to them, not only academically but also spiritually.

Sam finished high school when she was just sixteen. She was far too young to be considering university, but without hesitation she enrolled in psychology. To this day, she cannot tell you why she did, only that she had wanted to be so many things growing up—a lawyer, an interior designer, a drama teacher—but when the time came, she chose psychology. Her intuition, it seemed, was as strong as mine, as life events would soon play out that would influence which direction she would ultimately go. And much like my life—or anyone's actually—life never follows the plan we set out for it; rather, God leads us on this winding, somewhat unusual route, which takes us to exactly where we are meant to be.

Sometimes I imagine myself in my grandmother's shoes in the pleasant countryside and I laugh and think back to how many sayings and wives' tales I learned from her, and my mother, that I actually still use in my everyday life. There are times I convince myself that my children's academic success was purely built on my feeding them zaatar pizzas (thyme, oregano, sumac, sesame seeds, and salt with olive oil spread across thin dough), like my mother and grandmother used to do with us. They would advise us that, 'eating zaatar makes you smarter'—better able to memorise and recall things. While the scientific research is yet to determine if this is true, it's true to me.

Formally, Samantha secured two degrees—both bachelor and honours degrees—when she was just twenty.

Wanting to demonstrate our adoration and adulation of this achievement, along with a milestone birthday, Martin and I wanted to know what ideal gift Sam wanted for her twenty-first birthday. Jokingly and in true Sam fashion, she said, 'Oh, Mum, I don't want a big party.'

'What is it you'd like?' I wanted to know.

She gazed at me for a moment before replying, 'To go to New York.'

After talking it over with Martin, it was decided he would book everything for us. In November and December of 2010, we spent about three weeks in the first country I had called home after Lebanon. We visited Las Vegas, New York, New Jersey and Washington DC, before returning home through Los Angeles.

We arrived on Black Friday in New York City, with my birthday looming around the corner. Unbeknownst to me, my wonderful family had organised a surprise booking to see Phantom of the Opera on Broadway accompanied by an extremely luxurious dinner.

On the morning of the big day, while I was still happily dreaming in the land of nod, Samantha woke early and rushed out of the hotel to prepare my birthday gift. She bought me a lush and colourful bouquet of flowers, a card and my two favourite treats—a strawberry tart and chocolate éclair. Then my beautiful daughter awoke me from my slumber armed with the colourful and delectable gifts and a card from Martin and Alex, who were still back home in Australia.

I sat up in bed, wriggling across the sheets in my flimsy red nightie, crying with joy at such a beautiful gesture and, never one to miss an opportunity, Sam immediately grabbed a camera and froze me for eternity in my happy, dishevelled state. The gorgeous cards and touching words indeed made me ugly cry and my darling daughter caught it all on camera.

It didn't matter though—my family is used to me doing this and the three of them often make it a competition to see who will make me cry while reading cards on any special occasion. They would use the card itself, the words inside and the words they had personally written to achieve this. Whoever could make me cry the most or fastest would win.

On this particular occasion, I think they all won! It was such a lovely and memorable way to start my birthday and the rest of the day was equally magical.

There is nowhere on earth like Broadway. The lights and pulsing atmosphere truly have to be experienced to be understood and fully appreciated. Naturally, I wore my finest attire, along with my trademark high heels and lipstick—which, as anyone who knows me can tell you, that I do not leave home without.

Coming back from the restaurant, we were told that there were webcams almost everywhere in New York. We stood in front of one and spoke to Martin and Alex in Australia in real time. That particular webcam was positioned in front of one of New York's array of tantalising shopping boutiques—which, of course, Martin didn't fail to notice.

"Hey! Stop shopping!" he jokingly ordered me from across the planet. "Sam, tell Mum: no more souvenirs. No more buying, no more shopping." We both grinned and waved to the webcam. 'Sure, Dad.' Sam giggled. I was almost obedient, too. I only bought a few nice little items that day. Whilst talking on mobile, Martin and Alex watched us on the computer, and I remember thinking, even back then, that it's a small world after all.

At this point in time, Sam's ambitions were to continue her studies through to a Master's degree, to become a psychologist. However, God's plans always take a hold of our destiny, and so she finished one year of her Masters before deciding she needed a profession where she could help newly arrived migrants and refugees.

40

Returning to My Roots

In 2014, Samantha and I also had an incredible opportunity to visit Lebanon that inadvertently led her down the path to her chosen profession.

My nephew Lawrence had proposed to a beautiful Lebanese girl and, as such, we knew the wedding would take place in Lebanon. Even though our entire family was invited, it was decided that only Sam and I would travel back to my home country, because Alex was in the middle of university exams, and Martin would hold down the business while we were away.

It had been well over thirty-three years since I had been in Lebanon, but the opportunity to take my beautiful daughter back to our homeland and show her our roots was something that I couldn't wait to do.

It was a long and arduous journey by Emirates Airlines from Brisbane to Beirut, but once we made it—exhausted—through customs and were in the car, driving away from the airport, my memories of childhood flooded back and I burst into a river of tears. It seemed so incredibly different than the Beirut I had known. The streets were now so crowded that it felt like there was no room to breathe. I had a memory of the green hills in Beirut with few houses and buildings, but those green hills of my childhood were nowhere to be seen—there were buildings everywhere. What had happened to our homeland? Had the war so ravaged it? Had the population somehow exploded?

We arrived at our hotel and checked in swiftly for a most welcome shower and rest. Sam, of course, couldn't help but notice my profound reaction to being back in Lebanon. My children were born and raised in the freedom and security of Australia, and although I had always told them about my eventful childhood, hearing about it and seeing it are two entirely different things. For the first time, Sam now felt it.

Sam was understandably amazed by Beirut. It was so culturally diverse and physically and diametrically opposite to the lush tropics of South-East Queensland where she had been raised. It was a mixture of ancient beauty, exuberance and vitality, however still showing scars of its brutal past, an exciting hub of Middle Eastern and Western culture.

From the tenth floor of our luxury hotel, we were privileged to overlook the magnificent Mediterranean Sea and be bathed in the most stunning of sunsets. Yet everywhere my gaze fell it brought memories of both laughter and tears, causing me moments of melancholy and reflective meditation as each second of this long journey home unfolded.

My nephew Lawrence, sister Nada, brother-in-law Gary, niece Jo and her fiancé Ian, took Sam and me around in a rented 12-seater van, which included a visit to the area where we used to live in Beirut. As we drove, we provided commentary to Sam to explain and show where some of the stories I had told her had taken place: 'This is the corner where Aunty Nada was shot by the sniper. This is the intersection where your *tetah* (grandma) was injured by the bombs and explosions. This is where our neighbour Rami was killed and this is the building where we used to live.' I pointed, trying desperately not to burst into tears. However, as I looked over at Sam, I realised she had released tears for me. She wept in the back seat of the van as it dawned on her that all those stories she had heard growing up—the ones she would sometimes roll her eyes at and say, 'Yes, Mum, you've told me this before'—were, in fact, real.

So real.

More real than she had ever imagined.

'Look at the bullet holes,' Sam gasped.

'Oh, believe me,' I said with a sigh, putting my arm around her shoulder, 'that is nothing.' Although most of Beirut had been rebuilt since the end of the Lebanese civil war in 1990, there were still many areas that bore lasting marks of the war. As I looked at my daughter, I too became emotional. For over thirty years, I had repressed my painful memories and emotions associated with the war and loss. Sam's open and honest expression of her emotions allowed us all to realise that it was okay to release the pain we had been holding on to for decades.

'How did you all survive? And are still functioning?' Sam asked, in awe of our resilience and response to our trauma.

We all sat there silent. Not one of us answered Sam because, in all honesty, we had no idea how we had survived. There were so many occasions that we had been close to death and yet God had spared us, each and every time.

Soaking in the ancient history and the impact of the war, had a deeply profound impact on Sam. This was the first time she had been immersed in the culture of her bloodline and she felt a sense of both belonging and foreboding among the people who were her kin.

As I had told her and was typical, she found the Lebanese people to be friendly and generous. There were also fashionable areas where these days you would only see pedestrians attired in designer clothes. On the other side of the city and surrounding areas there were refugees—Oh my goodness were there refugees! Over 1.5 million of them—so my beautiful daughter had her eyes opened wide with the shocking and stark reality of the contrasts of my homeland.

We could both see that many Lebanese had masked themselves with the *façade* of happiness, yet the sense of sadness remained tangible in their eyes.

Certainly, there were Beverley Hills–equivalent suburbs, but there also existed poverty and hardship in many areas. We made a point of taking Sam to the mountains to assure her that the natural and timeless beauty of this ancient land remained. It was swelteringly hot in Beirut in the month of July, yet the further we distanced ourselves from the city, making the climb towards the peaks ahead, the more a chill in the air prompted us to rug up in warmer clothes.

Everything about this visit to Lebanon was something like stepping into a time warp. From the concrete jungle and poverty in the urban areas that were hot and humid, to the cool expanse of the mountain ranges and pure fresh air. It all felt completely surreal. Sam had never seen anything like it in her life, and despite what I had told her over the years, she had been unable to imagine the contrast and contradictions that Lebanon displayed and was now witnessing for herself.

It was a pivotal moment in her young life because it crystallised her decision as to what she was going to do next. She was connected to this country and its people. Despite never having lived there, she felt it was part of her—the pain and suffering, the search for hope, a better life—all part of her story.

The wedding we had crossed the planet to be a part of was absolutely magnificent. The church was built of sandstone and decorated with high windows of stained glass, depicting religious scenes and inside the expansive aisle was illuminated with oversized candles leading to where the bride and groom would kneel before the priest.

The wedding took place on the 31st of July and the bridegroom's family headed to the bride's home to pick her up and then drive around beeping horns so everybody would know about the forthcoming nuptials.

Sam was so excited that she was almost bursting. The bride's house was a mere walking distance from the church, but they took the scenic route, wanting to announce their joy to the entire area. Neighbouring children and adults alike would throw rice and confetti in celebration.

The views from the church and the bride's house were breathtaking, with rolling green hills and the ocean in the distance. The wedding was a sensational experience and it was so wonderful to see my daughter enjoying this part of her cultural heritage.

The day after the wedding, we returned to my old neighbourhood in Beirut, to enjoy local delicacies such as falafel. As much as falafel is common in Australia, nowhere makes it as delicious as *Joseph's Falafel*, the same shop I frequented as a child.

I also returned to visit the man who had helped me save Josephine, our neighbour's daughter, those few decades ago. He was now the mayor of his town. We didn't mention the incident in words, but as I handed him a small gift just to say thank you—something I never had a chance do before I left for the States, the silent exchange of our gazes said all that needed to be said. I can't believe how time passed surprisingly quickly, we only visited a few relatives in Lebanon, as well as historical landmarks throughout the region, including churches and natural wonders—my favourite being *Jeita Grotto* and the Cedar Forests. We went to my home town, Marjeyoun, in the South, and witnessed—from a distance—our ruined and neglected home. It was heartbreaking to see the remaining broken stone walls that marked the outline of our old house where it stood forlorn on the top of the hill. From this vantage point, the glorious mountain tops of Lebanon were clearly visible as were the various surrounding valleys and villages. Everywhere we looked were lush green hilltops, giving the impression of a vast landscape.

From there we decided to make a brief stopover in Dubai before we returned home. Dubai is indeed a stunning and amazing city—fresh, new and opulent everywhere one gazes. From our hotel window, we had a panoramic view of the exquisite architecture of the city, yet something felt lacking to me. As Sam and I shared a silent moment of reflection, I was the first to break the silence. 'What do you think?' I asked her.

'Mum, it's beautiful. The architecture is incredible and the people are extremely friendly, but…' she hesitated.

'Go on,' I urged.

'It just doesn't have soul like Lebanon.'

I smiled and nodded. I had been thinking exactly the same thing.

After returning from Lebanon in August 2014, Sam began working for a well-known organisation that helps refugees, asylum seekers, migrants and the local community. She was triggered, or should I say, 'called' to this work by what she witnessed with her very own eyes—the poverty and the suffering in a land she so easily could have been born in. She recognised the freedom and opportunity that Australia gave me and my husband as migrants, and she is determined to return the favour.

Now well established in the position, she is a competent and well-respected settlement and clinical services manager, with over seventy staff working under her. She is a diligent and dedicated worker, earning the respect of all around her. I am so proud and pleased that she has chosen this course of action as her life path, as in many respects I feel it has closed a *circle*.

In this work I have joined her on a couple of picnics that have been arranged for refugees, which take fifty or so people at a time from Brisbane to the Gold Coast beaches. To see the expressions on their world-weary faces as they gaze at the timeless waves lapping on our golden shores, I can see the reflection in their eyes of waves of hope. Who knows what horrors these people have come from; many of them, no doubt, have bigger and more heart-wrenching stories than mine.

I smile inwardly—perhaps with a sense of irony and reflection—when I hear my beautiful daughter telling some of them that her mother came from a similar situation and started slowly, not even owning a fridge in the beginning, just keeping her perishables preserved on a block of ice in an Esky.

These people are looking for an escape, looking for a better life for their children and the same chance we have been given to call Australia home, and my daughter is helping them find it.

41

Sunny

Alex—whom I've called Sunny since he was little—has always been a born performer.

He was a musically talented child—something he still does and is quite good at—as well as a whiz on the guitar. One of his highlight performances was as the Cowardly Lion in a school production of the Wizard of Oz. There was quite a large cast and crew in this lavish production. I cannot tell you how proud we were of him during the performances. He was made for the limelight. He was charismatic and charming, and absolutely hilarious, a standout. I often tell him it's not that I am a biased mother, but that he truly is very talented.

From a young age, he was curious, active and cheeky, giving him a wide appeal to an enormous variety of people. I was always worried about him as he has always been very friendly, trusting and believes in people too easily. On what seemed like a very usual visit to our local shopping centre, when Alex was three years old, we nearly lost him. I was standing at the cashier, ready to pay for my items, when Samantha shouted 'Alex!' and ran towards her brother who had been putting his lollypop wrapper in the bin about five meters away.

It took a moment to process what had happened, as Alex was next to me a second before. Sam returned holding his hand tightly and announcing, 'That person nearly took him away!' She pointed in the direction of a person making a rapid getaway.

Whether it was a woman or man, we couldn't tell as the would-be perpetrator was wearing a wig and sunglasses to disguise their appearance. 'That person, just took Alex by the hand and started walking away.' If not for Samantha's quick thinking and actions, it had almost been a kidnapping. How terrified I was to think that someone could so easily steal my child, but how relieved I was, at Samantha's tenaciousness in taking action. Kids are remarkably intuitive little creatures and Samantha had good instincts from a very young age.

When Alex was a toddler, he used to be somewhat of a nudist. In fact, he loved hats, but not clothes. Hats, hats and hats. His hats were mainly blue, of every shape and size, and scattered throughout his room in every nook and cranny you cared to look. In fact, it was never unusual to find him naked, but for one of his many, beloved hats, running around the house. Of course, prudence and discretion were qualities that I taught my children early, and thankfully this sank in with Alex and he dressed when it was necessary. Thankfully, he grew out of his nudist ways early on.

When it came to academics, Alex showed a penchant for languages early on, including a remarkable talent for mimicking accents. He was particularly interested in Chinese culture and studied the language in high school. Later, the school organized a trip to China and Hong Kong, which we knew would be a valuable learning experience—an opportunity for him to deepen his understanding of the culture.

After high school, Alex found his calling in architectural design at university. Although it was a far cry from his musical and performance-oriented interests, it proved to be a natural fit. He has a strong aptitude for and love of architecture, with an astute eye for what works both practically and aesthetically. His passion and skill in the field earned him university scholarships, which enabled him to return—now for the third time—to China and Hong Kong, as well as to travel to Italy to study architecture that is as ancient and spectacular as it is diverse.

As a child, Alex would spend hours building things with Lego and other materials. From a very young age, he was fascinated by the buildings in the cities we visited. He asked all sorts of questions about the shape, design, and strength of high-rises, always hungry for more information. Looking back, it's really not that surprising that Alex became an architect.

42

Reminiscing

"Chadia? Chadia?' I hear echoes of Martin's voice from inside our home and I smile as I transition back from my dreamlike reminiscence of my life—those moments that led me and my family to be exactly where we are today in our present life—a good life. I am completely mindful for a moment as I take it all in. This beautiful breeze gently brushing my face. I notice the glorious blue sky, and turn to see an even more glorious man opening the door and walking towards me.

Martin is, and has always been, a caring and loving husband. Like many marriages, we have our ups and downs—we are human, after all—but life would be boring without challenges. We work together nicely, but are far from perfect.

'Can I make you a cuppa? It's probably a good idea to start getting ready soon; we don't want to be late.'

I cannot help but beam with a smile and respond, 'Yes, thank you, Mart. I love you more than anything.'

Martin smiles back, most likely thinking his wife is being a little overly romantic about the simple gesture of making a cup of coffee. Little does he know the journey I've just been on down memory lane and my heart is happier than words can express. My life is so much richer with him in it and I'm forever grateful for our unexpected encounter at the Holiday Inn.

Life's cyclical and seasonal nature never ceases to amaze me. After all, who could have guessed that my connection to the

Holiday Inn—which began with a horror-filled memory of a burned-out shell of a building after the Battle of the Hotels in Lebanon—would also be my salvation and escape after a cold, abusive marriage in the States and would, ultimately, wind up bringing me the warmth of true love, a happy marriage and a beautiful family in Australia.

I follow him inside, give him a hug and proceed to the bathroom to get ready. We cannot be late.

We end up being early, which is a rarity for me. The venue is packed. People swarm to the occasion from all directions, taking very literally the title that has been given to this exercise of the 'Walk Together'. It is a national event held to celebrate the diversity that is Australia, that we are many people with one home.

The event commences at the opening of a new building for the organisation that my daughter works for. It hosts many politicians and media, but the most impressive is the exquisite range of cultures and religions—so much humanity represented in one place. Side by side there are Indigenous people, Australians whose ancestors came on the First Fleet, migrants whose families now call Australia home and newly arrived migrants and refugees.

As we walk, I am overwhelmed by the traditional dresses of those beside me. The colours are vibrant, with outfits so unique. People carry signs and banners with profound wise truths such as, 'If we're all people, we're all equal.' Police and local volunteers lead us through the streets of Logan, an area close to Brisbane; we are all together in this. Despite only being a 2.5-kilometre walk, it is symbolic of our life together as a nation. There will be times when differences will be highlighted and discrimination will be voiced in the community, but as long as we stand together, we will not be silenced. Multiculturalism and Australia are one and the same; they cannot be divided.

At the conclusion of the walk we arrive at the local park that has massive green space where the celebrations commence.

Different nationalities perform for the audience—from our First Nations people to our neighbours from New Zealand and those who have come from even further afield such as some of the African, Burmese and Middle Eastern refugees, who have fled their home due to persecution. There is a wide range of diverse foods and merchandise, and the aroma of exotic spices linger in the air. There are traditional games and activities, and children from all nations play together in harmony. As the Middle Eastern music starts, two young Syrian men began playing the drums (*derbake*). I look at my husband and, as if reading my mind, he smiles, grabs my hand and leads me to join others for the traditional dance, the *dabkeh*.

One by one, people from all walks of life and traditions begin to join us, forming a chain. As the chain grows to more than a hundred people, it closes into a circle and, inside it, people begin to dance. Ours is not the only circle—there are many more just like ours, all intertwined together with different dances from different cultures happening in each concentric circle. The significance of these circles full of people who have overcome adversity to begin life anew—exactly as the cyclamen I have loved since childhood—is profoundly evident everywhere I look. The energy is powerful and love and acceptance emanate from everyone around me until I am overwhelmed with feelings of joy and euphoria. Serendipitously, I find myself dancing under the banner 'If we're all people, we're all equal'. This event will forever be etched in my memory as I witness love and harmony in their purest forms.

Many of my family have come to support the event. We sit back down at our table and I look across at each of them, thankful that this is how our story ends. It is not ending on the killing fields of Lebanon, but the beautiful green pastures of Australia.

Across the field, I see a family—a husband, wife, daughter and son who have most likely fled from Syria. They are laughing and joking as their daughter chases her young brother around. I pause, realising why I am so mesmerised by this family and the simplicity of their enjoyment. It's then I realise it's because they remind me of my family, my children, my husband and me. They demonstrate immense emotion of joy and hope in this new country, their new home. The heartbreak they witnessed may not have melted away completely, but their future is looking brighter than ever. I can imagine their children grown and educated, contributing to Australian society. I imagine the stories they will share with those they encounter, the changing of stereotypes and discrimination. Without hesitation, I excuse myself from the table and approach. With the most heartfelt smile and tears welling in my eyes, I reach out my hand and say, 'Welcome home. I hope Australia is as kind to your family as it has been to mine.' As I chat with the beautiful family, we exchange details and I invite them to visit our home. It is then that I pause and smile to myself, realising that all those years before, the wonderful neighbours in Beirut had imparted something so profound within me—that we as humans feel we belong when we are welcomed and valued.

In recounting my life's journey to this point, I cannot express my gratitude and sense of being blessed to live on this exquisite land with my beautiful family. It is truly the best place on earth, and sadly far too many of us take it for granted. I acknowledge the traditional owners of this land and I'm thankful for their welcoming nature to those of us who came here for a safer and free life.

Samantha once said to me, 'I am a product of multiculturalism. I was born in Australia to a father from Zimbabwe and a mother from Lebanon. I couldn't be more of a mix and I will always remember my heritage, but ultimately, I am Australian. If not for Australia giving my parents, my brother and I opportunities, our life could have been very different. This is why I want to give back. The story of my parents—their will to survive and start afresh for their children to have a better life than their own—isn't too different from those who come here as refugees, escaping persecution and wanting to create a new life.'

I agree that the happiest people in the world are the givers and not the receivers, and that is what I see my daughter doing. She is so much like her *tetah*, who was a flame—perhaps burning herself out on occasion—but on the more positive side, always providing a guiding light. My son, Alex, is similar as well, as after completing his studies in architecture, his dream is to travel and build community centres, hospitals and homes for those less fortunate—namely those seeking refuge and those in developing countries. He hopes to use the skills that our God so generously gave him to make this world a better place. For someone still so young, I cannot help but be astonished by the wisdom beyond his years and his conviction to stand up for what is right, for what is true and worthwhile. He has a heart of pure gold, is highly intelligent, attractive and loved by all. I could not be prouder of the man he has become.

My children are now the ones who are carrying the family flame forward. With passion and vision, they form the link in our *circle* of life, wrapped in the eternal symbolism of that glorious bloom, the cyclamen, and its unerring destiny.

I could not ask for a better life than ours and I feel truly humbled, grateful and amazed that I lived through so much horror and overcame so much adversity to find such loving peace in this place I now call home.

Epilogue

This is an Australian story of hope, migration, successful resettlement and the perseverance of the human heart through even the hardest and inhumane situations. It is a story of survival and a beautiful but starkly real reminder that we are in the biggest refugee crisis this planet has ever seen. And, as such, we need to be more accepting of resettlement and multiculturalism than ever before in history. My hope is that, in reading this, it will open your heart and mind to a new future where colour, race, religion and country of origin are surpassed by love, diversity, kindness, and a willingness to embrace and learn from each other, to grow together in peace and harmony.

With God's will, it is also my wish that one day, my son, Alex, will design a building shaped as a cyclamen and, when it is my time to depart from this world and join those I love who have passed, that some kind soul will place a cyclamen on my grave.

With love from Lebanon, America and Australia,
Chadia Eva Chalmers

Acknowledgements

Writing *Cyclamen, A Journey of Hope* was harder than I expected. It was, at times, a difficult and stressful, yet rewarding experience. A journey I shared with many, who without their help, love and support, none of this would have eventuated. I am grateful to each and every one of you.

I would firstly like to thank Lynn Santer, Alexandra Nahlous, Samantha Moore, Dalyia Abu-Ghazaleh, Sarah Chalmers, Nadine Chemali, Labib Chemali, Jo Wilson and Jo Johnson for your guidance, support and editing.

I would like to thank the artists who were behind the illustrations, graphic design and photography. Thank you to Lucy Kochkina, Alex Chalmers and Bec Taylor.

I'm deeply grateful to my friends who have always been there for me, through all life's ups and downs. Thank you all for your love and for cheering me up during the harder seasons of life, and being there for my happiest moments.

I have always said "a life without family, is like a tree without roots or a bird without wings". I am so thankful to my family for allowing me to tell their stories as part of my own and would especially like to thank my wonderful siblings – Antoine, Nada, Walid, Jalil and John, for your unconditional love and support.

To my beautiful children, Samantha and Alex, who believed in me and supported me, thank you. You have always encouraged me to never give up. You brighten my days and are both the joy of my life.

Lastly, I would like to acknowledge my life partner, best friend and true love, my husband, Martin. Marty, you stood by me during every struggle and every success. You are my rock. I am beyond blessed to have found you and to share my life with you. I love you, thank you for everything and I look forward to writing many more chapters of life with you.

About the Author

Chadia Chalmers is an Australian migrant. Born in Beirut, she fled the brutal Lebanese Civil War in 1980 to the United States, and once more escaped domestic violence to Australia in 1986. Chadia is now a respected business woman on the sunny Gold Coast, Queensland, her home for over 30 years. She lives with her husband, Martin, and shares a happy life with him and their two adult children. Chadia takes joy in writing, gardening, oil-painting, travelling, cooking and spending time with family and friends.

www.ingramcontent.com/pod-product-compliance
Lightning Source LLC
Chambersburg PA
CBHW020547020726
47494CB00006B/1960